W9-CBB-988

Beautiful Storm

Center Point
Large Print

Also by Barbara Freethy and available from
Center Point Large Print:

The Way Back Home

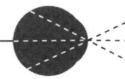

**This Large Print Book carries the
Seal of Approval of N.A.V.H.**

Beautiful Storm

A LIGHTNING STRIKES NOVEL

BARBARA FREETHY

CENTER POINT LARGE PRINT
THORNDIKE, MAINE

This Center Point Large Print edition
is published in the year 2016 by arrangement with
Fog City Publishing, LLC.

The text of this Large Print edition is unabridged.
In other aspects, this book may vary
from the original edition.
Printed in the United States of America
on permanent paper.
Set in 16-point Times New Roman type.
ISBN: 978-1-62899-852-8

Library of Congress Cataloging-in-Publication Data

Names: Freethy, Barbara, author.
Title: Beautiful storm / Barbara Freethy.
Description: Center Point Large Print edition. | Thorndike, Maine :
Center Point Large Print, 2016. | ©2015 | Series: Lightning strikes
trilogy ; 1
Identifiers: LCCN 2015043489 | ISBN 9781628998528
        (hardcover : alk. paper)
Subjects: LCSH: Large type books. | GSAFD: Mystery fiction.
Classification: LCC PS3562.O4474 B43 2016 | DDC 813/.54—dc23
LC record available at http://lccn.loc.gov/2015043489

Beautiful Storm

ONE

The clouds had been blowing in off the ocean for the last hour, an ominous foreboding of the late September storm moving up the Miami coast. It was just past five o'clock in the afternoon, but the sky was dark as night.

Alicia Monroe drove across Florida's Rickenbacker Causeway toward Virginia Key Park, located on the island of Key Biscayne. Most of the traffic moved in the opposite direction as the island had a tendency to flood during fierce storms. According to the National Weather Service, the storm would bring at least six inches of rain plus high winds, thunder and lightning.

Alicia pressed her foot down harder on the gas. As her tires skidded on the already damp pavement, a voice inside her head told her to slow down, that a picture wasn't worth her life, but the adrenaline charging through her body made slowing down impossible.

She'd been obsessed with electrical storms all her life. She'd grown up hearing her Mayan great-grandmother speak of lightning gods. Her father had also told her tales about the incredible blue balls of fire and red flaming sprites he'd witnessed while flying for the Navy and later as a civilian pilot.

Their stories had enthralled her, but they'd been an embarrassment to the rest of the family, especially when her father had begun to tell his stories outside the family. Neither her mother nor her siblings had appreciated the fact that a former Navy hero was now being referred to as *Lightning Man.*

A wave of pain ran through her at the memories of her father and the foolish nickname that had foreshadowed her dad's tragic death years later in a fierce electrical storm.

She'd been sixteen years old when he'd taken his last flight. It was supposed to be a typical charter run to drop a hunting party in the mountains and then return home, but after dropping the men at their destination, her father's plane had run into a massive storm. When the rain stopped and the sun came back out, there was no sign of her father or his plane. He'd quite simply disappeared somewhere over the Gulf of Mexico.

Everyone assumed he'd crashed. They'd sent out search parties to find him or at least pieces of the plane, but those searches had returned absolutely nothing. How a man and a small plane could completely vanish seemed impossible to accept, and she'd spent years trying to find an answer, but so far that hadn't happened.

What had happened was her increasingly obsessive fascination with storm photography.

Her sister Danielle thought she was looking for

her dad in every flash of lightning. Her brother Jake thought she was crazy, and her mother Joanna just wanted her to stop challenging Mother Nature by running headlong into dangerous storms. But like her dad, Alicia didn't run away from storms; she ran toward them.

While she worked as a photojournalist for the *Miami Chronicle* to pay the rent, her true passion was taking photographs of lightning storms and displaying them on her website and in a local art gallery.

It was possible that she was looking for the truth about her dad's disappearance in the lightning, or that she just had a screw loose. It was also possible that she was tempting fate by her constant pursuit of dangerous storms, but even if that was all true, she couldn't stop, not yet, not until she knew . . . something. She just wasn't sure what that *something* was.

Her cell phone rang through her car, yanking her mind back to reality. "Hello?"

"Where are you?" Jeff Barkley asked.

"Almost to the park." Jeff was the weather reporter at the local television station and had become her best resource for storm chasing.

"Turn around, Alicia. The National Weather Service is predicting the possibility of a ten-to-fifteen-foot storm surge, which would make the causeway impassable, and you'll be stranded on the island."

"I'll get the lightning shots before that happens. How's the storm shaping up?"

"Severe thunderstorms predicted."

"Great."

"It's not great, Alicia."

"You know what I mean," she grumbled. She didn't wish ill on anyone. But the more magnificent the storm, the better her pictures would be.

"You keep pushing the limits. One of these days, you'll go too far," Jeff warned.

"That won't be today. It's barely drizzling yet. The island is the perfect place to capture the storm in two places—over the ocean and then as it passes over Miami. Don't worry, I'll be fine."

"You always say that."

"And it's always true."

"So far. Text me when you get back."

"I will."

Ending the call, she drove into the parking lot. The attendant booth was closed, and a sign said the park was closed, but there was no barrier to prevent her from entering the lot.

She parked as close as she could to the trail leading into the park. She'd no sooner shut down the engine and turned off her headlights when lightning lit up the sky. She rolled down her window and took a few quick shots with her digital camera. She didn't have a great angle, so she would definitely have to find a higher point in the park to get a better picture.

Putting her digital camera on the console, she grabbed her waterproof backpack that held her more expensive film camera and got out of the car.

The force of the wind whipped her long, brown ponytail around her face. She pulled the hood of her raincoat over her head. It was just misting at the moment, but the sky would be opening up very soon. With tall rain boots and a long coat to protect her jeans and knit shirt, she was protected from the elements, not that she worried much about getting wet. She was more concerned with keeping her equipment dry until she needed to use it.

This was her second trip to the island, so she knew exactly which path to take, and she headed quickly in that direction. While the trails were popular with walkers, hikers, and bikers on most days, there wasn't another soul in sight. Anyone with any sense had left the park to seek shelter.

She was used to shooting storms in dark, shadowy places, but for some reason her nerves were tighter than usual today. The air was thick, almost crackling, and the atmosphere was dark and eerie. She felt a little spooked, as if someone were watching her.

A crash in the trees behind her brought her head around, and her heart skipped a beat at the dancing shadows behind her.

A second later, she saw two raccoons scurry into the woods, and she blew out a breath of relief.

The animals were just looking for shelter. Everything was fine.

Ten minutes of a rapid jog had her heart pounding and her breath coming fast as she traversed the hilly section of the park, finally reaching the clearing at the top of the trail. Instead of thick brush and trees, she was now looking at the churning waves of the Atlantic Ocean. But it wasn't the sea that sent a nervous shiver down her spine; it was the towering, tall clouds that the meteorologists called cumulonimbus clouds. These clouds were associated with thunder and lightning storms and atmospheric instability. Alicia felt both terrified and entranced by the potential fury of the stormy sky.

She pulled out her film camera. While she used digital more often these days, there was still nothing like capturing a storm on film.

She took several quick consecutive shots as lightning cracked over the ocean. She checked her watch, noting the lapse of fifteen seconds before the thunder boomed. That meant the lightning was about three miles away.

Eight seconds later, lightning split apart the clouds, jagged bolts heading toward the beach. The storm was moving in fast—the lightning less than a mile away now.

She had a feeling she knew where it would strike next.

Dashing down the adjacent trail, she headed

toward the old carousel with the shiny gold decorative rods that would more than likely attract the lightning.

As she moved through the thick brush, the rain began to come down harder, but she didn't slow her pace. She just wiped the water from her eyes and kept going.

When lightning lit up the park in front of her, she raised her camera and snapped two more photos before venturing farther down the trail. The carousel was just ahead.

The thunder was so loud it almost knocked her off of her feet.

She stopped abruptly as another jagged streak of lightning hit the carousel, illuminating the area around it. Captured in the glaringly bright light were a man and a woman engaged in a struggle.

The man raised his hand, something metal glinting between his fingers. A knife?

The woman screamed.

Alicia took a step forward, but the light disappeared and everything was dark again. She juggled her phone, trying to turn on the flashlight so she could see where to go.

Another boom of thunder.

Another flash of lightning.

She saw more dancing shadows. Then heard a long, penetrating scream. Closer now. The woman seemed to be running toward her.

She needed to help her. She moved down the

path, stumbling over some rocks, and then the lightning came again. The tree next to her exploded from the strike. A heavy branch flew through the air, knocking her flat on the ground. She hit her head on a rock, feeling a flash of pain that threatened to take her under.

She battled against the feeling, knowing she had to get away from the fire that was crackling around her.

Where the hell was the rain now?

It was still coming down but not enough to smother the fire.

She got to her feet, ruthlessly fighting her way through the flaming branches.

Finally, the skies opened up, and the rain poured down, putting out the fire and allowing her to get free.

She grabbed her backpack from under a branch and moved down the trail.

Using her flashlight again, she walked toward the carousel, her tension increasing with each step, but there was no one around. No man, no woman, no knife, no struggle. What the hell had happened? Where had they gone?

She looked around in bewilderment. It had only been a few minutes since she'd seen them—hadn't it? Or had she lost consciousness when the tree had knocked her down?

She didn't think so, but her mind felt hazy and her head ached.

Despite the fuzzy feeling, she couldn't forget the image of the tall man towering over the smaller woman. She could still hear the woman's scream of terror in her head.

She turned slowly around, seeing nothing of significance in the shadowy surroundings. Then something in the dirt brought her gaze to the ground. She squatted down and picked up a shiny, rectangular military ID tag.

Her stomach turned over. She had a tag just like this in her jewelry box at home, the tag that had belonged to her father.

But it wasn't her father's name on this tag; it was a woman's name: Liliana Valdez, United States Navy, blood type O positive, religion Catholic. Her birth date indicated that she was twenty-eight.

The name didn't mean anything to Alicia, but she still felt an odd connection to the woman who'd lost it. Had it been the woman she'd seen fighting for her life? Had that woman been wearing a uniform?

She couldn't remember. She had the sense that the woman had worn a long, dark coat, but the details escaped her. Maybe she'd caught them on film. That thought took her to her feet.

She needed to get home and develop the photographs. She walked quickly back to the parking lot, pausing for just a moment to get a few more shots of the lightning now streaking across the Miami skyline.

Then she got into her car and sped toward the causeway, hoping she hadn't waited too long to cross before the storm surge made the bridge impassable.

When she reached the bridge, water was splashing over the rail, but she made it back to Miami without incident. She felt relieved to be in the city, but the pain in her temple reminded her of what she'd seen by the carousel. Who were those people? Had something terrible happened? Had she been a witness to . . . what?

Alicia's gaze dropped to the ID tag sitting on her console—to the name Liliana Valdez. She needed to find Liliana; not just to return her tag but also to make sure she was all right, that she was still alive.

Alicia lived in the Wynwood Art District, a neighborhood just north of downtown Miami and known for its art galleries, boutiques and charming cafés. She lived on the second floor of a two-story building, and the bottom floor housed the art gallery where she displayed her storm photographs.

The owner of Peterman Art Gallery, Eileen Peterman, had leased her the apartment a year earlier, and Alicia was happy to be close to the gallery and in a neighborhood filled with artists and designers. She'd always been more comfortable among creative people who thought outside of the box, colored beyond the lines, and who put their emotions on display, whether it be in a sculpture or a painting or a photograph. She'd never been able to trust anyone who hid their emotions. It always made her wonder what else they were hiding.

After entering her apartment, Alicia dropped her backpack on the floor, set her keys and the ID tag on the side table, and then took off her wet raincoat and hung it on a hook by the door. She kicked off her boots and walked into the bathroom to grab a towel.

After drying her face, she pulled out the band from her hair and ran the blow-dryer through the damp dark tangles of her unruly mass of dark brown waves. Her hair was thick and long, drifting past her shoulder blades, and it was a constant battle to straighten the rebellious curls, which had gotten more out of hand in the wind and the rain.

As she stared at her face in the mirror, she was a little surprised at the size of the bump on her throbbing forehead. It was turning a lovely shade of purple and black and definitely stood out against her unusually pale skin. A dark-eyed brunette with olive skin, she usually had a vibrant, exotic look about her, but today was not one of those days. What little makeup she'd put on earlier that day had washed away in the rain, and the pain of her aching head injury had put strained lines around her eyes.

She set down the dryer, grabbed some ibuprofen from the medicine cabinet, took two capsules, and told herself she'd feel a lot better in about thirty minutes. Then she walked back to the living room.

She picked up Liliana's ID tag and took it over to the kitchen table. Opening her laptop computer, she typed in Liliana's name, age, and birth date. The Valdez surname would be common in Miami, a city made up of thousands of Cuban and Puerto Rican immigrants, so she was expecting her search to be complicated and long.

Surprisingly, it was neither.

The headline of the first article jumped off the page: *JAG attorney missing in Miami.*

As she read through the news story, she discovered that Liliana Valdez, a Navy lieutenant and attorney with the Judge Advocate General, had gone missing while visiting Miami in late July for the wedding of her sister. She'd last been seen in the parking lot outside of Paladar, a popular Cuban restaurant in Little Havana. The vehicle she'd been driving had been recovered from the parking lot, but there was no sign of a struggle or any other clues to her whereabouts.

Alicia let out a breath and sat back on the couch, staring out the window where rain now streamed against the panes.

Liliana Valdez had disappeared two months ago, and no one had seen her since.

Alicia picked up the ID tag, still a little damp and gritty with dirt, and ran her fingers over Liliana's name, feeling the same sense of connection she'd felt earlier.

She had a clue to a missing woman. She needed to take it to the police.

Jumping to her feet, she paused, struck by the thought that she might have more than one clue. Retrieving her camera, she took it into the walk-in closet off her bedroom that she'd turned into her personal darkroom.

Unfortunately, as the pictures developed, Alicia's enthusiasm began to fade.

The couple she'd seen by the carousel did not appear in any of the shots. The lightning was spectacular, but it was so close, so bright, it was impossible to see anything but shadows beyond the light, certainly nothing that clearly defined a person, which meant she had no other clue besides the military tag. Still, it was something. Hopefully, it would be enough to help find the missing woman.

TWO

It was after nine o'clock when Alicia sat down in a hard chair next to the desk of Detective Ron Kellerman of the Miami-Dade Police Department, Criminal Investigations Unit. The detective was a middle-aged, balding man with a few extra pounds around the gut. He'd been called away from his Friday night plans, and during the past hour he'd asked her many of the same questions two and three times. She was beginning to feel like she was more of a suspect than a witness.

"Let me get this straight," he said. "You were shooting storm photographs when you saw two people fighting by the carousel. Lightning hit the tree next to you and a branch knocked you on the ground. During that time, the couple disappeared. Is that right?"

She sighed. "Yes, yes, yes. How many times are you going to ask me the same questions?"

"As many times as it takes to get every detail correct." He gave her a sharp look. "How's your head?"

"I'm fine. I just want to help find Liliana."

His brows drew together, a speculative look in his eyes. "You say her name as if you know her."

For some odd reason, she felt like she didknow Liliana, but she wasn't about to try to explain

20

that odd feeling to this cynical and suspicious police detective. "No, I never heard of her before tonight. I looked her name up on the Internet when I got back from the park. When I realized she was a missing person, I thought I might have found an important clue to her disappearance."

"You said you were in the park between five and six. It's nine. What took you so long to come down here?"

"I wanted to develop the film I'd taken to see if I'd captured the fight. Unfortunately, I had not."

"Did you bring the photographs with you?"

"No. They didn't reveal anything, so I didn't think they were important."

He glanced down at the paper where he'd jotted down notes during their interview. "The man was wearing a hood and the woman had a long, dark coat. Is that correct?"

"I think so." She frowned, wishing she could provide a better description.

"Did you get a feel for size, weight, hair color?"

"The man was taller than the woman by at least six inches. That's all I could see."

"Were there any words spoken between them?"

"Not that I could hear."

"Did they see you?"

She hesitated, surprised by a new question. "I don't think so." Worry followed her answer. Had they seen her? She really didn't know what had happened in those few minutes when she'd been knocked off her feet. "Do you have any suspects? Can you tell me what's going on with the investigation?"

"I'm afraid I can't disclose details of an ongoing investigation. Thanks for coming in. We'll take it from here."

She frowned, wanting a lot more information than he was willing to give her. "Do you think the tag will help you?"

"I hope so. It's the first clue we've had in two months. We'll get a search party out to the park as soon as we can." He rose to his feet. "Have you spoken to anyone else about the tag or what you saw in the park?"

"No," she said, standing up.

"Not anyone at the *Chronicle*?"

"No. Why?"

"I'd like to release the information to the press without using your name—for your own protection."

A chill ran down her spine at his words. "Am I in danger?"

"I don't think so, but we don't know who we're dealing with, and one woman has already disappeared." He handed her his card. "Call me if you remember anything, or if you have any concerns."

"Thanks. You know, you're scaring me a little."

"Better to be scared and more cautious is what I always tell my daughters."

It's what her mother had always told her, but she'd never listened. Like her dad, she had a tendency to be more courageous and less careful than she should be, more determined to live her life than to protect her life. Maybe she should think about changing that . . .

The sixteenth floor of a building under construction was a dangerous place to be at night, especially when there were no walls, no windows and a storm with high winds and rain blowing across downtown Miami, but Michael Cordero walked off the elevator of what would one day be the Barkley Center Office Building with not a thought to the potential hazards.

As a project manager for Jansen Real Estate Developments, he'd become accustomed to walking through tall buildings in every stage of their development, and many of those buildings soared high into the sky. His grandfather William Jansen had built a company as big and as huge as his dreams, and his properties always reflected that same sense of grandeur.

The Barkley Building, with its decorative scalloped balconies and floor-to-ceiling windows, would be the cornerstone of a new outdoor mall that would encompass three city blocks and would eventually house a luxury hotel, convention space, upscale condos, restaurants, and retailers, all within view of the Atlantic Ocean. It would take two years to finish, but it would change the city of Miami forever.

Miami. He sighed as he looked out at the city where he'd been born, the city where he'd gotten into trouble—not once, but twice.

He should have known better than to come back. But it had been eight years since he'd been home for more than a weekend, so when the project had come up, he'd decided to take over the management for at least the first phase of the project. His grandfather had told him it was a bad idea. He'd said you can't go home again, and even if you can, you shouldn't.

He really should have listened to his grand-father, because three weeks after he'd arrived, all hell had broken loose. Not with the project. The construction of phase one was on budget and on time. His professional life was in sync, but his personal life was a mess.

All because of Liliana.

A gust of wind sent a chill down his spine. He'd felt restless all day, and the storm that had just ripped through the city had felt like an extension of his unsettled emotions.

During the daytime, he could work his thoughts away, but at night they always came back. With those thoughts came the guilt, the vicious circle of unanswered questions.

He'd tried to exercise his thoughts away, but the five-mile run he'd taken in the wind and the rain had done little to ease his tension, so he'd come here—to this tall, half-finished building that he hoped would open up his mind and ease his tension.

Drawing in several long, deep breaths, he tried to get Liliana out of his mind, but since she'd disappeared, her image seemed to permanently reside there. Every time he saw her in his head, her dark brown eyes pleaded with him to find her, to save her. But he didn't know where the hell| she was.

He hadn't actually seen her in person in eight years—since that one and only weekend trip home after his graduation from NYU. They'd texted and emailed since then, but not on a regular basis. Their childhood friendship had been left behind a very long time ago. Which was why it was so strange that she'd sent him a dozen texts the day she'd disappeared, telling him that she needed to see him, and he needed to say yes.

He had said yes, but he'd been late getting to the restaurant—twenty minutes late. In that time, Liliana had gotten out of her car in the parking lot of his father's restaurant and vanished.

The police had been all over him after her disappearance, asking him dozens of times about the nature of their relationship, what she wanted to talk to him about, why she'd been so determined to see him, why he'd been late—everything. He'd had no answers that satisfied the police or even himself. He didn't know why Liliana had asked to see him after so many years apart, why her texts had felt urgent and important.

He was thirty years old now, and Liliana was twenty-eight. A lifetime had passed since they'd run in and out of each other's houses in the neighborhood known as Little Havana. He'd left Miami when he was fifteen and Liliana had joined the Navy after high school so she could get a college education and eventually a law degree. Their lives had gone in completely different directions.

He didn't want to lose hope, but it had been two months, and the trail had been cold from the start, except for the trail that led to him. That was one the police kept going down. But no matter how many times they questioned him, his story wouldn't change, because there was no story, only the truth.

A sudden clanging of the elevator brought his head around, and he was startled to see a uniformed police officer step out. His tension dissipated as the officer walked forward, the flashlight from his phone illuminating his features.

"Diego," he murmured, seeing the familiar brown eyes of one of the few friends he had left in Miami.

He and Diego had run with the same bad crowd in middle school and gotten into a lot of trouble together. Michael had been forced to change his life when his grandfather had yanked him out of Miami and sent him to boarding school.

Diego had straightened out his life by becoming a police officer.

While Michael appreciated that Diego was now on the right side of the law, Diego's job was starting to put a dent in their renewed friendship.

Diego stopped a few feet away from him. He stood about five foot ten, and had a square, stocky build that had made him a really good linebacker back in the day.

"What are you doing here, Diego?"

"I was going to ask you the same question. I stopped by your apartment and your office. I should have figured you'd be up here. You always did like to get—high." He laughed at his own joke. "I'm talking about your love of heights, of course."

"Of course," he said dryly. "Why are you looking for me?"

At his question, the humor in Diego's eyes vanished. "I need to ask you a question. Where were you earlier tonight?"

His gut tightened. "Are you asking as a cop or as a friend?"

"Both."

"Something has happened." He saw the truth in Diego's eyes. "What?"

"Liliana's military ID tag was found."

His heart thudded against his chest. "Where?"

"First, you need to tell me where you were tonight, why you're soaking wet." Diego's gaze ran up and down his wet clothes.

"I went for a run after work. It's been raining."

"What time did you leave your office?"

"Around four. We closed up early because of the storm. I did some work at home, then went out when the weather improved."

"Anyone see you on your run or at your apartment complex?"

Every question made his nerves tighten. "I saw my neighbor in the elevator, Mrs. Spidowski from 12B. You can talk to her if you want. Now are you going to tell me where Liliana's ID was found?"

"Virginia Key Park."

He was more than a little surprised with Diego's answer. "That's nowhere close to any place we've been looking."

"I know. A woman came down to the station tonight. She told Detective Kellerman that she'd seen a man and a woman struggling by the carousel. When she went to investigate, she found the military tag with Liliana's name on it."

Adrenaline and hope shot through his system at Diego's words. "So Liliana is alive?"

"Unfortunately, the witness didn't get a good look at the woman. To make matters worse, she somehow got injured in the park and has a significant bump on her head. Kellerman isn't entirely convinced the witness saw anything more than shadows in the wind, but she did bring in the tag. That part is for sure." Diego sighed. "You know what I'm going to ask next—where did you run?"

"Nowhere near the park." He ran a hand through his wet hair, unable to believe that he was still a suspect. "If your department keeps looking at me, you're never going to find Liliana, because I didn't take her, and I don't know where she is."

"I believe you, Michael, but I know you. The detectives don't. And you were the last person to speak to Liliana."

"I didn't speak to her. We texted. So what happens next? Should I expect a visit from Kellerman?"

"Probably. He already spoke to the Valdez family, and he's notified the press of the new development. He wants to throw a wide net and see if anyone near the park today might have seen Liliana."

"I want to go to the park."

"So do I. Unfortunately, the causeway is closed for several more hours, but police on the island have already gone through the park. They didn't find anyone. We'll send out more officers and search dogs in the morning. I expect the family will be out there as well."

"God, I hope she's alive," he said, feeling a tiny seed of hope.

"Me, too." Diego paused. "You know I'm just trying to be a good friend and a good cop, Michael."

"Where I'm concerned, I'm not sure you can be both, but I appreciate the effort. You're one of the few people willing to give me the benefit of the doubt."

"A lot of people believe in you."

"You don't have to bullshit me, Diego. We both know that I'm the only suspect."

"Person of interest."

Michael shrugged. "Call it what you want."

"So how are things going around here? It looks like you're making progress."

"First phase should be done by Christmas."

"When does the next phase begin?"

"Sometime in January. That part of the project will run about eighteen months."

"You're going to be here awhile."

"I'm not planning on staying past Christmas. I need to get back to New York. I don't belong here. I never did. I don't know why I came back."

"You missed me," Diego said with a grin.

"I'd forgotten all about you."

"Ouch."

He smiled. Diego had always had a way of making him laugh, take life a little less seriously.

"How are things going with your dad?" Diego asked.

"Nowhere. Since Liliana disappeared, my dad

has been caught in the middle, and let's be honest, he's closer to Liliana's family than he is to me. Hell, Liliana's brother Juan works at my dad's restaurant. He's the son my father never had."

"It will get better. When we find Liliana, things will return to normal."

"I hope so. The tag is the first solid clue we've gotten. I just hope it leads somewhere."

"Me, too. Let me buy you a beer," Diego said.

He lifted an eyebrow. "You buy me a drink, and your cop buddies will be all over your ass."

"No. They'll think I'm playing you for information," Diego said with a wry smile.

Diego was teasing, but for a split second Michael wondered if Diego hadn't been sent to have this conversation as a *friend*.

"I'll pass on the beer tonight. Another time. Let's get out of here." The sky opened up with torrential rain as they ran to the elevator. The storm definitely wasn't over yet.

THREE

A licia returned home from the police station a little after ten. Since she'd missed dinner, she made tea and toast and sat down at the kitchen table to eat. Turning on her computer, she opened the search engine. She wanted to know more about the case she'd stumbled into and if the police weren't willing to give her more information, she'd find it for herself.

She'd only read through the first two articles on the subject earlier. Now, she intended to see what the other news reports had to say. There had definitely been quite a bit of coverage.

Liliana Valdez had been born in Miami, the second oldest of four children. Her father was a teacher; her mother was a homemaker. The Valdez family was loved and respected in their community, and they'd received an outpouring of support with hundreds of people showing up to search the area where Liliana had last been seen— the parking lot of a restaurant in Little Havana.

Over the weeks, the search had spread across Miami and reached other more remote parts of Florida, but nothing had come from any of the tips, and the trail had quickly gone cold. Part of the problem lay in the fact that while Liliana had grown up in Miami, she'd been living in Corpus Christi, Texas for the last three years.

At the mention of Corpus Christi, Alicia's spine straightened and a tingle shot through her body. Her family had moved to Corpus Christi when she was twelve years old. She'd left Texas four years ago, which was a year before Liliana moved there, but it was still another odd connection between them.

Accompanying that article was a recent photograph of Liliana in military attire, her black hair pulled back in a bun. She was a beautiful woman with strong cheekbones and serious brown eyes.

As Alicia stared into Liliana's eyes, she felt like the woman was sending her a plea to help find her. That was silly, of course, but Alicia couldn't shake the feeling that her part in this was not over yet. She needed to help, but how?

Reading through several more articles, she began to realize that there might not be any more information to find.

Liliana had come back to town for her sister's wedding. She'd been in Miami three days before she vanished. Her job, her friends, her life were in a state thousands of miles away.

There was only one person of interest in the case, an old friend of Liliana's by the name of Michael Cordero. The news articles stressed that the young, successful, wealthy real-estate developer was only being questioned because he'd had recent contact with Liliana, but it was clear in the subtext that he was under suspicion, despite the fact that he'd put up a $25,000 reward for information leading to Liliana's whereabouts.

There was one grainy photo of Michael Cordero, and Alicia stared at it for a long moment. The man was attractive, with dark hair and light eyes. But he didn't look very friendly or warm. There was a cool aloofness to his photograph, shadows in his gaze that were unreadable.

Had this been the man she'd seen in the park with Liliana?

She wished she could know for sure, but her brain wouldn't cooperate by producing a clearer and more detailed memory. In fact, her headache was getting worse by the minute. Her adrenaline rush had passed, and she was now exhausted and in pain.

Closing the computer, she headed for bed, hoping she'd be able to think more clearly in the morning.

Unfortunately, despite her exhaustion, sleep did not come quickly. Instead, images of Michael Cordero and Liliana Valdez ran around in her head. As she wrestled with sleep, she became less and less sure of what she'd witnessed in the park. She didn't want to doubt herself, but she really wished she'd been able to capture the moment on film. Then she'd have physical proof to back up her memories.

She gave up on sleep at five and took a long shower, where her thoughts continued to wander. By the time she'd dressed and drank her first cup of coffee, she knew what she needed to do—return to the scene of the crime.

She would go back to the park, walk around, see what she remembered and if there were any other clues she'd missed. She wanted to get there before too many people trampled through the area, although the police had no doubt already searched the ground around the carousel.

It was probably pointless to go back, but she couldn't stop herself from grabbing her keys and heading out the door.

It was a little after six and still very dark when she reached the causeway, which thankfully had reopened. As she drove toward the park, she turned on the radio, coming in at the end of a weather report. Forecasters were predicting a return of Miami's usual bright sunshine by midday.

She was actually looking forward to the sun. While stormy weather was her passion, today she felt like she needed the sun to shake the feeling that something bad had either happened or was about to happen.

When she reached the park, she found the parking area as empty as she'd last seen it. She wondered why the area wasn't filled with cops and search dogs. Maybe they were waiting for the sun to come up.

Using the flashlight on her phone to light the path, she walked toward the carousel, her nerves tightening with each step, and she couldn't help taking a look over her shoulder every now and then.

She told herself there was no one following her, but she had a prickly sensation at the back of her neck that she couldn't shake loose.

When she reached the spot where she'd found the ID, she squatted down and looked at the ground more closely. The dirt had turned to a thick mud and the grass was soaking wet. There were no footprints, no other clues.

With a sigh, she got to her feet, her tension increasing when she heard a rustle in the nearby bushes. She was expecting to see an animal, but the man dressed in jeans and a dark hooded sweatshirt paralyzed her with shock and fear.

He jerked when he saw her, as if he hadn't been expecting to see her, either. But that didn't make her feel any better when he came toward her.

She told herself to run. While dawn was beginning to lighten the sky, it was still very dark and she was acutely aware of the fact that there was no one else in the park. But the man stood between her and the parking lot, and he was so close now, she doubted she could dash past him.

Maybe he was a cop, she thought hopefully, but his clothes didn't seem to support that theory. He was tall and moved purposefully and confidently—a man who was used to getting what he wanted, she thought.

She pulled out her phone, punched in 911, her finger hovering over the keypad as she said, "That's close enough. What do you want?"

He stopped abruptly, his gaze narrowing. "I'm not going to hurt you."

"What are you doing here? The park is closed."

"I'm looking for my friend—Liliana Valdez. Someone found her military ID tag here last night." His gaze bored into hers. "Was that you?"

"Who told you about the tag?" Maybe he wasn't dangerous if he had information that she'd given to the police. On the other hand, he could have been the man in the park last night and had come back to cover his tracks. He was wearing a hood just like the man she'd seen, but as she searched for another defining characteristic, she came up empty.

"I have to go," she said abruptly.

"Hold on. You don't have anything to fear from me."

"If I did, I doubt you would tell me."

"Good point, but it's the truth. I heard about the tag from a police officer. As soon as the causeway opened, I came here to see if there was anything else to be found." He paused, his gaze meeting hers. "Is that why you're here before dawn? To look for a clue you might have missed? You're the one who found the tag, aren't you?"

There didn't seem to be much point to lying. "Yes. I couldn't sleep, thinking about what I'd seen, so I came back."

"What exactly did you see?" he asked, a sharper tone in his voice now. "I thought you just found the tag."

"And I thought you said the police filled you in."

"They told me the witness had a head injury and couldn't remember details." His gaze raked her face. "What happened to you?"

"Lightning struck the tree next to me and the branches came down on my head, but that was after I saw a couple struggling over what appeared to be a knife."

He stiffened at her words. "I didn't realize there was a weapon."

"I wasn't close enough to know for sure."

"Where were they standing?"

"Right here."

"And you? Where were you when you saw them?"

She pointed to the path through the trees fifty yards away. "I was up there. I was coming back from the beach."

"Will you show me?"

It was such a simple request. Yet, the idea of going into the dark trees with this man seemed like a bad idea. She preferred this clearing, where the early morning light was beginning to get stronger. "There's nothing to see. Maybe we should wait for the police. I'm sure they'll be here soon."

"If that's what you want, but I have to tell you that if I were going to hurt you, I could have done it already. You don't appear to have a weapon, and I don't think anyone knows you're out here."

She stared back at him, seeing determination in his eyes but not danger. Still, she needed to know more about him before she took another step. "You said you're old friends with the missing woman?"

"Yes. We grew up together. Liliana lived across the street. I don't remember a time when I didn't know her. Her brother Juan and I were the same age; Liliana was two years younger, but she was always around. Over time, I found I had more in common with her than with Juan. She was an amazing girl."

There was a heavy note in his voice now, as if he didn't think his friend could still be alive.

"Was?" she asked gently.

"Is," he immediately corrected. "The last two months have been difficult. I—we've been trying to keep hope alive, but as the days pass . . ." His voice trailed away. "It's rough."

Even in the shadows, she could see the pain in his expression. He seemed genuine and honest. She wanted to believe he was a friend and not an enemy. "Tell me something about her that only you would know, that wouldn't have been in the papers or the police reports," she said.

"Like what?"

"Something personal."

He thought about her request. "I don't know. There are probably lots of things about her that weren't in the papers."

"So give me one."

"Well, she almost got married when she was seventeen—she was so desperate to get out of the neighborhood. I don't think her parents even knew that she was that serious about the older guy she was dating. Luckily, she called me first, and I talked her out of it. Instead of running away, she joined the Navy, and she made a good life for herself as a military lawyer."

"Who did she almost marry?"

"Brad Harte. Did I pass the test?"

"You do seem to know her, although I have no way of knowing if you're lying to me."

"You're trying to figure out whether you can trust me—I get it. Maybe I'll just go down the path on my own. You were standing where a tree came down, right? That shouldn't be difficult to find."

"I'll show you," she said impulsively. They'd been alone for the past ten minutes. If he'd wanted to hurt her, he would have already made a move. She took him down the path, not stopping until she reached the tree that was sprawled across the trail. "I'd been at the beach, but I thought the gold rods on the carousel might attract the lightning, so I came here, and I was right. It was an incredible show of light. Flash after flash—I was shooting pictures like crazy. In one of the bright moments, I saw the fight between a man and a woman. I heard the woman scream and then the tree next to me was hit by lightning and the falling branches knocked me down. There was fire all around me. It took me a few minutes to get free. By the time I got down to the carousel, the people were gone."

"How long was it between the time you saw them fighting and when you reached the carousel?"

"Five minutes or so."

"Or so? You don't know, do you?"

"I was a little dazed, but it wasn't very long."

"What about the pictures you were taking? Do they show what you saw?"

"No. The lightning washed everything else out. All I could see were shadows."

He nodded, his gaze grim. "What happened next?"

"I went to where they were standing, and I found the tag in the dirt. After I got home, I looked up Liliana's name on the computer. When I realized she was a missing person, I developed the film to see if I had captured the scene, then I went straight to the police. I told the detective on the case everything I just told you. They assured me someone would start looking for her right away. I must admit it's a little disappointing not to see anyone here now."

"The police here on the island searched the park last night, but there will be another search this morning."

"Good. I hope the tag will help to find her."

"It certainly gives the detectives a new lead to follow, and God knows they've needed one. It's been the longest two months of my life. You have no idea what it's like to live through something like this. The uncertainty kills you."

"I have an idea." Reading about the search for Liliana had triggered painful memories of the night her father's plane had gone down and the days of questions and worry that had followed.

"You lost someone?"

"I did—a long time ago. He's partly the reason I came back here this morning. I know what it's like to wait for answers, and I haven't been able to get Liliana out of my mind. I read everything I could find about the case last night. I watched a video of her parents pleading for her safe return. I saw her sister crying and her friends with sad hope in their eyes. If I can help bring her home, I have to try. I have to find a way to get her scream out of my head."

His face paled at her words. "Tell me about the man you saw. What did he look like?"

"He was tall. His clothes were dark. He wore a jacket or a sweatshirt with a hood."

His hand moved to the strings of his hooded sweatshirt. "The sweatshirt. That's why you jumped when you saw me."

"I thought for a moment . . ."

"It wasn't me. I wasn't here last night. I would never ever hurt Liliana. She was a good friend to me at a time when I really needed one. I don't know what happened to her, but I intend to find out." He stopped talking, his gaze turning down the path.

She was happy to see police gathering by the carousel, some of them with dogs. "It looks like the search party has arrived." She felt relieved that she was no longer alone with this man. A part of her wanted to trust him. Another part of her was afraid. She'd never had such an intense reaction to a stranger. She blamed it on the circumstances, the spooky early morning light, the events of the night before, the bump on her head; anything that would explain why her stomach was churning and her palms were sweaty.

"We should talk to them," she said.

"Before you go—you may hear things about me, but they're not true."

"What do you mean? What would I hear?" It suddenly occurred to her that she'd never asked him his name. "Who are you?"

"Michael Cordero."

A shiver ran down her spine. "You were the last person Liliana texted and—"

"A person of interest." He gave her a direct look. "Which means I want to find Liliana more than anyone else. Not just to make sure she's all right, but—"

"To also clear your name."

"Yes."

Now she knew why he'd come to the park before daybreak, why he seemed so intent on persuading her that he was innocent. What she didn't know was how she felt about his story. There was a chance Michael Cordero was innocent, but there was also a chance he was a really good liar.

She didn't believe him, Michael thought as he stood in the shadows of the trees watching Alicia Monroe talk to the police. He'd learned her name when Detective Kellerman had quizzed her on her presence in the park. That was, of course, after the detective had asked him the very same question, but with a lot more hostility.

During his exchange with Kellerman, Alicia had watched him with a sharp, speculative gaze. He'd thought he'd won her trust earlier, but it was clear that the detective's suspicions were now coloring her thinking.

He probably shouldn't have come to the park and put himself in yet another vulnerable position, but he hadn't been able to stay away, and in truth, he didn't give a shit what Detective Kellerman thought of him.

Changing the detective's mind wasn't important. Finding Liliana was all that mattered. Then the truth would come out—whatever that was.

He wanted to believe that Liliana was alive after what Alicia had told him she'd seen the night before. But the ferocity of the storm, the huge tree that had knocked Alicia to the ground, and even the doubt in Alicia's own voice gave him pause. While she'd obviously found the tag, and she seemed quite certain about the rest of her story, there was a gap in time when Alicia had been on the ground and the couple had disappeared.

The fact that Liliana hadn't already been found was also disturbing. Had they come so close only to be thwarted again?

Crossing his arms in front of his chest, he blew out a breath of frustration.

He hated being out of control, not knowing what would happen next, feeling helpless to make a change. Those feelings reminded him of his childhood when life had been chaotic, unpredictable, and lonely. When he'd left Miami at fifteen, he'd left those emotions behind him. He'd become the kind of person who set goals and achieved them, who knew what he wanted and went after it.

He was good at fixing things. He was a builder. He put things together. He executed a vision every day of the week, but he couldn't fix the problem with Liliana. He couldn't find her. He couldn't bring her home, and it was driving him mad.

Hopefully, today's search would yield something new, but the fact that there was no sign of Liliana didn't bode well for that outcome. Still, they had something new to go on—because of Alicia.

His gaze moved back to the woman who had recharged the investigation.

Now that the sun had come up, he could see her more clearly. She was young, mid-twenties, he thought, slender and fit in her jeans and jacket. She was pretty, too, in a natural, not-really-trying kind of way. Her dark hair was pulled back in a thick ponytail that hung halfway down her back, and her brown eyes were wide and framed with long black lashes. While the bump on her forehead and the shadows under her eyes made her look tired and beat-up, there was a fighting spirit, a curiosity, a determination that came through in her gaze and in her actions.

How many random witnesses came back to the scene of a crime to look for more clues? And she hadn't even waited for daylight. She'd come to the park before dawn.

But he also had to ask himself why she was so interested in an unsolved mystery. She didn't know Liliana, and she'd already turned in the military ID, which would make her eligible for the reward, so the money couldn't be driving her.

Maybe it was guilt. She'd seen a woman being attacked, and she hadn't been able to help her. Now she wanted to find that woman and make it right. It made sense, but he still came back to his original question: how many witnesses would return to the scene of the crime to help out a stranger?

Probably very few.

Alicia shifted her gaze from the police detective to him, and even from a distance he could read the wary suspicion in her eyes. No doubt Kellerman had warned her away from him. He wondered if Alicia would listen.

He got his answer a moment later when Alicia said something to the police detective and then started walking toward him.

She had her back to Kellerman, so she didn't see the police detective watching her, but Michael was acutely aware of Kellerman's gaze following her steps, those steps leading straight to him. He had a feeling Alicia's action was only going to add another complication to his life, but right now he was more interested in finding out if Kellerman had shared any information with her.

"What did the detective have to say?" he asked as she stopped in front of him.

"He had more questions than answers. He wanted to know if I'd met you before this morning. I said no, but I'm not sure he believed me, which was strange. Why would I lie?"

"He's suspicious of everyone, especially if they're seen with me."

"He told me not to trust you."

"I'm not surprised," he said evenly, but her words still burned through his soul. He'd straightened out his life a long time ago, and he wasn't used to people doubting his actions or his intentions.

"I know you and Liliana exchanged texts on the day she disappeared, that she was supposed to meet you, but that doesn't explain why the detective is so suspicious of you."

"He has no other leads. And he's never been a fan of mine."

Her eyebrow lifted in surprise. "What do you mean?"

"A long time ago, when I was a teenager, I had a few run-ins with the police, with Kellerman in particular."

"Like what?"

"Vandalism, theft," he said with a shrug. "I was fifteen and running with a bad crowd. Kellerman was a beat cop back then. He still thinks of me as that punk kid, but I'm not that person anymore. Hopefully, this new clue will take the investigation toward whoever is responsible for Liliana's disappearance. That isn't me."

"Good to know." She paused, looking back toward the police. "They're getting ready to search the park. I offered to help, but the detective suggested I stay out of it. I don't know why. It's as if he suddenly doesn't trust me."

"Don't take it personally."

"It felt personal." She looked back at him. "I can't forget what I saw last night. That woman needed help, and I was the only one around, but I didn't get to her in time."

He wished Alicia had gotten to Liliana, too, but they couldn't change what had happened. "Well, you found her tag. That's something. You got the police out here. They'll search every inch of this park."

"I still wish I could do more."

He thought about her words for a moment. Like Alicia, he'd been sidelined, and he was feeling just as frustrated as she was. "Maybe you can help me. I'd like to see the pictures you took yesterday."

"There's nothing on them. I already told you that."

"Could I see them anyway? Just in case you missed something."

"I didn't."

"Then what's the harm in showing me the photos?"

She hesitated, her gaze moving once again toward the police and then back to him. "I'm not sure I should. You're a suspect."

"But I'm not guilty. If you researched the case last night, I'm sure you learned some things about me. What did you find out?"

She gave him a long assessing look, and then said, "You left Miami when you were a teenager, went to prep school and have a master's degree from NYU. Since college, you've been working in real-estate development with your grandfather William Jansen, who is a very rich and successful man."

It was odd to hear his life encapsulated in such a succinct way, but she'd at least saved him the trouble of a lengthy explanation. "Do I sound like a guy who would kidnap a girl I used to share peanut butter and jelly sandwiches with?"

"Appearances can be deceiving."

"I just want to look at your photographs, Alicia. It will take a few minutes of your time. You said you wanted to help."

It had been awhile since a woman had been reluctant to spend five minutes with him. In fact, he couldn't remember when it had ever happened. But Alicia was obviously still uncertain about him, and he couldn't blame her. He'd had two months to try to wrap his head around this horrible situation, and he hadn't been successful. Alicia had had less than twenty-four hours.

"All right." She glanced down at her watch. "It's almost eight. Why don't I meet you at Il Piccolo Café on Bryant Street around ten? I need to go home and take a shower and pull myself together."

"I'll be there."

"So will I."

After Alicia left, Michael turned his attention back to the police officers. There were almost two dozen men and women gathered by the carousel now; some from the police department, others from the park service. They were about to start another search of the park, this time using dogs to try to pick up Liliana's scent.

He turned his head as a man called out his name. The voice belonged to Juan Valdez, Liliana's older brother and someone he had once called a friend.

Juan was a tall, skinny man with long, dark hair pulled back in a short ponytail. He had on black sweatpants and a long-sleeve T-shirt. With his bloodshot eyes and unshaven beard, he appeared to have rolled out of bed a few minutes earlier. He looked exhausted and stressed, which was how everyone in the Valdez family had looked the past two months.

Next to Juan was Rico, Liliana's younger brother. Rico was as different from Juan as night was from day. While Juan was a hardworking chef who was creative and kind, Rico was a short-statured bulldog who was perpetually in between jobs and whose numerous scars represented his willingness to fight about anything.

He'd never been a fan of Rico's, even though Liliana had tried to tell him that Rico's cocky attitude just covered up a lot of insecurity. That

51

might be true, but he still knew an asshole when he saw one.

Behind the Valdez brothers, he could see the rest of the family coming in from the parking lot; Liliana's younger sister Isabel and Isabel's fiancé David, along with her parents and extended family of aunts, uncles and cousins.

"Have the police found anything, Michael?" Juan asked.

"Not as far as I know, but you might be able to get more information."

"I'll go," Rico said, shooting Michael a distrustful look. "I wouldn't believe anything this guy has to say."

"Did you go through the park?" Juan asked, as Rico headed toward Detective Kellerman.

"Briefly. I didn't see anyone. I'm sure the police won't leave any stone unturned."

"You're right. I want them to find her, but . . ." Juan's voice trailed away as he dug his hands into his pockets and stared at the shrubs all around them. "I can't imagine it will be the result we want."

"Yeah, I know." They both wanted Liliana to come walking out of the thick trees alive and well. "How are your parents doing?"

"They're hanging in there, more optimistic now that there's a lead. I don't think anyone slept last night after the detective called us." He paused. "Your father and Veronica are planning to help with the search today."

He wasn't surprised. His father and Liliana's father had been like brothers for years. "Good."

"I just don't know what Liliana would have been doing out here," Juan said. "We've wanted a new place to search for the last few months, but I never thought it would be this park, miles away from where she disappeared." He paused. "I can't understand why she didn't turn to me for help. I'm her big brother. I've always been there for her. Why did she text you? Why reach out to a man she hadn't seen in years? Why couldn't she talk to someone in her own family— if not to me, then to Rico or Isabel or Mama or Papa?"

"I don't know, Juan. Everyone assumes she had a problem to discuss with me, but she may have just really wanted to see me." If Liliana had had a problem, the only reason he could think of for her going outside the family was that the problem had to do with her family, but he couldn't point that out now, not with everyone's pain so raw.

"It looks like they're getting ready to start," Juan said. "Are you coming?"

"No. Detective Kellerman suggested I not be involved. I'd appreciate it if you'd let me know if they find anything."

Juan's gaze narrowed, as if Michael's words had just reminded him that he was still a suspect. "Of course."

As Juan went to join the search party, Michael headed to his car. He might not be able to search the park, but he could at least look at the photographs Alicia had taken. Maybe there was another miracle clue hiding somewhere in the shadows.

FOUR

Alicia sat at a window table in the Il Piccolo Café, sipping a latte and eating the last of a blueberry muffin just before ten. After leaving the park, she'd gone back to her apartment, showered and changed into white jeans and a rose-colored tank top under a thin white sweater. She'd also taken another look through the photographs, wanting to make sure she hadn't missed anything before she showed them to Michael Cordero.

Aside from the fact that she'd gotten some of the most spectacular lightning shots of her life, there were no other clues to the fight she'd witnessed. If the images hadn't continued to flash through her mind, she might have been able to believe it was all in her imagination, but the memories were relentless. It was as if her brain was telling her to pay attention, to see something she wasn't seeing.

Perhaps it would be good for Michael to look at the photographs. She'd stared at them so hard and so long, they were blurring in her mind. She needed an objective eye.

Thinking about Michael made her question why she'd agreed to meet with the only known suspect in the case. The police were suspicious of him. So why was she giving him the benefit of the doubt? Wasn't it possible he just wanted to see the photographs to confirm that he wasn't in them?

A shiver ran down her spine at that thought.

Michael had surprised her in the park, scared her a little with his hooded appearance, but as they'd spoken about Liliana, there had been so much pain in his voice that she just couldn't believe he was guilty of harming the woman he'd grown up with.

Did that make her highly intuitive—or a fool?

Whichever it was, she knew that one reason she'd agreed to meet with him was that she wanted more information. The detective had made it clear that her part in the investigation was over. Since they weren't interested in sharing information with her, she'd have to get it from another source.

She straightened as the café door opened, and Michael walked in.

He still wore jeans, but he'd traded in the hooded sweatshirt for a short-sleeved polo shirt. He'd also shaved and showered and seeing him in the light of day, her gut tightened for an entirely different reason than it had earlier.

The man was more than a little good-looking with his black hair, olive skin and light blue eyes that seemed to see straight through her. As his gaze met hers, nervous anticipation made her stomach flutter and her palms sweat. It had been a long time since she'd felt such an intense physical and emotional attraction to a man.

That was both a good and a bad thing. While she'd often lamented the fact that it was difficult to find a man she could really connect with, she didn't want to connect with *this* man in *this* situation.

Michael pulled out the chair opposite hers and sat down. "I wasn't sure you'd come."

"I said I would. Do you want to grab a coffee first?"

He glanced back at the counter where a long line had formed. "I'll wait. I'm more interested in looking at the photographs." His gaze moved to the large envelope on the table. "May I?"

"Yes." She pushed the envelope across the table.

As he opened it, he said, "I'm surprised the police didn't ask you for these."

"They did. I'm going to drop them off at the station later." She still had the negatives so she could print out additional copies for her display at the gallery. Some of the photos were definitely worth framing.

Michael pulled out the photos and began to look through them, his expression changing as he went through the stack.

He lifted his gaze to hers. There was a gleam of admiration in his eyes. "These are amazing, Alicia. You got so close to the lightning. I know you said it was right there, but I didn't imagine it like this. You could have been killed."

"I wasn't."

"But you took a big risk."

"Sometimes that's what it takes to make something incredible happen."

His gaze bored into hers and she saw what looked like understanding. "That's true. So this is your job? You chase lightning? I've heard of storm chasers, but I've never met one before. I have to say, I pictured some crazy-eyed guy in a van with a lot of weather equipment."

"I've been in a van like that with those crazy-eyed guys," she admitted. "But I chase storms on my own time. In my day job I'm a photojournalist with the *Miami Chronicle* where I spend most of my time taking photographs of ribbon cuttings, car accidents, fires and local community events."

"Interesting."

"Not really," she said with a little laugh. "But it pays the bills so I can do what I really want to do. Florida is a hotbed of lightning strikes. It's been a busy summer."

"I'll bet. You must be fearless to do what you do."

"Or crazy," she said lightly. "Many people have questioned my sanity. But while I do push the envelope, I also respect the power of the lightning. I know there is danger behind the magnificent beauty. I never forget that."

"When did you start chasing storms?"

"Eight or nine years ago."

"What got you started?"

She hesitated, not sure how the conversation had turned to her, but maybe her explanation would help him to understand why she sometimes risked her life. "My father was a pilot. About ten years ago, his plane went down in an electrical storm somewhere over the Gulf of Mexico."

"I'm sorry." Sympathy filled his gaze. "Before, at the park, you mentioned you'd lost someone close to you."

"That was my dad. What made the loss even worse was that neither his plane nor his body was recovered. Search parties went out several times to look for him without any luck. I know what it's like for someone to vanish in a second. I know what it feels like to live without answers to a loved one's disappearance. I was sixteen years old when my dad died. It's been ten years, and I still don't really know what happened to him, what he thought in those last moments, whether he knew he was going down, whether he survived for a few minutes or was killed on impact." She took in a shaky breath at the painful memories. "The questions have haunted me. I think that's why I feel so emotionally connected to Liliana. I haven't been able to find my dad, but maybe I can help find her."

"That makes sense."

"Good," she said with a smile. "It's nice to make sense once in a while. After my father died, my mother sent me to a shrink for almost a year. Unfortunately, therapy was not at all successful. She wanted me to talk about my feelings. All I wanted to talk about was lightning. Ever since then, when lightning strikes, I run toward it. There's something inside me that wants to understand it."

"What's to understand? It's a weather phenomenon. Certain forces cause lightning to happen. It's not a mystery."

"I know the science behind electrical storms, but I think there's more than science involved."

He raised an eyebrow. "Like what?"

"You wouldn't understand."

"Try me."

"Why? You came here to look at my photographs."

"I'm curious."

"Lightning is majestic. It's a heavenly show," she said with a wave of her hand.

He rested his forearms on the table as he gazed at her. "So it's a spiritual thing?"

"It's a lot of things."

It had been a long time since anyone had really asked her about her passion. Most men got bored, made a joke, or changed the subject when she started to ramble on about lightning.

Her obsession to chase storms had broken up more than one relationship, so she'd learned to keep her mouth shut, which is what she should have done now.

"What else?" he pressed. "I know there's more."

She didn't know how he knew, but of course he was right. She sipped her coffee, then set the cup down. "My father was born in southern Mexico, in the Yucatan. He grew up in a small village near the remains of ancient Mayan sites. His mother and grandmother raised him in the traditions of their ancestors. To my father's family, lightning ties the earth to the heavens, the living to the dead, the past to the present. My great-grandmother used to say that the lightning comes down from the sky to show you what you need to see."

Michael leaned forward in his seat, his expression a mix of skepticism and interest. It was actually a more positive response than she usually received. "I thought your father was a pilot. Surely, he had to understand weather in order to fly planes. That didn't change some of his mystical beliefs?"

She nodded. "He was always torn, not just about lightning, but about everything. He used to tell me that he'd lived his life in two parts. He was born in Mexico, but while his mom and her family were Mayan, his dad and his dad's family were American. My grandfather was an engineer. He was working in the Yucatan when he met my grandmother, so he was a man of science."

"Your grandmother's beliefs must have been a challenge for your grandfather."

"I'm sure they were, and it's possible that their marriage wouldn't have lasted, but my grandmother died very young. My dad was only ten when she passed. After that, my grandfather moved my dad back to the States. So my father had this early upbringing that was rather magical and then the rest of his childhood and life was about science. He joined the Navy, became a pilot, and had a very good career before he retired and flew charter jets. But even with all his knowledge of weather, the one thing that still amazed him was lightning. He would tell me stories about things he'd seen in the sky; blue dancing sprites, orange balls of fire. He got as close as anyone could get to a power unmatched in nature. His stories made me want to see what he saw."

"Why didn't you become a pilot?"

"Fair question. It never interested me. My brother Jake is a pilot. He, however, does not believe there's anything mystical about lightning."

"Interesting." Michael stared back at her in a thoughtful, speculative way.

"What are you really thinking?" she asked as the silence went on.

"Really?" he asked with a smile.

"Yes, I can see something going on in your eyes."

"To be honest, I was thinking that your father's story reminded me a little of myself. I think of my life in three parts: one with my mom, one without her, and then the life I lived after I left Miami. I'm also a mix of cultures—half-Cuban, half-Caucasian. My fair-haired, blue-eyed mother died when I was eight."

"I'm sorry," she said, understanding now where he got his striking blue eyes.

"I've always felt like I had one foot in each world, but I never fit perfectly well into either one."

"My dad used to say that, too." It was odd that her father's background ran parallel to Michael's. Besides the clash of cultures, they'd also both lost their mothers at an early age.

"You know what else struck me about your story?" he asked.

"The Navy connection?" she returned.

He nodded. "Your dad was in the Navy and so was Liliana."

"When I first saw her ID in the dirt, I was taken right back to my father. It's the one thing I still have of his."

Michael sat back in his seat. "I'm surprised that you're not afraid of lightning, considering what happened to your father."

"I know. But don't you feel something powerful and inexplicable when you look at these photographs?" She tapped her fingers on the

63

picture in front of him. "I actually felt the heat of this strike. And it was shocking in its intensity. The lightning calls to me. I don't know if it will always be that way, but right now I can't resist the call."

He stared down at the picture, then looked back at her. "I don't know if you're crazy, but I can say that I've never met anyone like you, Alicia."

She smiled. "Good. I like being one of a kind. And you can call me crazy. My father was nick-named *Lightning Man*. It made him laugh, but my mother hated to hear the locals call him that. He was a decorated fighter pilot before he retired. But hardly anyone remembered that when he started talking about dancing blue sprites in the sky. He became a joke, but he wasn't a joke, and I don't believe he made anything up."

"It sounds like he wasn't just a Navy hero; he was *your* hero."

"That's true. We were very close. I was the youngest of three kids, and my dad and I probably spent the most time together. Sometimes it feels like a lifetime ago, and sometimes it feels like just yesterday."

"Are you still close to your mother—your siblings?"

"No. They're all in Texas. I came to Miami four years ago because I needed to build a life somewhere new, and Florida has the highest number of lightning strikes. I figured I could do photojournalism anywhere, so why not here?"

"Texas?" he queried, his brows drawing together.

"Corpus Christi." As she said the words, shock flashed through his eyes. "I know. Liliana lives in Corpus Christi, Texas. It's another weird link between us. Sometimes I wonder if anything really happens by chance."

Michael frowned at her words, then lowered his gaze and flipped through the rest of her photographs without saying another word. She didn't know what he was thinking, but she was grateful to have a minute to gather her own thoughts.

"Where are the others?" Michael asked, slipping the photos back into the envelope.

"What are you talking about? There are no others. This is the roll I took in the park."

"You didn't shoot anything when you first got to the island, drove into the parking lot, got out of the car . . ."

She suddenly remembered the digital camera she'd used when she first arrived. "Oh my God."

"There is another roll, isn't there?"

"Not film, but I took a few shots on my digital camera when I got to the parking lot. I don't know why I didn't remember that before."

"Where's your camera?"

"At my apartment."

"Let's take a look," he said, jumping to his feet.

"Hold on," she said, rising more slowly. "Maybe I should just bring the camera here."

Disappointment tightened his lips. "You still think I'm going to hurt you?"

"I'm trying to be smart and cautious."

"You? The woman who runs toward lightning? I thought you were fearless. I also thought you wanted to help Liliana."

He had a point. She'd already gone this far with him, why was she holding back now? "Fine. I'll show you the pictures. I live just around the corner."

"Okay, good. You can trust me, Alicia."

"I'm counting on that."

FIVE

As they walked out of the café, Alicia was surprised by the blustery wind. The clouds had passed and the rain was gone, but the breeze was surprisingly strong and shockingly cool for late September. Miami was usually warm well into October and sometimes throughout the entire winter season.

Despite the weather, Bryant Street was packed with tourists enjoying the mix of cafés, art galleries, antiques shops and sidewalk stands of artists selling everything from jewelry to wood carvings and abstract metal sculptures. She loved the vibe of Bryant Street, and she was getting to know some of the local vendors, many of whom gave her a wave and a smile as she passed by.

"You're popular," Michael commented.

"Everyone is very friendly around here. And I love artists. It's inspiring to see people's dreams come to life, whether it's in a painting or a sculpture or a knitted sweater."

"You find knitted sweaters inspiring?" he asked doubtfully.

"They can be," she said with a smile. "Anyway, I like it here."

"It's charming. I didn't realize so many of the

warehouses had been converted into design space and lofts."

"My landlord says the area has really changed in the last year. All I know is that it feels a lot different than downtown with all those trying-too-hard skyscrapers." She stopped abruptly, realizing what she'd said. "Sorry. I forgot that you're a builder."

"The new city center is going to be amazing," he said, pride in his voice. "It's not trying too hard to be great; it just is. Have you seen the drawings online or downtown?"

"No. I've heard that it's a really interesting development, but I don't spend a lot of time in that area. I guess I haven't paid attention."

"You should come down there sometime. I'll give you a tour. Have you ever stood on the top of a skyscraper before the walls are in?"

"I can't say that I have."

"It's an incredible feeling, like you're on top of the world. Someone who chases lightning would like the perspective."

"I'd like it even more if an electrical storm was moving through the city."

He tipped his head. "It always comes back to that, doesn't it?"

She shrugged and opened the gate in front of her building. Three steps led to another door, which she unlocked, and then she led him up a narrow stairway to the second floor.

As she ushered Michael inside her small one-bedroom apartment, she said, "It's not much. My furniture was either left behind by the previous tenant or picked up at the consignment store." She dropped her keys on the side table as Michael wandered around the room, pausing to look at her framed lightning shots. Then he moved on to the bookshelves, running his finger along her books. He glanced back at her. "You have a lot of books on weather."

"I told you that I understand weather."

He moved across the room to a map she'd hung on the wall earlier that week. "What's this?"

"It shows all the lightning strikes in the U.S. over the past eighteen months. You can see that Florida gets quite a few."

"I can definitely see that," he said with amusement. He picked up an antique camera that she'd bought at an estate sale a few years back. "How old is this?"

"About fifty years. It's cool, isn't it?"

"Do you ever shoot anything besides lightning?"

"Of course I do. In my job with the *Chronicle*, I shoot many different things. I've also picked up side jobs: weddings, bar mitzvahs, anniversary parties."

He looked through the lens of the camera. "When did you fall in love with photography?"

"When I was a very small child. I've always liked being able to capture moments in time. You never know if you'll ever see that exact moment again."

He set down the camera and gave her a thoughtful look. "You're an observer of life."

"Some of the time. But as you know, I also like to put myself in the picture."

His smile lit up his amazing blue eyes, and she found herself unable to look away from him. She would love to capture him on film. He had the kind of face that a camera would like: strong features, mesmerizing eyes, an expression that showed confidence, maybe a bit of arrogance and definitely pride. But behind all of that strength, she saw a hint of vulnerability, an uncertainty that came from the situation he found himself in, a situation he was determined to fix.

He took up a lot of space in her apartment, she thought, but she didn't feel afraid.

No, it definitely wasn't danger that was putting her nerves on edge; it was attraction—unexpected, wrong place, wrong time, wrong man attraction. Her pulse leapt at the realization.

"Where's your camera?" he asked. "Your digital camera."

"What? Oh. In my backpack." It took her a moment to remember why they'd come to her apartment. She walked over to the backpack she'd hung by the door and pulled out her camera. She then sat down at the kitchen table and connected the camera to her computer, importing the new photos.

Michael stood behind her, looking over her shoulder as she clicked through the first few photos.

"Those are downtown," he commented.

"I stopped a few times on the way to the park." She moved quickly through the next few city shots, finally getting to the parking lot. "I shot these out the window of the car." She paused, looking for some clue she'd forgotten, but there was nothing but a dark cloudy sky, tall trees, dozens of shadows and an empty parking lot.

"Nothing," she said, feeling disappointed. "Ever since you asked me about what other photos I'd taken, I had the feeling that I'd seen a car coming out of the lot when I was going in, but I was so focused on getting into the park before they closed it that I wasn't paying that much attention. But there's no car in the lot."

Michael sat down across from her and for a moment there was nothing but silence. "I guess that's that," he said heavily.

"Sorry."

"It's not your fault."

"I feel like there's something in my mind, but I can't get to it." She put a hand to her temple, running her fingers gently over the bump. "Did I see something that I can't remember?"

"I don't know. How does your head feel?" he asked.

"It aches, but it's not as bad as it was."

"Did you see a doctor? You might have a concussion."

"I'll be fine," she replied. "I just want to remember the details of what I saw last night. I want to be able to offer more help. I feel like every minute counts."

His expression turned grim. "I know what you mean."

Now she felt like apologizing for another reason. Michael obviously cared about Liliana. He was torn up inside, and while she was discouraged because she wanted to help, he was devastated because there was a good chance his friend had been hurt or was still in danger.

"What was Liliana like?" Alicia asked curiously.

"She was serious, intelligent, outspoken, a little bit self-righteous at times. She always wanted things to be fair. If there was a fight in the neighborhood, Liliana would jump in and try to mediate. Usually, her help was not well received, especially by her brothers, but she'd try anyway." He paused, his expression much softer now. "She read a lot. She loved books. I'd be playing baseball in the street with her brothers, and Liliana would be on her porch reading. Sometimes she'd join us; she was a good athlete, but she loved a story more than anything else. I thought she might grow up to be a writer, but instead she went into law."

"You lived across the street?"

"Yes. Our families were very close. My father and Liliana's father both came over from Cuba in the 80s. They were part of something called the Mariel Boatlift."

"I've never heard of that."

"It was a rare moment in time when thousands of people were allowed to leave Cuba. My father came over with two of his siblings. His parents were in ill health and stayed behind, but they encouraged their children to go. They wanted the next generation to have a better life."

"Does your father have a better life?"

"He does now. There were a lot of lean years early on. After my mom died, he was in a dark place. I couldn't talk to him at all. Liliana was a good friend to me during those years. She was one of the few people I could really talk to."

Alicia realized in that moment that there was absolutely no way that Michael had hurt Liliana. There was too much pain and guilt in his eyes. "Have you told the police about your relationship with Liliana?"

He started, as if she'd just pulled him out of the past. "I told them we were childhood friends, which was confirmed by numerous other people, but they were more focused on the fact that Liliana seemed desperate to talk to me and that I was twenty minutes late for our meeting."

"That doesn't seem like enough to make you a suspect."

"They were grasping for something and that's all they came up with. Plus, my history with Kellerman didn't help."

"Did you start getting into trouble after your mother died?"

"I definitely ran wild without her influence on me. Things got worse when my dad remarried when I was eleven. He was very happy with his new wife. Veronica was a local woman of Cuban descent. They had a lot more in common than my parents had had. My father and Veronica quickly added three girls to the family, each born a year apart. I ended up sleeping on the couch for a while."

She was beginning to see what he'd meant when he'd said he'd lived his life in three parts. In the middle part, he'd basically lost his family and had been drifting. Liliana had been more than his friend; she'd been his anchor.

"Did Liliana get into trouble with you?" she asked. "You said you started going down the wrong path when you were a young teenager."

"No, when I went off the rails, Liliana was doing her own thing. She wasn't too impressed by my swagger," he said with a rueful smile. "She thought I was turning into a criminal. She was afraid for me. She was very happy when my grandfather stepped in. I didn't feel the same way."

"What did your grandfather do?"

"After I got arrested for stealing, he got me an

attorney who negotiated a plea deal. I finished out that school year, did community service, paid restitution and then my grandfather convinced my father to send me to prep school. He said I was out of control, that I needed to be with kids who had drive and ambition that extended beyond building a criminal record. It was the same school my mother had gone to—a boarding school outside of Boston. It was the first time my father and grandfather ever agreed on anything. Next thing I knew, I was on a plane."

"So that began part three of your life."

"Yes. My life changed dramatically. I hated that school at first, and the weather sucked. It was cold all the time."

She smiled at that. "Miami does bring the heat."

"Yeah, I didn't appreciate that at the time. At the new school, I broke every rule I could."

"So you would get kicked out? So you could go home?"

"Part of me didn't want to go back, because my father had finally shown how much he did not want me to be in his new family. So why would I want to return? I didn't fit in there. But I didn't fit in that well at prep school either."

She was beginning to see that Michael had never really fit in anywhere. "But you stuck it out."

"Didn't have a choice, really. Eventually, it got better. In the end, it was the best move of my life.

My grandfather offered me opportunities that I wouldn't have had if I'd stayed in Miami. Now my life is good. The only mistake I've made recently was to come home, but when the development project came up, I had a moment of temporary insanity. I thought it might be interesting to see everyone again. Bad decision. If I had stayed away, Liliana wouldn't have tried to meet me, probably wouldn't be missing, and I wouldn't be a suspect."

"I don't think you can make that assumption, Michael. She might have still gone out that night, maybe even to that same restaurant. I know what it's like to play the *what-if* game, but it doesn't get you anywhere. I used to ask myself what if I had asked my dad to stay home that day. What if I'd told him I was sick and I didn't want him to go, would he have cancelled his flight? Or what if the group hadn't booked their charter flight that day, what if they'd left a day earlier, would he still be alive?" She gave him a compassionate smile. "It becomes a never-ending loop. You can't go back in time. You can't change what happened."

"No, but I can try to make things right. I need to find Liliana."

"I'm sure you've been looking as hard as you can."

"Yes, but we ran out of places to look. Thankfully, because of you, we now have somewhere new to focus on."

"I'm glad about that, but I want to do more. I realize that I don't know her, and I'm not family or a friend or anyone with investigative experience, but I still feel this driving need to help find her."

"I feel the same way, but the police don't keep me in the loop, and my own family seems to have trouble trusting me with information."

"But someone told you about my discovery at the park, so you're not completely out of the loop."

"That was a friend, someone who would probably get into trouble for telling me, but he wanted to give me a heads-up that I might need an alibi for yesterday evening."

"They wanted to know where you were at the time I saw Liliana." She hadn't considered that Michael's whereabouts might have been questioned by the police.

"Yes. But my neighbor was able to verify that I was in my apartment building at the time you were in the park. Not that that has completely cleared me of suspicion since Kellerman works hard to hang on to his only person of interest," he said, his voice edged with anger.

"Well, hopefully, he finds someone else of interest soon." She cleared her throat. "There have to be some other suspects."

"Not that I've heard mentioned for more than a split second."

"The police must have created some sort of a timeline from when she landed in Miami until Friday night. I would think they would have talked to anyone she came into contact with."

"Like I said, the police don't share their investigation with me, but I would make the same assumption."

"Maybe you should ask your friend—the one who wanted you to have an alibi."

"I don't want to involve him. He's taken too many chances already for me." Michael paused. "Do you have any coffee? I should have grabbed one at the café. I could use a caffeine boost."

"I can make some," she replied, getting to her feet.

"Great. The night is catching up with me."

"No sleep, huh?" she asked as she started the coffeemaker.

"Not even a minute."

"I didn't get much, either. I kept thinking about what I'd seen. I couldn't wait for it to be morning. I had to get back out there."

"You were there early. I didn't expect to see anyone before dawn."

"I didn't notice your car when I pulled into the lot."

"I parked on the ocean side. I didn't know exactly where you'd found the tag, only that it was somewhere in the park."

She pulled out two mugs, thinking she might

need more caffeine, too. "Did Liliana have a history of going to that park?"

"Not that I know of. We never went there together. It was not the nicest park when we were growing up. They've fixed things up in the last few years." Michael paused. "I don't know why she would have been there last night. It was storming. What the hell were they doing out there? They certainly weren't taking photographs."

"No, they weren't doing that." She poured coffee into two mugs then took them both over to the table and sat back down. "If you want cream or sugar—"

"Black is fine," he said, taking a sip. "Nice and strong—just the way I like it."

"Me, too. I've never seen the purpose in turning my coffee into something that looks like a milkshake. I'd rather just drink a milkshake."

Her words eased the tension in his face. "I feel exactly the same way."

"Really? No fancy cappuccino or latte maker in your home?"

"I wouldn't go that far. My company stocked the kitchen with everything I could possibly want."

"Lucky you."

"Not feeling that lucky these days," he said, raising the mug to his lips.

"I guess not. So getting back to the case. What's your next move?"

"I'm out of moves."

"Are you sure?"

"What do you have in mind, Alicia?"

She thought for a moment. The police had probably talked to everyone who had ever spoken to Liliana. But was it possible there had been gaps in the timeline? Could Liliana have tried to connect to any other old friends besides Michael? "When I asked you what you knew that no one else knew about Liliana, you told me that Liliana almost ran off to get married when she was a teenager."

"Yeah, so?"

"Do you know if she kept in touch with that man? Is he someone she might have seen when she came back to town for a few days?"

Michael's brows knit together. "Possibly. Why?"

"I was just thinking that if Liliana reached out to you, perhaps she reached out to other old friends as well."

"She mentioned to me a few years ago that Brad had gotten married, and she was happy for him, that it seemed like he'd finally moved on with his life."

"Does Brad still live in Miami?"

"I think so."

"Did the police talk to Brad when Liliana disappeared?"

He frowned. "I would doubt it. Unless there was some evidence that she connected with him.

I've never heard anyone in her family mention him, not that I specifically asked."

"Maybe you should ask. Or maybe we should see what we can find out about him on our own."

He stared at her with a gleam in his eyes. "Are we working together now, Alicia?"

It was probably the worst idea she'd ever had. On the other hand . . . she wasn't ready to walk away from the mystery. "Well, the police don't seem interested in keeping either of us up to date, and we both want to help find Liliana, so I'm thinking we should join forces and see if we can come up with a new perspective. It's not like we can hurt anything by digging around a little. We can only help, right?"

"Right." He gave her a searching gaze. "But I need to ask you something first."

She knew what he wanted to know. "Yes, I believe you're innocent."

Relief flashed through his brilliant blue eyes. "I think that's the first time anyone has said the words with actual certainty. And it's you," he said with some degree of amazement. "A woman I only met a few hours ago, not a family member or a friend. How can you trust me when people who've known me since I was born have doubts? It sounds a little—"

"Crazy?" she put in with a laugh.

The smile spread across his face in a very attractive way changing his whole expression, lightening his demeanor. "You said it; I didn't. But seriously, Alicia . . ."

"When you talk about Liliana there's pain in your eyes. If you're faking it, then you're really good at it. But I don't think you're pretending."

"I'm not," he said quietly.

"My gut tells me to trust you. So far, it hasn't steered me wrong. I hope this won't be the first time."

"It won't be."

"Good. Let's see if we can find Brad on the Internet. What's his last name?"

"Harte," he said, spelling it out for her.

She opened her computer and typed in Brad's name. "What do you know about him? Do you have any idea what he does for a living?"

"He always liked motorcycles. I think I heard that he worked for a dealer or was a mechanic."

"So you knew him when you were a kid?"

"I knew who he was. He had a younger brother who was a year ahead of me in school. I remember Brad used to speed through the neighborhood on his motorcycle and the older neighbors were pissed about it. That's the extent of my knowledge of him."

She typed some words into the search engine, but the results were not promising. "Let's try social media." She started another search, and this time the results were better. "I think I found him." She turned the computer screen around so

Michael could look at the photograph of a man on a bike.

"That's him," Michael said.

While most of Brad's profile was private, there were a few public facts, including the name of the motorcycle shop where he worked.

"We've got an address," she said with excitement.

Michael gave her a rather impressed look. "That was fast. Maybe you should have been a cop instead of a photographer."

"I may have found nothing more than a motor-cycle dealership, but it's a place to start."

"A good place," he agreed, getting to his feet. "Shall we go now?"

She couldn't think of a reason not to go. "All right."

"I'll drive. I'm in a two-hour spot, so I need to move the car anyway."

"Sounds good."

As she stood up, Michael's gaze met hers. "Thanks, Alicia."

"I haven't done anything yet."

"Yes, you have. You've given me hope."

Her heart warmed at his words. "I'm glad, but I have to say this could all lead nowhere."

"Even if that's the case, it's something to do, and I've been wanting to take action for a long time, but whenever I attempted to get involved, I was shut down. It's been incredibly frustrating."

She couldn't even imagine how he'd felt when the police had turned their suspicion on him. "Well, you're not on your own anymore. You've got a partner." She grabbed her jacket as they headed out the door. "Hopefully, together, we can make something happen."

SIX

*H**e had a partner,* Michael thought in bemusement, as he opened his car door for Alicia. He hadn't started out the day that way, but things had definitely taken a turn for the better. And he liked that his partner was a beautiful, curious, and fearless lightning chaser . . . He liked it even more that she'd instinctively trusted him.

Alicia hadn't needed a lot of information to make a decision. He didn't know if that made her too trusting, but it certainly made him happy. It was nice to talk to someone who wasn't eyeing him with suspicion every time he made a suggestion. Alicia's belief in his innocence had re-energized him. He didn't know if Brad Harte would be able to provide any new information but at this point he was willing to give it a shot.

"It's an eight-minute drive," Alicia said, checking directions on her phone. "Just stay on this road for another mile and then I'll tell you where to turn."

"Got it."

She settled back in her seat, running her hand over the smooth wood console between them. "This is a nice car. Is it new?"

"New to me. The company leased it for me when I got to Miami. And, no, I did not ask for a convertible. But somehow I ended up with one."

"If you're going to have a convertible, Miami is a good place for it. Of course, you have to actually put the top down to enjoy it," she said lightly.

He grinned in return. "It was raining yesterday. I have had it down on occasion."

"So where do you live when you're not here?"

"New York City. I have a condo on the forty-second floor of a high rise. There's a great view of the city and the Hudson River."

"Sounds impressive. I've always wanted to live in a high-rise, but apartments with a view are usually out of my price range. And convertibles like this—also out of my price range."

"What do you drive?"

"A ten-year-old Honda Civic that belonged to my boss's grandmother," she said with a laugh. "It's not sexy like this car, but it gets me where I need to go."

He didn't think she needed a car to be sexy. Since they'd left her apartment, she'd pulled the band out of her hair, and thick, dark waves now tumbled around her shoulders. Her eyes were intelligent and wide-set, with long, sweeping black lashes, and aside from the bruise on her forehead, her skin was flawless. She also had a really sexy mouth, full lips, and a warm voice that seemed to steal the chill out of his body.

His nerves tightened as he realized how much he'd noticed about her, what a strong connection he felt to a woman he'd met only a few hours earlier. It was the circumstances, he told himself. Every emotion was heightened and Alicia was now caught up in his nightmare. But her entrance into the situation had given him optimism. He would hang on to that as long as he could.

"Take a left at the next street," Alicia said, adding, "You'll be on this road for about three miles."

As she finished speaking, his phone rang through the car's audio system. "That's Diego. It's probably best if you don't let him know you're in the car."

"Who's Diego?"

"The cop who has been helping me." He answered the phone. "Diego, how did the search go?"

"Unfortunately, we did not find any other evidence that can be connected to Liliana."

His heart sank. He'd really hoped there would be something besides the ID tag.

"What happens next?"

"We keep looking. I heard you were at the park this morning. You shouldn't have gone out there, Michael. You just drew more attention to yourself. Kellerman thinks you were there trying to cover your tracks."

"He should think I was there because I have nothing to hide," he retorted.

"It would be better for you if you just stayed

out of the investigation. For once in your life, take my advice. I'm trying to keep you out of jail."

"I appreciate that. Call me if anything new comes up."

"I will."

He ended the call and glanced over at Alicia. "Nothing else in the park."

"That's disappointing, but maybe it's a good thing. Liliana could have gotten away."

"Or she was taken somewhere else."

"Or that," she said with a sigh. "So who's Diego? Why is he helping you?"

"I grew up with Diego. He's one of the kids I got into trouble with when I was a teenager. Like me, he was also arrested, but that experience made him want to be a police officer. They definitely scared him straight."

"So you both got on the right track."

"We were lucky to get caught for something small. It didn't ruin the rest of our lives."

"Turn right at the next corner," she said, glancing down at her phone. "And then it's a quick left on Baker and we're there." She paused. "Why didn't you tell Diego about Brad?"

"You heard him tell me to stay out of the investigation."

"True, but maybe the police need to speak to Brad as well."

"They may have already talked to him, and I

just don't know about it. Let's see if we can get anything out of him. Then we'll figure out what to do with the information, if there is any." He gave her a quick smile. "Okay, partner?"

She smiled back at him. "You like that word, don't you?"

"It's nice to have someone on my side."

"Don't make me regret it," she warned.

"Right back at you, partner."

"The shop is there." She tipped her head toward the large building on the right.

"Got it." He pulled into a parking spot in front of the motorcycle dealership.

As they walked through the display area, the shiny and expensive bikes impressed him. Brad Harte was obviously still living his passion for motorcycles.

"Have you ever ridden a motorcycle?" Alicia asked.

"I have, but not in a long time."

"I don't see the appeal."

He raised an eyebrow. "Seriously? You, the fearless storm chaser, don't see the appeal of a motorcycle?"

"I like going up against nature, not traffic. Plus, I look really bad in a helmet."

"Somehow I doubt that."

"I think that's him," Alicia said, her voice suddenly tense.

He followed her gaze to the man making his

way out of the showroom. His sandy brown hair was thinning on the top of his head, and he had gained a few pounds since he was a kid, but it was definitely Brad.

"Can I help you?" Brad asked, giving them a cheerful smile. "Are you looking for a bike?"

"Actually, we're looking for a little conversation," Michael said.

Brad's gaze narrowed as it settled on Michael's face. "Wait a second—I know you. You're—you're Michael Cordero."

"Good memory."

Brad's smile faded. "I think I know why you're here." He drew in a shaky breath. "Has Liliana been found?"

"No, but you obviously know she's missing," Michael returned, wondering about the sudden pallor of Brad's skin, the nervous gleam in his eyes.

"I saw it on the news. It's a terrible thing."

"When did you last talk to Liliana?"

Brad swallowed hard and cast a quick look toward the showroom, where an attractive blonde woman was walking outside with a young couple. "I can't speak to you here."

"Why not?" Michael hadn't really expected anything to come from meeting Brad, but his behavior now was a little suspicious.

"I'm busy. I have work to do."

"This won't take long," Alicia interjected. "And

it's really important. Michael said you and Liliana were close. Surely you want to help find her."

Brad licked his lips, cast a quick glance at the blonde and then said, "I can meet you tonight. Javier's at eight o'clock." He turned abruptly at the end of his sentence and went over to join the other group.

Michael watched as Brad slid his arm around the waist of the blonde and then urged her and the couple back into the showroom. "That must be his wife," he said.

"And he didn't want her to hear our conversation," Alicia murmured. "Why not?"

"Good question. I didn't think Brad had talked to Liliana in years. Now, I'm not so sure."

"What is Javier's?"

"It's a bar in South Beach."

She met his gaze. "Looks like we have a date tonight."

"Looks that way," he said, as they walked back to the car. "I just hate having to wait until tonight. Who knows if Brad will show up? He could just be buying time, and we could be wasting another seven hours."

"So, let's not waste them," she said as she got into the passenger seat.

He walked around the car and slid behind the wheel. "What did you have in mind?"

"Well, we could have lunch. It's after one, and I'm starving. What about you?"

His stomach rumbled at her words. "I could eat. Where do you want to go?"

She hesitated for a long moment. "We could make it a working lunch. Didn't Liliana disappear in the parking lot of a restaurant?"

"Paladar," he said, his muscles tightening. "I don't think we should go there."

"Why not?"

"Well, for one thing, the Valdez family tends to spend a lot of time there, and I suspect that's the first place they went after finishing the park search this morning."

"Even better. We might be able to learn something." She paused. "What's the other thing?"

"My father owns the restaurant."

Her eyes widened with surprise. "I didn't know that. There wasn't any mention of that in the news articles I read."

"Well, it's a fact. He and my stepmother opened the restaurant about eight years ago. It's their dream come true. Liliana's older brother Juan is one of the chefs. Both he and my father usually work on Saturdays."

"We have to go there, Michael."

"It will be awkward."

"So what? We might be able to get new information."

"No one talks to me, Alicia."

"Well, they might talk to me. I'm the one who provided the break in the case."

She had a point. And since she was quite possibly the only person who'd seen Liliana since she disappeared, the Valdez family would probably be thrilled to speak to her.

"They'll grill you," he warned her.

"I can handle their questions. I meant to ask you what happened with Liliana's sister's wedding— did it take place before Liliana disappeared?"

"No, it was scheduled for Sunday afternoon. Liliana went missing on Friday night. Isabel has postponed her wedding plans until her sister comes home."

"That's rough."

"It is. I don't think her fiancé is too happy about it, but at this point it wouldn't be much of a celebration."

"I suppose not. I would like to see where Liliana disappeared, Michael."

The glint of steel in her eyes told him that she was not going to be dissuaded. "Fine, we'll go to Paladar."

"Good." She paused. "There's something else I've wanted to ask you. Do you have a copy of the texts that you and Liliana exchanged?"

"They were on the phone that the police confiscated, and I haven't gotten it back. I had to get a new phone."

"Do you remember what they said?"

"Pretty much. There were ten texts in total. The first two came in on Thursday asking me to meet her that night, but I didn't get back to her. I was tied up in meetings that day. The rest came in between eight AM Friday morning and one o'clock when I finally started answering texts. Liliana told me it was important that we get together. I asked why. She said she didn't want to get into it on the phone, but that it was urgent."

"What did you think it was about?" Alicia asked.

"I had no idea. She suggested we meet at Paladar. I resisted, because it's my father's restaurant, and I hadn't been there yet. Then she said, 'You've been back in Miami for a few weeks, and you still haven't eaten at your dad's restaurant? What is wrong with you? You need to break the ice, put the past behind you.' So I agreed. We set the time. She said great. Then she sent one more text asking me not to mention our meeting to anyone until I saw her. I thought that was odd, but I was busy, so I just said fine. That was it."

"So she picked the location."

"Yes. That didn't surprise me. She was always after me to call a truce with my dad. I used to tell her that I wasn't fighting with him, but she said a cold silent war didn't make it any less of a battle."

"So you did talk to each other? I had the impression you hadn't spoken in years before you returned to Miami and she came home for the wedding."

"We hadn't seen each other in person in eight years, but we'd exchanged texts and emails occasionally, maybe three to four times a year, but not much in the last twelve months. I knew she was an attorney, but I didn't know much else about her life in Texas, and she didn't know much about my life in New York. We'd drifted apart as childhood friends often do."

Alicia nodded. "Which is why it was unusual that she was suddenly so intent on seeing you."

"I really thought she just wanted to connect. We were both in the same place at the same time and that hadn't happened in forever."

"But she did say that she had something important to talk to you about that she didn't want to get into over the phone."

"True. I've never figured out what that was. No one in the Valdez family has a clue, either."

"It is pretty cryptic," she admitted. "I need to think about it."

"Think all you want. Believe me, I'm open to new ideas. You've already given me one new possible lead in Brad Harte. Who knows what you'll come up with next?"

"I'm just asking questions—questions you've probably already answered a million times."

"Not all the same questions," he said, thinking it was good Alicia was now in the mix. She was shaking things up, making him look at everything in a different way. She was like the strong wind that had come with yesterday's storm. She was blowing cobwebs off dusty old facts, and he was feeling more hopeful than he had in a very long time.

They arrived at Paladar just before two. There were only a half dozen cars in the lot, which wasn't unexpected since they were past the lunch rush.

"Where was Liliana's car parked?" Alicia asked as they got out of the car.

"Over there." He pointed across the lot to the third spot in from the entrance. It was about thirty yards from the front door of the restaurant. "Unfortunately, that spot is not in view of the security camera by the front door, so there was no video of when she arrived or when she got out of the car."

"That is unfortunate," Alicia murmured, her gaze sweeping the lot. "What kind of car did she drive?"

"That night she was in her brother Rico's car, a flashy red Mazda Miata convertible. When the police arrived, the doors were locked. There was nothing belonging to Liliana inside the vehicle. It's believed that she had her purse and her phone with her when she disappeared."

"Did you see the car when you drove into the lot?"

"If I did, it didn't register. I was running late, so

I was in a hurry to get through the front door. When I entered the restaurant, there was a line at the desk, so I went into the bar and made my way through the dining room, thinking she'd already gotten a table, but I didn't see her. I went back to the reception area and waited there. I couldn't believe she was later than me. I was going to text her, but when I pulled out my phone, I had some texts from the foreman on my job. I spent a few minutes answering his questions before I sent off a text to Liliana." He let out an angry breath. "I wasted a lot of time."

"What happened next?"

"When I didn't get an answer from Liliana, I went into the kitchen. It occurred to me that Liliana might be talking to her brother Juan. But she wasn't in the kitchen. Juan said he hadn't seen her. In fact, he hadn't been aware she was going to meet me that night. He thought she was spending all her time with her sister, getting ready for the wedding. I think that's when I first got worried." His stomach twisted with the painful memories.

"What did you do after that?"

"I texted Liliana again. Juan called Rico, who said he'd lent Liliana his car. He'd last seen her around six when one of his friends had picked him up to go to dinner. Liliana's mother said she'd last seen Liliana at seven. She'd mentioned she was going to run an errand before she met me.

No one has been able to figure out if she actually ran that errand or what it might have involved."

"Okay. So Liliana drove here, parked over there, got out of her car and—"

"Vanished. We called the police around nine o'clock. Actually, we called Diego. He was on duty that night. He and his partner came by to find out what was going on. We searched the alley between the restaurant and the office building and went around the back area that leads to another alley. But we found nothing. Because there was no evidence of foul play, there wasn't a full-press search immediately launched. Diego was on patrol, so he looked around the neighborhood and the family started calling Liliana's friends."

"When did the police start to look for her in earnest?"

"Not until the next day. It bothers me that it took so long. Those first few hours were crucial. The family was looking for her, but if we'd had more manpower, maybe we would have found her."

"Or not," Alicia said gently. "It doesn't sound like you had anything to go on."

"But if I hadn't been late—"

"Stop. I know you've been on a guilt trip since that night, but you have to stop going around and around."

"That's easy to say, but—"

"But what? You were twenty minutes late. That

happens. Liliana parked in a crowded, lighted lot in front of the restaurant where her brother worked. This isn't a dangerous neighborhood, and it wasn't late at night. No one could have anticipated that she'd run into trouble here. She obviously didn't. She got out of the car and locked it behind her."

"And then someone grabbed her."

Alicia stared back at him. "It is weird that no one saw anything, because it would have been a popular time for people to be going in and out of the restaurant."

"I know. It doesn't make sense. She wouldn't have gotten in the car with a stranger without a struggle. She was the kind of woman who would fight for her life."

"Maybe she knew the person who approached her. She didn't fight because she wasn't afraid."

"Which is how I came to be the main person of interest," he said.

"Oh, right. I get it now. I don't know why I keep thinking I'll come up with something new. It's not like the cops don't have a lot more experience than me unraveling mysteries."

"I appreciate that you're trying, Alicia. It certainly can't hurt."

He looked around the lot, wishing there was some hidden answer just waiting to be found, but if it was there, he couldn't see it.

"One scenario," he said, pointing across a five-foot wide plant divider to the parking lot next door, "is that whoever approached Liliana parked over there and walked toward her from that direction."

"There's a camera on that building. I can see it from here."

"Yes, but it was broken, and the business closed at five, so there was no one around there, either."

"It was broken? For how long?"

"The owner said it had happened the day before. She hadn't gotten around to fixing it."

"That's odd timing—the day before."

He nodded. "I thought so, too."

"So Liliana parks in a spot that can't be seen from any camera that's working. Is it possible someone disabled the camera?"

"It's possible. Or it could have just been broken. Do you want to go inside or do you want to eat somewhere else?"

"I want to go inside." She gave him a thoughtful look. "Have you been back here since that night?"

"A few times. Not to eat, though. The restaurant became ground zero for the search. My father has been feeding volunteers for months."

"Is your dad working today?"

"He usually works Saturdays," he said, his lips tightening. "It's the busiest day and night of the week."

"Maybe I'll get to meet him."

"Maybe you will. I hope you like Cuban food."

"I couldn't live in Miami and not like it," she said, as they walked toward the front door. "I love spicy food, and sometimes the Cuban dishes remind me of Texas. There were a lot of Latino influences on the menu in Corpus Christi."

And just like that, he was reminded of the Texas connection between Liliana and Alicia. Were all the little connections coincidence or something else? But what else could they be? It was the lightning that had drawn Alicia to the park the night before, not Liliana.

Alicia's earlier words rang through his head. *My great-grandmother believed that the lightning comes down from the heavens to show you what you need to see.*

Had the lightning given them a valuable clue, or was he just letting Alicia's passion for the mystical get into his head?

Probably the latter, he decided, opening the restaurant door for her.

As she walked past him, her scent stirred his senses, but he had enough trouble in his life. He needed to think of Alicia as a partner and not as a beautiful, impulsive, fearless woman who had already gotten past his usual line of defense. Unfortunately, he had a feeling introducing her to his father was only going to bring her deeper into his life.

SEVEN

Paladar was a cozy, charming restaurant with hardwood floors, tall ceilings, spinning fans, and the fragrant air of Cuban spices wafting through the large dining room. The hostess was a petite, dark-haired young woman who appeared to be in her late teens. She gave Michael a big smile. "I can't believe you're here, Michael. Papa will be so happy." She gave Alicia a curious look. "Is this your girlfriend?"

"No, this is my friend Alicia. This is my sister, Violet."

"Hi," Alicia said as the girl gave her a speculative look.

"Nice to meet you," Violet said. "Do you guys want to eat?"

"That's why we're here," Michael replied. "Do you have a table?"

"Lots of them, but . . ." She hesitated, taking a quick look over her shoulder. "The Valdez family is here, just so you know."

Michael nodded. "That's fine. Is there any news?"

"I don't think so. Everyone is pretty discouraged after the search this morning."

Violet grabbed two menus and led them down a short flight of stairs.

Michael moved closer to Alicia as they made their way past a large crowd of people in the center of the room. Some of those people she'd seen at the park earlier in the day—obviously, Liliana's family.

Conversation seemed to hush as they drew near.

Then a short, stocky man jumped to his feet and blocked their path.

"How can you show your face here, Michael?" the man demanded.

"Get out of my way, Rico."

"Why should I? You don't belong here," Rico said with a hateful look. "You never did."

"Stop it, Rico," a woman said firmly, getting up from the table. She appeared to be in her late fifties or early sixties. She had piercing black eyes, dark hair and a commanding manner. "This is a time for us to draw together, not fight with each other. Sit down."

Her words got Rico to shuffle back into his seat. He settled down, crossing his arms in front of his chest.

"Michael," she said, moving around the table.

"If it bothers you that I'm here, I'll go," he said.

"It only bothers me that Liliana's disappearance has caused pain between our families. Please sit down with us. You and your friend." She gave Alicia a strained smile.

Michael hesitated. "We don't want to interrupt."

"You're not interrupting. We've been talking

for hours, around and around in circles," she said wearily. "We were just about to order. Please sit." She turned toward the group of five seated at the table. "We can make room," she said, making it a statement rather than a question.

"Are you sitting here?" Violet asked her brother.

Michael gave Alicia a pained look. "What do you want to do?"

"Your call." While she didn't like the attitude Rico was giving them, it might be beneficial to talk to Liliana's family.

"We want to talk to you about the search," the woman added, obviously sensing Michael's hesitation. "Please join us."

"All right. We'll join you." They walked over to the table and Michael introduced her to the family: Liliana's mother Theresa, who had invited them to the table, her husband Dominic, son Rico, daughter Isabel and Isabel's fiancé David Kenner.

"How did the search go?" Michael asked as they sat down between Isabel and Theresa.

"Not well," Theresa said. "We'll try again tomorrow. It's a big park."

"But there's probably nothing else there," Isabel put in, a discouraged note in her voice. "We don't even know how long the tag was in the dirt. I know the woman who found it thinks she saw Liliana by the carousel, but it all sounds very vague."

Alicia tensed. Obviously, Isabel did not know she was that woman. She glanced at Michael. He gave her a subtle nod.

"I'm the woman who found the ID tag in the park," she said.

Isabel's jaw dropped. "You? I don't understand. I thought you were a friend of Michael's?"

"We met this morning. I went back to the park to see if there was anything I missed," she explained. "Michael was there. We started talking."

"You saw my daughter last night?" Theresa interrupted.

"I saw a man and a woman fighting by the carousel. I didn't see their faces, unfortunately." She didn't want to crush their hope, but she had to be completely honest. She couldn't lead them on.

"You said they were fighting?" Dominic asked, a question in his eyes.

"The man had a hold of the woman's arm. She was struggling to get away. I couldn't hear any words being exchanged."

"Why didn't you help her?" Rico demanded, his glare burning through her.

"I tried," she said defensively. "The tree next to me was hit by lightning and the branches fell on top of me. When I got up, they were gone. I saw the tag in the dirt, and I took it to the police. I'm sorry I couldn't do more. I can't imagine what you're going through. I really want to help you find Liliana. Her scream echoes through my head."

"You heard her scream?" Theresa asked, putting a hand to her mouth, fear in her dark eyes.

Dominic put a comforting arm around his wife. "Liliana is a fighter, Theresa. She's tough. We have to keep believing."

"I'm trying to have faith, but it's been so long." She looked back at Alicia with watery eyes. "Thank you for taking the tag to the police."

"Hold on a second," Rico interrupted. "I still don't get why you're with Michael now. You met hours ago. Why are you still together?"

"We've been talking, trying to figure things out," she said, feeling a little intimidated by his forceful glare.

"That's enough, Rico," Dominic said, giving his son a stern look. "Alicia helped us by taking the ID to the police."

"I wonder," Rico muttered, doubt in his eyes. He shoved back his chair and stood up. "I'm out of here."

Rico stalked away from the table, leaving silence in his wake.

"Please forgive my son," Theresa said, an apology in her gaze. "He's worried and scared. That's no excuse, but it is the truth."

Their conversation was interrupted by the arrival of large platters of food. Alicia hoped that the meal would ease the tension, but when an older man with pepper-gray hair, olive skin and dark eyes came to the table, she could feel Michael stiffen. Seeing the similarity in their features, especially the gleam of stubborn pride in each of their eyes, she had to assume he was Michael's father.

The man's gaze fell on Michael and a long look passed between them, the substance of which she could not read, but there were definitely a lot of emotions involved.

"Michael," he said. "I didn't know you were here."

"I just got here. This is Alicia."

"She's the one who found Liliana's tag," Theresa put in.

"It's nice to meet you. I'm Ernesto Cordero."

"Alicia Monroe," she said.

"Well, I hope I have brought enough food to sustain you all on this difficult day," Ernesto said, waving his hand toward the large platters. "We have filete salteado, pernil asado, croquetas con jamon, a salad with avocado, watercress and pine-apple, rice and beans. Are we missing anything?"

"You've outdone yourself once again, Ernesto, thank you," Theresa said.

"You are always welcome. Please enjoy." He paused, moving around the table to where Michael was sitting. "May I have a word?"

Michael hesitated, then nodded. "I'll be right back," he told Alicia. "This won't take long.

We don't have anything to say to each other."

"Take your time."

As Michael left the table, an older couple paused by the table to speak to Theresa and Dominic, so Alicia turned toward Liliana's sister.

Isabel handed her a platter of beef tenderloin strips sautéed with peppers. "This is one of Ernesto's most popular dishes," she said.

"Thank you." Alicia dished some beef onto her plate, then said, "Michael told me that you had to postpone your wedding."

"Yes, it's been very hard on David," she said, casting a quick glance at her fiancé, who was reading something on his phone. "But I can't get married without my sister."

"That's understandable."

"So what do you think of Michael?" Isabel asked as she handed Alicia a bowl of rice.

"I don't know him well, but he seems genuinely upset and worried about Liliana. He told me that they were very good friends when they were young."

"Very good friends," Isabel agreed with a nod, her brown eyes filled with sadness. "Liliana always said that Michael would do wonderful things with his life. I didn't believe her when we were kids, because he was a troublemaker. He was always getting into fights at school. But after he went away, he changed his life, and Liliana's prediction came true."

It didn't sound like Isabel disliked Michael as much as some of the other members of her family.

"Isabel, I have to make a call," David said, drawing Isabel's attention back to him. "I'll be back in a moment."

"Don't you want to eat first?"

"This can't wait." He glanced back at his phone and then headed out of the restaurant.

"David has been so stressed the last few months," Isabel said. "Not just about the wedding but also about his business. He started a computer software training company a few months ago, and he's been working a lot. Sometimes I wonder why we ever thought getting married and starting a new business at the same time was a good idea."

"That does sound challenging."

"Things would have been better if we'd actually gotten married. Now, we're stuck in limbo. David is getting more and more impatient with me. I feel like he's given up, but I can't do that." She paused. "We've been at this restaurant a lot since she disappeared. It always makes me feel conflicted. Knowing this was where she came last makes me feel close to her, but then again it also reminds me of everything bad that's happened."

"Did you see Liliana the day she disappeared?" Alicia asked.

"Yes. We had brunch, got our nails done, tried on our dresses; it was wonderful. I thought we were going to spend the evening together, too, but Liliana decided to meet up with Michael. She said she hoped I wouldn't mind, but she really needed to see him. How could I say no?" Isabel asked, guilty tears in her eyes. "She was only home for a few days, and I had some of my other friends spending the night with me, so I said go and have fun." She dabbed at her eyes with the corner of her napkin. "That's the last thing I said to her."

"It was a nice sentiment," Alicia said with a compassionate smile. "I'm sure she appreciated your support."

"I hope so. I've been a little self-absorbed the past year, caught up in my wedding plans. I feel like Liliana and I drifted apart. When the police started asking me questions about Liliana's life, I realized how little I knew."

"That's only natural. You were in love. And Liliana lived far away."

"I should have stayed in better touch with her, but sometimes our conversations were not that good . . ."

Alicia frowned at Isabel's odd words. "What do you mean?"

"Liliana and David didn't get along very well. It was awkward between us at times."

Alicia's pulse sped up at that piece of information. "Why didn't they like each other?"

"David said some things about the Navy that

110

rubbed Liliana the wrong way. He's not big on the military. His father was in the Navy. He was injured in a friendly fire incident, and David thought the Navy covered up what really happened. He asked Liliana to look into it, and she did. When she told him that there wasn't any evidence to support his theory, he thought she was covering up, too. I was caught in the middle." Isabel drew in a breath. "I should shut up so you can eat. I don't know why I said all that."

"Because you're worried about your sister."

"I feel like I should have tried to smooth things out between David and Liliana. Maybe then Liliana would have stayed with me that night instead of going off to meet Michael."

"But you weren't with David that night. You said you were with your friends."

"That's true." Isabel sighed. "I don't even know what I'm saying. I'm going to be quiet so you can eat."

"You should eat, too."

"I haven't felt hungry in a long time." Isabel picked at her food. "I was so worried about getting skinny enough for my wedding that I worked out like a maniac. Since Liliana disappeared, I haven't been to the gym, and I've lost ten pounds."

"You need to stay strong for your sister. And this food looks amazing."

"It's good. Ernesto is an excellent chef."

Alicia bit into a delicious piece of steak, whose flavors almost made her swoon. "I can see that," she murmured, spooning some rice into her mouth. "This is delicious."

"Ernesto is like a second father to me, but he and Michael have been at war for as long as I've known them. I hope they're calling a truce. Everyone needs to realize that family is important, no matter our differences."

"Very true." Alicia's gaze drifted across the dining room. Michael had been gone a long time for a man who'd declared he had little to say to his father.

Michael sat across from his father in the small office next to the kitchen. His dad was rarely in this office. He usually left the business management to Veronica.

Ernesto had always preferred to be at his stove, supervising the other chefs, and focusing on new recipes to try. But today his father had taken a seat in the black leather chair behind his desk.

"What do you want to talk about?" he asked abruptly. He couldn't remember the last time he'd felt comfortable in his father's presence, and today was no exception. They did a lot better when there were people around them to act as buffers.

"I'm worried about you, Michael. The police continue to look at you as a suspect."

He shrugged. "I'm used to it."

"Your grandfather called me the other day."

His muscles tightened. Whenever his grandfather and his father spoke, it was never good for him. "About what?"

"You, of course. We have nothing else to discuss," Ernesto said, a bitter edge in his voice.

Michael couldn't completely blame his father for his attitude. William Jansen had never made any pretense of caring about or respecting the man who had married his daughter. He'd always told Michael that his mother had been far too good for Ernesto. Michael had never wanted to take sides, but as his father distanced himself from him, it had been a lot easier to stand on his grandfather's side. It was Will Jansen who had turned his life around, who had put him on the right path, paid for his education, and given him the job he had today. But despite all that, he was not unaware of the fact that his grandfather could be a cold and ruthless man.

"Will said you sent the attorney he hired for you back to New York," his father continued.

"I don't need a lawyer; I didn't do anything wrong." He paused, hating the uncertainty in his father's eyes. If anyone should be able to trust him, it should be his dad. And yet it wasn't. Why was he surprised? Ernesto had so rarely given him what he needed, even if what he needed was just his attention.

"Even so, you should be careful."

"Even so?" he queried. "Does that mean you believe I'm innocent? Because I sure as hell haven't heard those words come out of your mouth."

"Of course I believe you're innocent. You wouldn't have hurt Liliana."

"It's only taken you two months to say that out loud."

"Well, you don't give me a chance to say much of anything," Ernesto retorted. "I've called you several times. Veronica and the girls would like to see you. But you haven't called me back."

"I've been busy. And we both know that you don't really care if I show up or not. Let's be honest. Once you married Veronica, I was out. I get it. You moved on. And you have a great family, but I haven't been part of your family since I was fifteen—hell, since I was eleven."

Tight lines formed around his father's tired eyes. "I made some mistakes. So did you, Michael. Perhaps it's time we let go of the past and start again. You're here in Miami now."

"Only until Christmas. Coming back to Miami was a bad idea. As soon as this job is finished, I'll be returning to New York."

"We still have some time. Why don't you come over to the house one day? Your sisters want to spend time with you, to get to know you better. They don't deserve to be blamed for my sins."

"I don't blame them." He let out a breath. "I'll try to see them next week, but right now I'm focused on working this new clue."

"What can you do that the police can't?"

"Look for a suspect who isn't me."

"Be careful, Michael. I know you won't believe me, but I do worry about you. I want you to be happy, to be safe. I hope one day you'll forgive me, that we can start again. Is that possible?"

His father was asking him for something he couldn't give—at least not now. "I don't know. We'll see."

EIGHT

E verything okay?" Alicia asked when Michael returned to the table. He looked pale and tense.

"Fine," he said shortly, reaching for the nearest platter. "How about you?"

"Good." She wanted to tell him what Isabel had said about the discord between Liliana and David, but she couldn't do that with the Valdez family surrounding them.

"I'm glad you're talking to your father," Dominic said. "He's missed you a great deal over the years."

"His choice," Michael said shortly.

"There are always two sides to a story," Theresa said gently.

"I know both sides."

Michael's words cut off whatever Theresa was going to say next. She exchanged a look with her husband and then reached for the dessert tray.

"Who wants one of these treats?" Theresa asked.

"None for me," Alicia said. "I'm stuffed."

Michael waved on the tray as he quickly cleared his plate. Then he said, "We should get going."

"Before you leave," Dominic interrupted, "I

wanted to let you know that we're going to hold a special Mass and candlelight vigil tomorrow night at St. Peter's Church at five PM. We've put in some calls to our friends in the press and hopefully we'll get some media coverage on the news. The more people we can reach the better. We need to find anyone who was anywhere near the park yesterday."

"We'd love for you both to come to the vigil," Theresa said.

"I'll see," Michael said.

"I'll try," Alicia said.

"Good." She turned to her daughter. "Isabel, if you speak to Rico, tell him that Michael comes with my blessing."

"I'll talk to him," Isabel said. "But I can't promise he won't be a jerk. He's so angry all the time now."

Theresa nodded. "I can barely get him to talk to me. He seems to blame himself for lending his car to his sister." She let out a sigh. "It's strange," she continued, a sad smile on her lips. "I worried so much about Liliana when she went into the Navy. She had assignments that took her into dangerous countries. I never imagined that coming home would be the most dangerous thing she could do."

"Or coming to my wedding," Isabel said, her voice cracking. "Excuse me." She got to her feet and quickly left the table.

"Oh, dear." Theresa's eyes crinkled with concern. "I didn't mean for Isabel to take it that way."

"She'll be all right." Dominic patted his wife's hand. "We all have guilt."

"But none of you are guilty," Alicia put in. "The only person who's guilty is the person who took Liliana. You were just having a wedding."

"And the wedding should have been Liliana's focus," David said, a harsh note in his voice. He turned his gaze on Michael. "Why she had to run out and see you that night, I will never understand. Couldn't you have met her after the wedding?"

"She pushed to meet me that night," Michael said. "You know that."

"I know it; I don't understand it," David replied.

"Well, join the club," Michael said, irritation in his voice. He put his napkin on the table. "Are you ready to go, Alicia?"

"Yes," she agreed, reaching for her purse. "Let me give you some money—"

"My father won't let anyone here pay," Michael told her.

"He's right," Dominic said. "Ernesto is always very generous."

"I hope someone will tell him thanks for me. It was nice to meet all of you."

"Hopefully we'll see you tomorrow," Theresa said.

She nodded and followed Michael out to the car.

"Are you okay?" she asked as he buckled his seat belt, then gunned the motor.

"You need to stop asking me that," he replied, as he sped out of the parking lot.

"Then don't act like you're not okay." She put her hand on the side of the door as he took a sharp turn. "Michael, if you're not going to slow down, then let me out."

He eased his foot off the gas. "Sorry."

"Do you want to talk about whatever is bothering you?"

"No. I just need a minute." He blew out a breath. "We'll go back to your apartment and regroup. We still have a few hours before we can meet Brad at Javier's."

"All right. That sounds like a plan," she said lightly.

"Does it? It sounds more like another few hours of spinning my wheels in the same deepening rut."

His frustration was understandable. Michael had been stuck in limbo for two months. She'd been involved less than twenty-four hours and felt stymied by the lack of clues. But there had to be a way to break something loose. While she was sure the police detectives had done every-thing they could do, she was bothered by the fact that they were so zeroed in on Michael. Had the police missed something or someone else because they were fixated on the wrong man?

By the time they got back to her neighborhood, it was after four, and the streets were so crowded with tourists that Michael had to park a couple of blocks away.

"Everyone is out today," she commented as they walked down the crowded street. "Yesterday it was a ghost town with the storm coming. But the tourists came back with the sun."

"It's Florida. What do you expect?"

"True." They paused at an intersection. "What did your father want to speak to you about?"

"He thinks I should come by the house more often and get to know my sisters better."

"Violet seems to like you a great deal."

"She's a good kid. Her sisters are, too. But while we may share a bloodline, we're not family. I left the house when Violet was three years old. And my youngest sister wasn't even born yet. They don't remember me being around."

"They might remember more than you think. Why not get to know them? They didn't treat you badly. They're not responsible for their parents' actions."

"I don't hold them responsible." He gave her a hard look. "Don't try to fix me and my family. We have a history together that you can't begin to understand."

She thought she understood more than he knew,

but she decided not to argue. It was his family, his business, and she should stay out of it.

They crossed the street and walked down the next block in silence. When they reached her building, her landlord Eileen Peterman was just coming out of the gallery.

At fifty-nine, Eileen was a beautiful platinum blonde with a bohemian style of dress, who had never married and loved to travel.

Eileen liked having Alicia upstairs so she could keep an eye on the building while Eileen was off on her many adventures, an arrangement that suited them both well. In fact, in Eileen Peterman, Alicia had not only found an enthusiastic buyer for her photographs, she'd found a mother figure and a kindred spirit, someone who understood her far better than her own mother ever had.

"Alicia," Eileen said with a smile. "I can't wait to see what photographs you took last night. Tell me you did not miss that amazing storm. I just got back from visiting my sister in Charleston, but we saw the news reports. The lightning looked amazing."

"I got some good shots. I'll bring them down tomorrow or Monday."

"I can't wait." Eileen gave Michael a curious smile. "And who's your friend?"

"This is Michael Cordero—my landlord Eileen Peterman. She owns the building and the gallery and is kind enough to sell my photographs."

"They fly off the walls." Eileen's speculative gaze took in every inch of Michael. "It's so nice to meet you, Michael. Are you also a photographer?"

"No, I'm a builder."

"His company is putting up the new city center," Alicia interjected.

"I saw the plans for that. I like the style of the development, the integration of local culture and artists," Eileen said approvingly.

"We try to build in a way that works with the existing landscape but also improves upon it," Michael replied.

"Well, if your designers need any art, I have some wonderful pieces."

Alicia inwardly groaned at Eileen's blatant sales plea but she could hardly complain. If Eileen weren't so good at taking every opportunity she could, Alicia's photographs would not have made her nearly as much money as they had.

"I'll definitely pass on your name," Michael said. "It's not my area, but I'll make sure the designers take a look at what you have to offer."

"Excellent." She looked back at Alicia. "By the way, a reporter stopped by a half hour ago, looking for you. She said you were involved in some missing person case and she would like to speak to you. I have her card inside. Shall I get it for you?"

"No. I don't need to talk to any reporters. Where was she from?"

"ABC News."

"I wonder how she got my address." She was a little dismayed by her lack of privacy, not that she'd ever worried that much about protecting her address. It wasn't as if she had a lot to steal. But now that she might have witnessed something dangerous, she was more concerned.

"She didn't say." A frown moved through Eileen's eyes. "Do I need to be worried about you?"

"I'm fine. I found a military ID tag at the park when I went to shoot the photographs yesterday. It belonged to a missing person. That's all. Hopefully, it will help find her."

"You always have had a sharp eye, Alicia. Probably not many people would have noticed an ID tag lying about or thought it was important."

She shrugged, not wanting to get into the fight she'd witnessed. "We'll see if it helps bring the woman home. Were you just leaving?"

"Yes, I have a date tonight with a very distinguished gentleman," Eileen said. "Handsome and rich, my favorite combination."

She laughed. "Good for you. I want to hear all about it. I have to live vicariously through you."

Eileen's wicked smile turned to Michael. "I don't know that I believe that anymore. You have such an attractive companion. You two have fun."

123

As Eileen walked away, Alicia gave Michael an apologetic smile. "Sorry about that. She loves to try to find me dates. I'm the single daughter she never had."

"I know what that's like. My assistant is a fifty-six-year-old woman who feels compelled to try to match me up with someone whenever she can, usually the daughter of one of her friends."

She smiled, doubting that Michael had trouble finding dates on his own. "Have you ever let her set you up?"

"Twice, under duress. She wouldn't let up on me, and I knew she was trying to be nice, so I went. One woman wasn't bad, but she was really hung up on her ex-boyfriend. The other was a fanatical conservationist who basically told me building projects were destroying the planet. Needless to say, we didn't have much to talk about."

She laughed as they walked up the stairs to her apartment. "I've had worse dates than that."

"Oh, yeah? Like what?"

"Like the guy who wouldn't stop crying."

Michael gave her a skeptical look. "You're making that up."

"I'm not. He'd just sold his '76 Mustang that he'd apparently inherited from his grandfather, and he was mourning its loss. Everything I said and did reminded him of that car. I mentioned I liked the beach and he broke down in sobs, saying the first time he ever drove that car, he took it to the beach. The smell of salty sea air would stay with him forever."

"Hey, women always want us to show emotion and when we do, you don't like it," he said with a grin.

"Not when you're crying about your car," she said, letting him into her apartment.

"A '76 Mustang is a sweet ride."

"It's just a vehicle, something that gets you from point A to point B."

"No, a car is always more than a car to a guy. It's like a purse to a woman. It's a sign of status. It represents your personality. And it shows off your flash."

She raised an eyebrow. "Okay, but you're driving a leased convertible that you didn't even pick out for yourself, so if a car is so important to you, then what's the deal?" She tossed her keys down on the side table and took off her jacket.

"That car is just part of the job. It's not me."

"So what do you drive in New York?"

"I don't drive in the city."

"Then you don't own a car?"

"I do," he said, a sheepish smile on his face.

"What is it—a Porsche? A BMW. Wait, it isn't a Mustang, is it?"

"No, it's an Infiniti sports car. Nice speed, great handling, and all-wheel drive takes me wherever I want to go."

"And where does it take you?"

"Upstate New York sometimes. My grandfather has a place in the Adirondacks, sometimes down to Cape Cod or farther south to Martha's Vineyard."

"Where I assume your grandfather also has houses?"

"He does own a lot of real estate," Michael admitted. "It's his business, and he's been buying and selling for half a century."

"Sounds like you have a nice inheritance in your future."

"Only if I prove myself. Otherwise, he claims to be leaving everything to his favorite charities."

She gave him a doubtful look. "Seriously?"

"Yes. Will Jansen doesn't give anybody anything unless they earn it, and part of earning it is being unconditionally loyal and following the path he wants you to follow."

She sat down at her kitchen table. "Is that what you're doing, following his path?"

"While trying to make it my own—yes. Unfortunately, making it my own doesn't always make my grandfather happy." He paused as he sat down across from her. "But we got off topic. We were talking about your bad dates."

"I'd rather talk about you. You told me your dad came to Miami from Cuba. And I've now heard a little about your grandfather, but I don't know anything about your mother. How did your parents meet?"

"My mother was twenty years old. She was going to school at Yale, but she and a friend came to Miami for the summer. She wanted to suntan and make some money by the beach, so she got a job waitressing. My father had only been in Miami three months when he met her. He was working as a bus boy at the same restaurant."

Michael paused for a moment, his gaze reflective. "They both told me that they fell in love at first sight. They had a whirlwind romance. I think their relationship also went faster than normal, because they knew she would go back to school soon. By the end of the summer she was pregnant. She dropped out of Yale, much to her parents' dismay and she married my dad."

"And had you," Alicia said.

"We had a good life. Those early years, I just remember as being really happy. She was a free spirit, nothing like her father—my grandfather. She didn't care about money or ambition. She was a dancer and a singer, and she liked to have fun. I think her parents disowned her when she got married. They thought my dad was after her money, but he wasn't. He was in love with her."

"It sounds very romantic."

"I think it was."

"How did she die?"

"She had a difficult time with my birth. I guess there was scarring or something that made it risky for her to have more kids. But she thought she could beat the odds."

Alicia's heart turned over. She knew where this was going. "Oh, Michael."

"I was eight years old when she got pregnant again. She was really happy about it. She kept telling my father that everything would be fine, but it wasn't fine. She died from a late miscarriage," he finally said. "Both her and the baby."

"That's so sad. You and your father must have been devastated."

"It was horrible. My dad got so quiet after she passed. It was like we were living in a tomb. Everything was silent. I thought I would never hear him laugh again. But it turned out I was wrong about that. He met Veronica and life was good again—at least for him."

"What's Veronica like?"

"She's great," he said with a shrug. "She's devoted to my dad. She's a good mother. She treated me well enough. But she didn't like me to talk about my mom. She's not a bad person. And my dad isn't bad, either. They just didn't need me in their lives. I'm sure life was a lot easier when I left. My dad made it sound like going to prep school was all about me, saving me from crime and bad influences, but it was also about him having the freedom to show his love for his new family without any restraint."

She thought about his words for a moment.

"Your family history is definitely complicated."

"Like I said, it wasn't that bad."

She had a feeling he was making light of some painful memories. "You don't have to pretend with me, Michael."

"I'm not pretending. I'm also not crying. So that should make you happy."

She made a face at him. "It was a car, Michael, a thirty-plus-year-old car with peeling paint and bad upholstery. I'm not a mean person. I have compassion."

"Just not for old, sad cars."

"Okay, you've got me there."

He settled back in his chair. "So, did anyone in Liliana's family have anything interesting to say while I was away from the table?"

"Yes, as a matter of fact. Isabel told me that Liliana and David were not very friendly with each other. Did you know that?"

He shook his head. "No, I've never heard that."

"She said that David's father was injured in a friendly fire incident while he was in the Navy, but that the Navy covered up the true facts of the incident. He asked Liliana to look into it, which she did, but she came to the conclusion that there was no cover-up. David didn't agree."

"Why have I never heard that before?"

"Isabel probably didn't want to make a point of it since she was caught in the middle between her fiancé and her sister."

"Liliana loved being in the Navy. It wasn't just that the Navy got her through college and into the career that she wanted; she was also a patriot. If David attacked the Navy and/or her integrity, she wouldn't like it," Michael said.

"But she did come back for Isabel and David's wedding, so she must have put negative feelings aside for her sister's sake. Isabel also mentioned that David is really unhappy about the indefinite postponement of their wedding."

"I can see why he would be frustrated about that. He's definitely got a temper. I've seen that over the last couple of months."

"Maybe we should look into David."

Michael raised a brow. "You think he'd try to get rid of Isabel's sister? Why?"

"Perhaps he thought she was going to tell Isabel not to marry him. Liliana wanted to speak to you and not her family, which would support the theory that her problem had something to do with her family."

"I get where you're going, but if Liliana had something to tell Isabel, she would have just told her. She wouldn't have held back."

"Her sister was getting married in two days. It would have been really difficult to crush her sister's dreams at that point."

A frown spread across Michael's face, but she could see that he was considering her idea. "Maybe we should take a closer look at David."

"Isabel said he recently started his own computer software training company." She opened her computer. "What's David's last name again?"

"Kenner."

She typed in his name and hit Search. She got an answer on the first page of results. "Kenner Computing. They offer software training for mid- to large-sized businesses covering the usual office software programs." She looked at Michael. "It sounds pretty boring. But just because David appears to be on the dull side doesn't mean he doesn't have a secret. I wonder whether the police questioned him about his whereabouts the night Liliana went missing."

"I know they talked to all the family members, but whether that was just a few cursory questions, I couldn't tell you."

"We'll have to find out."

He nodded, a long yawn following that motion. He absentmindedly ran his fingers through his hair.

Despite his weariness, she couldn't help thinking how attractive he looked with a shadow of beard on his cheeks, the waves of his hair deliciously mussed. She wouldn't mind running her hand through those thick strands, maybe offering a kiss to soothe his furrowed, worried brow. Then she might see something else in those amazing blue eyes of his besides exhaustion. A pack of butterflies flew through her stomach at that thought.

What on earth was wrong with her? She felt suddenly nervous, restless.

If she leaned across the table, and if he did the same, she could make this tantalizing daydream come true.

And then Michael's voice broke through her reverie.

"Can I use your shower?" he asked.

"What?" she asked, still a little dazed by the sexy thoughts running through her head.

"To clear my mind. I need to wake up. Or, I could run home and come back."

"You don't have to do that. You can shower here. There are clean towels under the sink."

"Thanks."

After he left the room, she let out a breath, thinking maybe she was the one who could have used a shower—a cold shower.

She looked at her computer, yawned and then decided to take her laptop over to the couch.

She settled in among the comfortable cushions and then realized she'd made a huge mistake. Her eyelids seemed suddenly extremely heavy.

Maybe she'd take just a short nap. Then she'd come back at full strength.

Michael turned the shower first to hot and then to cold, needing something to douse the unexpected attraction he'd felt for Alicia a few minutes earlier. For a second there, he'd thought about kissing her, and the expression on her face seemed to support that possibility as a good idea. But it wasn't good; it was bad, very bad.

Alicia was one of the few people who believed in his innocence and was trying to help him get to the truth. The last thing he needed to do was ruin that. He needed her.

It was an odd thought to have about someone he'd met only hours earlier, but deep down in his soul, he felt like she was going to be the answer to all the unanswered questions. She was going to be the way out of the darkness.

Shaking his head at the ludicrousness of that belief, he stepped directly under the spray, letting the cold water run through his hair and over his shoulders.

Alicia was just a photographer who'd happened to be in the right place at the right time or maybe it was the wrong place at the wrong time—who knew? She thought the lightning had shown her something she needed to see—the ID tag. It didn't make sense to him, but he couldn't argue with the results. Nor could he discount all the little connections between Alicia and Liliana.

There was the Texas connection for one; the Navy for another. And what about the similarities between her father's background and his? Her dad had had a Hispanic mother and a Caucasian father. He'd had just the opposite, but they'd both grown up in families that had a clash of cultures.

He and Alicia were one step removed from the clash, but he often felt like he still had a foot in each world. He didn't think Alicia had been so profoundly impacted by her ethnic background, probably because her parents had provided a stable home until she was a teenager. Although she still liked to think that lightning had some mythical powerful quality, a belief she traced back to her Mayan great-grandmother.

There was something else they had in common. Alicia had lost her father, and he'd lost his mother.

So it wasn't that uncommon for people to suffer loss, but when he put that similarity with all the others, he felt goose bumps run down his arms. Maybe there was something to her idea that the lightning had brought them together for a reason.

Or maybe her craziness was rubbing off on him. He usually relied on his brain not his emotions. In fact, he preferred not to have too many emotions. In the past, they'd always messed up his life. So he'd chosen logic and reason, which made his life more solid, less unpredictable.

Perhaps a little boring . . .

Had he gotten complacent? Had he started to turn into his grandfather, a man who had never done anything on a whim in his life? Had he turned so far away from his father and his father's values that he'd lost all the color, all the excitement, all the joy?

That was a disturbing thought.

What was also disturbing was that he was even questioning his life. He'd thought everything was pretty damn good until he'd come back to Florida.

That had certainly changed.

His thoughts turned back to David. He had had no idea that David's father had been in the Navy, or that he'd been injured, or that Liliana had looked into the case.

But even if David and Liliana had hated each other, so what? Liliana wouldn't have tried to stop her sister's wedding. Unless . . .

Was there something she'd found out about David? But what could she have found out? That David was cheating on her sister? That his business wasn't on the up-and-up, that he was a liar? What?

He could be completely off base. Maybe she hadn't wanted his advice. Perhaps she'd just wanted to see him and thought those few days would be their best chance at catching up in person for years to come.

That seemed more likely.

One thing he'd always known about Liliana was that she was headstrong. She went after things. She didn't wait for someone else to take action; she stepped up when she needed to. If she thought her sister was making a terrible mistake, she would have said so.

Unless, she hadn't had the chance. Which brought him back to David being a person of interest, at least in his mind. He needed to find out more about the man.

Shivering, he stepped out of the shower and dried off. He dressed and then headed back into the living room, ready to get to work.

Alicia wasn't sitting at the kitchen table anymore, nor was she looking at her computer. She was stretched out on the couch and fast asleep.

He sat down in the armchair across from her and smiled to himself at the pretty picture she made. Her dark hair tumbled around her shoulders. Her cheeks were pink, her lips slightly parted as she breathed in and out, her soft breasts moving with each inhale and exhale.

There was a part of him that really wanted to lie down next to her and dream whatever dream was making her look so peaceful. She'd managed to escape the anxiety and tension of the past twenty-four hours. He wished he could do the same.

But he was awake now. And he couldn't undo the cold shower he'd just taken, so he turned her computer toward him and decided to do a little digging himself.

He went onto various social media sites, looking for personal photos and information. He finally got lucky when he linked through mutual friends to find David's personal profile.

He flipped through the photographs, many of which had been taken during the past year: the engagement party, bachelor party and other wedding-related events.

He scrolled down the page, clicking on the previous year. He wanted to go further back in time. He didn't know exactly when David and Isabel had gotten together, but he thought it had only been a year ago. He distinctively remembered someone telling him that they'd fallen in love hard and fast.

Sure enough, there was David getting cozy with a redhead a year and a half ago, and there were other photos of women and friends that he didn't recognize. He was beginning to realize that in his mind David had just been an appendage, Isabel's fiancé. He hadn't thought much about who he was outside of that role.

David loved hunting and fishing. He apparently spent a great deal camping as well, which surprised him. Isabel didn't seem like much of an outdoor girl.

But what did any of it mean? Nothing, as far as he could tell.

He clicked through several more photos, his breath catching in his throat when he saw David standing in a bar with another man. They were raising their beer glasses to the camera and appeared to be very good friends. "Damn," he said aloud.

"What?" Alicia woke up with a start, jolting into a sitting position, her eyes dazed and startled. "Did you say something?"

"Sorry. I didn't mean to wake you."

She blinked a few times, then said, "I didn't realize I fell asleep."

"You were out like a light."

She ran a hand through her hair, tucking the strands behind her ears. "What are you looking at?"

"A picture of David Kenner." He turned the computer screen around, so she could see the photograph of the two men holding beers at a sports bar. "Look who he's with—Brad Harte."

Her jaw dropped. "They're friends?"

"Looks like it. I'm surprised. Harte is at least nine or ten years older than David. This was taken over a year ago."

Alicia stared back at him with puzzled brown eyes. "What does it mean?"

"I have no idea, but we just came up with another question to ask Brad."

NINE

Two hours later, Michael had come up with quite a few more questions he wanted to ask Brad, but first Brad had to show up. They'd arrived at Javier's, a trendy, touristy bar in South Beach ten minutes before eight and it was now almost eight thirty. They were already finishing up their first round of drinks, mostly because they were both impatient for the time to pass.

"I don't think Brad is going to show," Alicia said, running her finger around the rim of her wine glass as she scanned the crowd.

"Let's give him a little more time."

He lifted his beer bottle to his lips and took a swig. If Harte didn't show up, Michael didn't know what the next move would be. They would have to go to David, but that wouldn't be easy. If they started asking him questions, the Valdez family would no doubt circle the wagons around him.

"This is a beautiful bar with beautiful people," Alicia murmured. "Not really my scene."

He raised an eyebrow at her words. "You don't like beautiful?"

"Not when it feels fake. I prefer raw, natural beauty, the kind that's unexpected."

"Like the kind you find in lightning."

139

She smiled back at him. "Exactly. There's nothing more incredible than nature showing what it can do."

"A lot of what nature does is destructive."

"I know."

"Do you?" he challenged. "Because it seems to me like you have a rather idealized view of storms. The aftermath of tornadoes, hurricanes, earthquakes, and flooding can be devastating. Or maybe you don't stick around long enough to see what the lightning brings with it."

She frowned and set her glass down on the table. "I stick around. I've volunteered many times to help people displaced by storms. I don't just take my pictures and vanish into the wind. I wouldn't do that. I *couldn't* do that. And you should know that better than anyone."

"I do. Sorry. I definitely know that you don't disappear when someone is in trouble. I don't know why I said that."

"Because you think my obsession with storms is a little weird, and that's okay, because it is. But it's part of me, and I'm not interested in pretending that it's not. I already tried that, and it didn't work."

"What does that mean?"

"I lost a pretty serious boyfriend because he didn't like the way I dropped everything when the weather changed. I hid my passion at first. I didn't rush off when the weather changed. I tried not to care. I stopped taking as many photographs. I just went to work and tried to be a good girlfriend. But I wasn't happy. I wasn't me. There's something about the lightning that speaks to me. It calls me to come. It wants to show me something. I really believe that."

He was beginning to believe it, too. "So you broke up with your boyfriend so you could chase storms?"

"No, he broke up with me. I left him in the middle of a party, and he didn't like it."

"Well, you can see why he wouldn't."

"It was a hurricane, Michael. It wasn't just any storm—it was the storm of a decade."

"I didn't think lightning came with hurricanes."

"Not usually, but sometimes it does. And besides that, my boyfriend had left me plenty of times when he needed to work. He just didn't view my lightning photography as work. He thought it was a stupid hobby. But you know I actually make more money selling my photographs at the gallery than I do working at the newspaper."

"That's impressive. And the boyfriend doesn't sound like he was the right man for you."

"He wasn't. Not that I know who the right man is," she said with a little sigh. "It's so difficult to find someone you really connect with, where it's instantly easy. You're not trying to talk yourself into anything. It's just good."

He nodded, her words resonating within him. He hadn't felt that kind of connection in a very long time . . . until now.

The unexpected realization unsettled him. He chugged down the rest of his beer.

"So what about you, Michael? I know you've had some bad dates, but what about serious relationships? When was the last time you had a girlfriend?"

He had to think about that. "Three years ago."

"What happened?"

"The usual stuff."

"As in . . ."

"She thought I cared about my work more than her. And she wasn't wrong. I've spent the last several years committed to getting ahead in my grandfather's company. I was usually thinking about my job instead of her."

"Or maybe she just wasn't the woman to make you think about her instead of work," Alicia suggested.

He met her gaze, thinking that he hadn't thought about work at all since he'd met Alicia. "You're right."

"Did you always want to be a builder?"

"No. When I was a lot younger, I wanted to be a baseball player. I was a great Little League shortstop."

"That's a hard position."

"I liked the challenge. But baseball wasn't really

an option at prep school. And summers after that were spent working at one of my grandfather's job sites. I ended up getting a master's degree in construction management and then worked my way up through his company. It's good. I like building things out of nothing. Every project has different challenges, and my grandfather's company has sent me all over the world."

"That sounds great, but it's still just a job, and you know what they say—a job won't keep you warm at night."

"I could probably say that about lightning, too," he said dryly.

A smile entered her dark eyes and spread across her face. "Actually, lightning can be kind of a turn-on for me."

His body stiffened at that piece of information. "Really?"

She laughed and nodded. "All that magnificent power gets your heart pumping."

She got his heart pumping. Not just with her words but also the look in her eyes. He had a feeling when Alicia let go, she would be pretty magnificent, too.

"You're staring at me," she said, her cheeks warming under his gaze.

"You're beautiful, Alicia."

"Today?" she said, doubt in her eyes. "I can look good, but that usually involves makeup and hair products."

He laughed at her candor. "You don't need anything, Alicia. Not when you have raw, natural beauty, not like the other women in this bar."

She grinned back at him. "You're in a better mood. What was in that beer?"

"I can't give the beer any credit; that goes to you."

"What have I done?"

"You believed me."

Their gazes clung together for a long moment, and he couldn't stop himself from putting his hand over hers. A jolt of heat moved between them. It wasn't lightning, but it felt a little like it. His fingers curled around hers and he very much wanted to lean across the small table and see if her lips tasted as sweet as they looked.

But Alicia suddenly started. "Brad's here."

He'd almost forgotten why they were in the bar. He let go of her hand and got to his feet as Brad approached the table.

Brad looked nervous with beads of sweat dotting his brow.

"Thanks for coming," Michael said.

"You didn't give me much choice. I figured if I didn't meet you, you'd come back to the dealership, and I couldn't have that."

"Probably right." He took his seat while Brad sat down across from them. "So, we might as well get straight to it. What do you know about Liliana's disappearance?"

"All I know is what I heard on the news and around town."

"Then why wouldn't you talk to us before? Why set up this meeting if you have nothing to say?" he challenged.

"I didn't want to talk about Liliana in front of my wife. She gets jealous. I'd told her that I cut off all contact with Liliana years ago."

"But you hadn't?"

"Not exactly. I mean, nothing was going on with us," he amended quickly. "But we kept in touch over the years. I think you know I was in love with Liliana. We almost got married. And even though that didn't happen, I've always cared about her."

"She told me back in high school that you'd asked her to marry you," Michael said.

"I had to propose. I was terrified of losing her. I knew she was going to enlist. She wanted to go to college, and there wasn't any money in the family to pay for it. I thought if we got married, she would put that idea out of her head. We'd take care of each other, and we'd both find our way to a better life. But she turned me down." Brad took a quick breath, painful emotion running through his eyes. "I really loved her. I would have tried to make her happy, if she'd given me a chance."

"You said you kept in touch. How often did you talk to her?" Alicia asked.

"We didn't speak for about six years after we

broke up. Then I ran into her one day and we started talking. After that, we'd email or text, occasionally meet for coffee. I liked having her back in my life, but my girlfriend at the time, who later became my wife, found out I was talking to Liliana and asked me to stop. I told her I would, but I didn't, because honestly there was nothing more going on than friendship."

"Why didn't you tell your wife that?" Alicia interjected. "Why lie about it?"

"I did tell her we were just friends, but she didn't believe me. She'd read a couple of my texts and thought that I sounded too admiring of Liliana. She accused me of still being in love with her. And maybe I was—a little—but I wasn't doing anything about it. I was faithful."

"When did you last speak to Liliana?" Michael asked.

"The day she arrived in Miami for her sister's wedding. She came by the shop, and we spoke for a few minutes."

"I assume your wife wasn't there."

"No, it was after we closed. She'd gone home for the day."

"What did you talk about?"

"The wedding, Liliana's job—we were just catching up."

"Did the police speak to you about your chat?" Michael asked.

"No."

"They never came by or called you?"

Brad shook his head. "I guess they didn't know we met."

"Why didn't you tell them after she disappeared?"

"Because I didn't have any information. Liliana and I met on Tuesday afternoon for about a half hour. She disappeared Friday night, and I didn't know anything about that."

Michael didn't like Brad's answer. He knew why Brad hadn't said anything; he wanted to protect himself. He wanted to keep his friendship secret.

Why the police hadn't figured out that Brad and Liliana had met was another question. He'd thought they'd constructed a timeline from when Liliana got off the plane, but they'd obviously missed that stop. What else had they missed?

"Look, I'm sorry about Liliana. I've been shaken up since it happened, but I don't know anything that can help."

"Do you know why she wanted to talk to me?" Michael asked. "Did she tell you that she was going to try to set up a meeting with me?"

Brad hesitated. "I've thought about that question a lot, especially when I heard you were a person of interest. I was surprised the police considered you a suspect. You and Liliana were good friends when you were kids. Then again, things change, people change. I hadn't seen you in years."

"I didn't hurt Liliana," he said sharply. "Can you say the same?"

"Of course," Brad said quickly. "You think I had something to do with it?"

"It crossed my mind. You were still in love with someone who didn't love you. Maybe that bothered you more than anyone knew."

Brad's face paled. "I would never hurt Liliana. I cared about her, yes. But I'm in love with my wife."

"Are you? She seems like your second choice."

"I knew I shouldn't have come here. You want to get yourself off the hot seat by pinning this on me."

"I'm just asking questions."

"You're accusing me of doing something unspeakable."

"He's not doing that," Alicia interrupted. "You both need to calm down and work together. This is about finding Liliana, remember?"

Michael nodded, crossing his arms in front of his chest. "Sorry for the accusation, Brad. Getting back to my question, did Liliana tell you that she wanted to see me while she was in town?"

"Yes. She said she was excited you'd come back to Miami and that she hoped you would make peace with your family."

"Was that it?"

"I remember her saying she wanted to talk to you about something, that maybe your grandfather could help."

"My grandfather?" he echoed, surprised at that piece of news. "What could my grandfather know?"

Brad gave a shrug. "No idea. I thought it might have something to do with her job. She said she was working on a case that had a lot of twists and turns. She was pretty excited about it. She said she felt like a detective more than a lawyer, and you know she always liked a good mystery."

"What was the case?"

"She didn't get specific, and I didn't ask. I didn't want to waste the time we had talking about her job."

"Do you know what she was working on, Michael?" Alicia asked, turning to him. "Do the police?"

"They went to Texas. They interviewed her employer, her coworkers, a few of her neighbors. As far as I know, they didn't feel there was any link between her life there and what happened here. But I am now curious to find out what she was working on, especially if it was something she wanted to talk to me or my grandfather about."

"Did she have a relationship with your grandfather?" Alicia asked.

"No. She never met him, but I talked about him a lot."

"What's going on?" Brad interrupted. "I thought Liliana's disappearance was random. Are you saying you think someone deliberately kidnapped her?"

Michael looked into Brad's eyes and saw what appeared to be genuine curiosity. Or was Brad just playing them to see what they knew?

"No scenario is off the table," he replied. "What do you know about David Kenner?"

"David?" Brad echoed in surprise. "We have some mutual friends. Why?"

"Isabel said that David and Liliana didn't get along, that David was very critical of the Navy," he said. "Did you know that?"

"Yes. David has a lot of resentment toward the Navy. He talked about his father's case all the time. I haven't seen him in over a year so I don't know what his relationship was with Liliana. Obviously, he was going to marry her sister, so I assume everything was all right." He paused. "Are we done?"

"One second. I'm confused as to how Liliana met with you without anyone knowing about it. She must have contacted you in some way, but the police have her cell phone records, and they've followed up with everyone who had texted or met with Liliana that week."

"She called me before she left Texas. Maybe it

was on her home phone or office phone. I have no idea. She told me she'd come by on her way home from the airport. That was it." Brad slid out of his chair. "I have to go. I'd appreciate it if you didn't come by the shop again. I don't need problems with my wife, and I really don't know anything else. I hope Liliana is found soon and that she's well," he said, taking a deep breath at the end of his sentence. "She's a special woman. I can't imagine this world without her in it."

"He's still in love with her," Alicia said, as Brad left the restaurant.

"But she wasn't in love with him. I can't help but wonder if the realization of that didn't send him over the edge."

"Now? After all these years?" she asked skeptically. "Seems like a reach."

"He hadn't seen her in a long time. Maybe he had hopes when she agreed to meet him the Tuesday before the wedding that he could get her back."

Alicia's steady gaze clung to his. "It's a possibility. Should we tell the police to talk to Brad? Although, like you, I'm a little surprised they weren't able to figure out she met with him. That doesn't sound like very good police work. What else did they miss?"

"I have the same question." He paused. "But to be honest, I wouldn't have even thought of Brad if you hadn't asked me so many questions about

Liliana and her past. You've definitely stirred things up, Alicia."

"The dust is flying, but we still don't know where Liliana is."

"We should call it a night. You're exhausted." The shadows under her eyes were getting darker. "Let's sleep on what we've learned and talk about it tomorrow. Maybe one of us will have another brainstorm. I'd rather not contact Kellerman until we have something solid to tell him." He picked up the billfold and slipped a twenty-dollar bill into it.

"I can pay for my drink," she protested.

"Don't worry about it."

The drive back to Alicia's apartment was quiet. He was mulling over what Brad had told them, and he suspected Alicia was doing the same. He double-parked in front of her building and pulled out his phone. "Give me your number. I'll call you in the morning."

They exchanged numbers and then she got out of the car. As she was about to shut the door, something inside him turned over. He was afraid to let her go, to break the connection between them. The feeling was so strong, he said, "Alicia, wait."

"What?"

"You're not done with this, are you? You're not going to wake up tomorrow and decide you're through? I wouldn't blame you if you wanted to get back to your life, but I would be disappointed."

She met his gaze and shook her head. "I'm not done, Michael."

"Are you sure? This isn't your fight."

"It became my fight the minute I saw Liliana in the lightning. And besides, we're partners. Call me in the morning. We'll figure out what to do next. I already have a thought, but it's probably crazy."

"What is it?"

"I'll tell you tomorrow. I need to sleep on the idea, see if it sounds better in the morning."

He had a feeling he knew exactly what her idea was, and it did merit some serious thought. He watched her get safely inside and then headed for home.

TEN

Alicia got up Sunday morning with the same outlandish thought that had been running around her head the night before. She tried to tell herself that she was getting carried away. It was one thing to ask questions, to try to help, but was she seriously considering taking vacation time to continue searching for a woman she had never met?

She was in the thick of a mystery, and she really wanted to solve it. Still, she needed to think about it, and today was a good day for that. She had no pressing obligations, just her usual weekend catch-up stuff.

After starting some laundry, she tidied up her apartment, made some breakfast, and then went on her computer to answer emails.

There was a note from her mom asking her how she was doing and saying she hoped that Alicia would consider coming home for Thanksgiving or Christmas. The suggestion made her feel guilty. She'd missed the holidays last year because of work commitments and a series of big storms over the Southeast.

She really should try to stay in better touch with her family, but the truth was she felt very disconnected from her mother and even her siblings. The break with her mom had come with her father's death, and the distance between herself and her siblings had grown when she moved to Florida.

Her phone rang, startling her. She thought it might be Michael, but it was her assignment editor at the *Miami Chronicle*.

"Hi, Ron, what's up?"

"Are you free this evening? Jamie's kid is sick with the flu, and I need a photographer."

"For what?"

"A candlelight vigil for a missing Miami woman. Apparently, there's been a break in the case. Shelly is interviewing the family for the article, but I'd like some photographs of the vigil to go with it."

Her gut tightened with each word. It wasn't another sign that she was meant to stay connected to Liliana, she told herself. She was a photojournalist. She covered these kinds of events all the time.

Still . . .

"Alicia?" Ron queried, impatience in his voice.

"Sorry. Yes, I can cover the vigil."

"Great. It's at five o'clock at St. Peter's Church. Send me the photos as soon as you're done. We want to get the story online tonight."

"Will do."

"I appreciate the help. I owe you one."

"Speaking of that," she said quickly. "I need to take a few days off this coming week."

"Why?"

"It's a family issue," she said vaguely. "I have vacation time available."

"How long will you be gone?"

"Two or three days."

"Well, Jamie promised to be back to work tomorrow, so do what you need to do."

"Thanks. I'll let you know my plan as soon as I finalize it."

As she set down her phone, she had a feeling she'd just taken the first step to putting her crazy plan into motion.

Step two was next. She punched in Michael's number.

He answered on the first ring, his deep baritone voice stirring her senses in a way that had nothing to do with the mystery they were trying to solve. Her mind ran back to the night before when he'd covered her hand with his. The heat between them had been intense.

Michael was under her skin, no doubt about it. He was like no one she'd ever met before. She couldn't totally read him. Most of the time he was dark, moody, angry, and frustrated, but then she caught glimpses of another man, one who was lighter, who smiled more. She knew he was capable of deep emotions. She'd seen how he felt about Liliana. She'd also seen how his family's rejection had hurt him. He might be reserved on the surface, but he had all kinds of emotions simmering underneath.

"Alicia, are you there?" he asked impatiently.

"I just got a call from my assignment editor. He wants me to take photographs of the vigil tonight for the *Chronicle*."

"Then I guess you're going."

"Are you?"

"Yes. Do you want to go together?"

"I'll meet you there. Maybe we could talk afterwards."

"About your idea?" he asked. "Why don't you tell me now?"

"Okay, here goes. I was thinking that we should go to Texas and find out what Liliana was working on."

"I think we should do that, too. Ever since Brad told me Liliana might want to talk to me about her case, I haven't been able to think about anything else. Can you get time off work?"

"I can take a few days. What about you?"

"I'll make it work. We can leave tomorrow and come back Tuesday night or Wednesday. I'll look into getting us airline tickets."

"Okay, good." She paused. "Are we nuts?"

"Probably. But at the worst, it will just be a waste of time. At the best, we figure out where Liliana is."

"Right. I'll see you tonight."

As she ended the call, she hoped the worst would be nothing more than wasted time, but there was a part of her that wondered what would happen if they kept stirring the pot. Because someone had taken Liliana, someone who wanted to do her harm—maybe had already done her harm. If they got too close to finding out who that someone was, they might be in danger, too.

The candlelight vigil started with the lighting of hundreds of candles, a procession around the two blocks surrounding St. Peter's Church, followed by a Mass.

Alicia shot over two hundred frames, taking care to get as many of the participants on film as she could. She'd seen Michael arrive just as the Mass began. She'd actually been watching for him during the procession and had wondered if he'd changed his mind when he didn't show up, but he'd obviously wanted to make a less conspicuous entrance.

He slipped into the last pew in the church, giving her a nod as he did so. She'd set up her camera on a tripod at the other end of that row. She didn't really need to shoot the Mass. She'd already sent two dozen digital shots to Ron, and was quite sure he had whatever he needed for the story, but since she was here, she wanted to stay until the end, see who was in the crowd, hear what everyone had to say, and maybe see if she could find another clue, something that could only be seen by an outsider looking in.

As the Mass continued, her gaze drifted back to Michael. He wore a black coat, gray shirt, maroon-colored tie and dark slacks, looking more like the successful businessman that he was than the man she'd first met in the park dressed in jeans and a sweatshirt. But she liked both versions of the man. In fact, she liked the man way too much. She'd actually missed him today. How ridiculous was that?

She turned her gaze back to the front of the church. The priest had started Communion and long lines of people made their way down the aisle. Liliana certainly had been well-loved by many.

Alicia couldn't imagine that she could draw a crowd this big. Her family, sure—maybe some coworkers—but who else would come? She'd lost track of most of her childhood friends, and the past few years she hadn't made many new friends outside of work.

It was her fault she'd become isolated. She'd put her storm photography ahead of everything else. She was beginning to realize that shooting life as it occurred wasn't the same as living life.

As Communion came to an end, she noticed a few people slipping out of the church as the priest said his final words. Standing in the shadows was Detective Kellerman, wearing a gray suit and open-necked white dress shirt. His gaze swept the crowd, lingering on the back of Michael's head, then it moved on to her. She blinked in surprise as he gave her a speculative look.

Why did she suddenly feel guilty? She wasn't doing anything wrong. In fact, she'd been assigned to come here.

Turning away, she snapped a few more photos as the Mass ended, then took down her tripod and put her equipment away.

The crowd filed outside, their candles to be relit once more in preparation for another processional journey around the church. She didn't need to shoot that trek since it would be no different than the one done earlier.

Detective Kellerman came over to her. "Miss Monroe. I didn't expect to see you here."

"I was assigned to cover the vigil for the *Chronicle*. They want to get the story online tonight."

"Do they know you're part of the case now?"

"I didn't mention it."

"Why not?"

"I'm hardly part of the case. I just found her tag."

"And yet you're extremely interested in the abduction of a woman you never knew."

"You sound suspicious of my motives."

He met her gaze head on. "I'm suspicious of everyone's motives. You've certainly gotten friendly with our primary suspect. A word of advice—don't be taken in by expensive clothes and a smooth smile."

She stared back at him, not sure what to say to that. It was clear that Kellerman disliked Michael. His personal feelings were definitely clouding his professional judgment.

"Michael told me that you arrested him when he was a teenager."

"I did. His rich grandfather got him off."

"You don't like him very much."

"That doesn't matter."

"It sure seems like it does."

"And it seems to me that it would be quite convenient for Michael if there was a new clue that pointed away from him."

"You think Michael set all this up? That he's using me?" she asked in disbelief.

"Or you could be working with him."

"You're wrong. That isn't what happened. And Michael is innocent."

"We'll see. People don't change," Kellerman replied, shooting Alicia a hard look. Then he turned his head toward Michael, who was walking toward them. "Once a punk, always a punk."

Michael didn't respond to the taunt, but she could see the anger in his eyes.

"I've got my eye on both of you," Kellerman added. Then he turned and left.

She blew out the breath she'd been holding. "I don't like him."

"Join the club."

"He thinks you put the tag in the dirt and I discovered it to throw the search in another direction."

"I don't care what he thinks. We know that didn't happen."

"True. I'm glad I didn't tell him we were going to Texas. He might have tried to stop us."

"Speaking of Texas, there's a nonstop at nine-twenty in the morning. Should we be on it?"

She nodded, even though her stomach was twisting now with the realization that she'd just agreed to go back to Texas. "Yes."

Michael must have read something in her hesitation, because he said, "You don't have to go, Alicia. I'd prefer if you did, because you have good ideas, but I know you have a job here."

"I can take time off. I have a lot of days saved up. I just wish Liliana hadn't been living in Corpus Christi. Going back to Texas, to my hometown, could be a little problematic."

He raised an eyebrow. "Why is that? Do you have outstanding parking tickets?"

"No, but I have a mother living there, and I don't see how I can go to Corpus Christi and not see her."

He shrugged. "So you'll see her. We'll make time for it. I'd actually like to meet your mother. Is she like you?"

"Not in any possible way. We're not close at all."

"It looks like Liliana's disappearance is bringing both of us back to our families." He gave her a dry smile. "Still happy with the lightning strike that started this whole thing?"

"I don't know if I'd say happy, but lightning lit up the trail. Now we follow it and see where it goes."

"Only a storm chaser would say that. Most people would run the other way."

She smiled. "Obviously, neither one of us is like most people. Do two crazy people make one sane person?"

He grinned back at her. "I think we're going to find out."

ELEVEN

They landed in Corpus Christi just after noon on Monday. They rented a car at the airport, then drove to a hotel near the naval station and checked into two adjoining rooms.

After stowing her overnight bag and taking a moment to freshen up, Alicia went into Michael's room and found him on the phone. She paused, wondering if he needed privacy, but he waved her inside. As he went over what appeared to be construction questions for his job, she walked over to the window.

The hotel overlooked Corpus Christi Bay, Padre Island, and the Gulf of Mexico. The water sparkled in the bright early afternoon sunlight. Like Miami, Corpus Christi enjoyed warm temperatures most of the year. Today it was already in the high seventies with a high of ninety expected. Also like Miami, Corpus Christi saw its fair share of hurricanes and was known as the *other windy city*. In fact, most people thought this part of South Texas had more wind than Chicago, but it was a different kind of wind, a wind that had always made her feel restless; a wind that often fore-shadowed a bigger storm.

She felt like that now—on edge, eager but uncertain.

She'd had time to rethink her decision to come to Texas with Michael, and while she believed it was important to learn what Liliana had been doing in Texas, she also worried that they were headed straight into a hornet's nest.

Then there was the issue of her family. She loved her mother and her siblings, but she didn't want to tell them why she was in Texas. They would shake their heads in despair if she said that she'd followed a lightning strike straight into a criminal investigation. Maybe she'd find a few moments to stop by right before she got on the plane back to Miami. For the moment, she was going to concentrate on finding information on Liliana.

Michael finished his call and walked over to the window. "Sorry about that."

"No problem. What do you think we should do first?"

"I called the JAG offices. The receptionist passed me on to a woman who said she'd worked closely with Liliana and would be happy to talk to us."

"That's great. It almost sounds too easy."

"Which probably means we're not going to find anything, but at least we have a place to begin."

"Should we go now?"

"She said she had a lunch but would be back at two. I'm thinking we should grab a bite and then meet her. Do you know any good places around here?"

"Let's see. The last time I was in this particular part of Corpus Christi was my first year in college. I went to Texas A&M."

He raised an eyebrow. "I didn't know that."

"Don't be too impressed. I didn't finish school. I got a job working for a photographer my senior year, and I was so in love with what I was doing that I took the year off, thinking I'd go back sometime, but sometime hasn't come."

"Do you need a degree for photojournalism?"

"Not really. Now that I have a big portfolio, my work speaks for itself. But sometimes I think I should go back and finish, because you should finish what you start."

"That sounds like someone else's voice coming out of your mouth."

She made a face. "My mother. She always complained that I was like a butterfly, flitting from one leaf to another, never settling down, never finishing what I started. She's not totally wrong."

"Am I going to get to meet her while we're here?"

"We'll see. Let's concentrate on Liliana. We should come up with some good, leading questions for her coworker."

"We'll do it over lunch. Shall we go?"

She nodded. "I'll take you to what was my favorite burger place. Hopefully, it's as good as it used to be."

. . .

Half an hour later, they were enjoying burgers smothered with onions and guacamole at a restaurant called Burger Bob's. It was three blocks from the university and filled with college students.

"Excellent," Michael commented as he finished his burger and wiped his face with a napkin. "Good choice."

"Probably not as fancy as you're used to."

"You think I'm fancy?" he said with a grin.

She laughed. "Maybe not so much. At least, not when it comes to food. You have a few crumbs on your lip."

He wiped his mouth with his napkin. "I prefer a good burger over an overpriced steak. I like food that's not pretentious. I like my friends that way, too."

"So do I."

As the air warmed between them, she felt a spine-tingling dance of butterflies in her stomach. Michael was attractive, smart and, when he let down his guard, very likeable.

But nothing was going to happen. Not now anyway.

"Another place, another time," he muttered.

"What?"

"You and me."

She saw the same awareness in his eyes, felt an almost irresistible pull toward him, but somehow she resisted leaning across the table. It was getting more and more difficult not to give in to temptation.

She'd always followed her passions, but this time she had to be smart. She had to think before she jumped. "We should talk about what we want to ask Liliana's coworker."

"Yes," he agreed, his lips tightening.

For a moment, it looked like he wanted to say something else, but then he picked up his glass and drank what was left of his beer.

"We need to find out what case Liliana was working," she said.

He nodded. "And who she was working with, whether there were any problems with her associates at work."

"We should ask about Liliana's personal life, too: friends, boyfriends, where she lived."

"I have Liliana's home address in my phone. When she first got the job, she gave me her address and I sent her flowers."

"We can go there after our meeting." She paused as the waiter set down their check and took their empty plates away.

"Good idea." He put some cash on the table to cover their bill. "Ready?"

"Michael?"

He gave her an inquiring look. "What?"

"*Maybe* another place, another time—*maybe* you and me."

His gaze met hers, and a smile played through his eyes. "No *maybe* about it, Alicia."

His words stopped the breath in her chest. She didn't know what to say. The silence reminded her of the calm before the storm. She had a feeling Michael could be as magnificent and as dangerous as the lightning she chased.

But she wasn't going to chase him, not now anyway . . .

Michael's pulse was racing way too fast. He wanted to blame it on the fact that he was walking into the JAG offices where Liliana had worked, but he was also amped up from talking to Alicia, from acknowledging the attraction between them. Now, all he could think about was taking their future *maybe* plan and making it happen now.

But he couldn't do that, and he felt a little guilty for getting sidetracked from their mission.

He opened the office door for Alicia, and she preceded him down the hallway and into the lobby.

The receptionist gave them visitor passes and took them through another door and into a conference room where she told them to wait.

Michael felt almost too wired to sit. He hoped this trip to Texas wasn't going to be a wild-goose chase. This next meeting would probably be a good indicator of what was to come.

"Breathe," Alicia told him.

Her words made him let out the breath he'd been subconsciously holding. "You're very good at reading my mind."

"I know there's a lot at stake, Michael, but whether this meeting turns out to be filled with good information or not, it isn't going to be the end of anything. It's just a step we have to take."

"You're right, but I'm hoping for a break."

"Me, too."

The door opened and a woman in her early thirties walked into the room. She was in uniform—navy blue skirt, white blouse—and her blonde hair was pulled back into a bun.

"Sorry to keep you waiting. I'm Lieutenant Erin Hodges."

"I'm Michael Cordero. This is Alicia Monroe."

After they all shook hands, Erin waved them back into their chairs.

"How can I help you?" she asked. "I already told the police everything I know."

"You spoke to Detective Kellerman?" Michael asked.

"Yes. He interviewed a number of us. I thought he'd come to the conclusion that there was no link between Liliana's life here in Texas and what happened in Miami?"

"We're just following up," Alicia interjected. "The case has gone cold, so we're reviewing all the facts in hopes of finding a lead that was previously overlooked. We really appreciate you taking the time to speak with us."

"Of course. Liliana was one of my best friends. I can't believe she's still missing."

"Do you know what Liliana was working on before she left Texas?" he asked.

"It was a murder appeal. Last year a female Navy lieutenant, Melissa Bryer, was convicted of murdering her husband and another woman. Her appeal made its way back to our office about three months ago. Liliana was reviewing the trial transcripts, the evidence and witness testimony to see if there was any merit to the appeal.

Michael's nerves tightened with that piece of information. "It was a double homicide? Who were the victims?"

"The lieutenant's husband, Thomas Bryer, a professor at Texas A&M and his alleged lover, Connie Randolph. The lieutenant was believed to have killed them in a fit of rage after finding them together in her house. The Bryers were living in Navy housing, and since the case involved a naval officer, Lieutenant Bryer was tried in military court."

"What was the basis for the appeal?" Alicia asked.

"Incompetent defense counsel. Lieutenant Bryer had two attorneys work on her case. The first attorney left JAG halfway through the trial to accept a civilian offer. Her replacement attorney was a younger, less experienced counselor. The appeal claims that mistakes were made because of the change in representation and the level of experience of the second lawyer who had not defended a murder case before."

"Why didn't a more experienced lawyer get the case?" he asked.

"We were low on manpower. Some of our attorneys were overseas at the time. It was an unfortunate set of circumstances." She paused for a moment. "But I don't see how the case could be connected to Liliana's disappearance in Florida."

"It may not be, but we need to check it off the list," he said. "Did Liliana find any merit to the appeal?"

"The day before she left town she told me that she thought the lieutenant deserved a new trial, but she didn't say why. I was busy on another case, so I wasn't paying much attention to what she was doing. I wish now that I'd asked her more questions."

"She must have been keeping notes," he said. "Where are those?"

"Detective Kellerman was given access to her computer, and I believe all relevant information was copied and sent back with him as well."

"Could we see that information?" Alicia asked.

Lieutenant Hodges immediately shook her head. "I'm sorry, but I'm not authorized to provide that information to anyone but the police."

Michael was discouraged but not surprised. "Tell me this then—was that case the only one Liliana was working on?"

"There were other smaller pieces of litigation, but that's where she was spending the majority of her time."

"Is there anything else you can tell us?"

"I don't think so. What's happening in Miami?"

"The police investigation has come to a grinding halt," he said.

"I'm sorry to hear that. I was hoping for better news."

"You said you were a friend, not just a coworker."

"Yes."

"Then you need to help us. The police have no more leads to follow and aren't interested in looking into what happened here in Texas, but we're not going to overlook any possible clue. We're going to keep digging and pushing until Liliana comes home."

Lieutenant Hodges suddenly smiled. "I would expect nothing less. Liliana told me about you, Mr. Cordero."

"Please, call me Michael."

"She said that you were her best and most stubborn friend, but that's probably why you got along so well, because she was just as bull-headed."

He was touched that Liliana had spoken to her friend about him.

"She also said that you'd always known her better than anyone else. That you gave her the best present for her thirteenth birthday."

"A second edition of Jane Austen's *Emma*," he murmured. "I can't believe she told you that."

"You gave her *Emma*?" Alicia asked curiously.

"It was her favorite book. I saw an edition online that was really old, and I thought she'd like it," he said, feeling a little awkward about the present now.

"She told me because she brought the book to our book club one night," Lieutenant Hodges added. "She said you'd told her she was a lot like Emma, nosy and meddling."

"That's true. She was both of those things, but she was also smart and caring."

"She was," Lieutenant Hodges agreed, sadness filling her gaze. "I thought it was just a random attack, that someone grabbed her off the street, Michael. Now you're making me think it wasn't that at all."

"That might have been what happened," he admitted. "But on the chance that it's not, I can't leave any stone unturned. If the situation was reversed, I know Liliana would keep looking for me."

"I'm sure she would."

"Did she tell you that she wanted to see me when she got to Miami?" he asked.

The lieutenant shook her head. "No, she didn't say anything beyond the fact that she didn't care much for her sister's fiancé but she was going to have to be nice now that he was going to be family. She also seemed a little irritated that she was going to have to put her investigation on hold for what she called a week of silly wedding events. She's not the type to enjoy the big bridal show."

"No, she definitely didn't care about that kind of thing."

"Is there anything else you can tell us about the case?" Alicia asked, bringing the conversation back to the appeal. "Were there any other suspects besides the wife? If she didn't do it, does she have any thoughts as to who did? What about someone connected to the woman who was killed? Did she have a boyfriend?"

"Everyone believed Ms. Randolph's boyfriend was Professor Bryer," Lieutenant Hodges replied. "She had an ex-husband, but they'd been divorced for about a year and he wasn't in town when she was killed. He had a strong alibi, too." She paused. "The police spoke to a lot of people: the Bryers' housekeeper, the neighbors, people at the university and also at the company where Connie Randolph was employed. Very few people had any relevant information. Lieutenant Bryer's sister, Cheryl Alton, was, however, quite vocal in defending her sister. She also didn't believe that there was an affair. But she had no proof."

"We really need to see the case file," Michael said. "It sounds like there were a lot of players."

"There were. It was a double homicide, so the investigation had to cover both victims in great detail. One thing is for certain. The bodies were found in the Bryers' house, so whatever relationship Thomas Bryer had with Connie Randolph, they were together the night they were killed. I'm sure you can find a lot of the details on the Internet. The press was very interested in the case. Love triangles are always media headlines, especially when the military and the university are involved. Just about everyone here in Corpus Christi knows someone who's either in the Navy or going to Texas A&M. It's that kind of town."

"Did Connie work at the university?" Alicia asked.

"No, she worked for MDT, which stands for Mission Defense Technology. They're a defense contractor. That's where she met Professor Bryer. He did some consulting work for them."

"What kind of technology?"

"They have many different product lines, electronics, radar systems, weaponry, GPS trackers and other military devices. The company has over ten thousand employees around the country, and at least seven hundred here in Corpus Christi. I know Liliana spent at least two days there talking to people. She came back pretty excited about some of the new technology they were working on." Erin smiled fondly. "Liliana loved gadgets. I think she had a secret desire to be a spy, not a lawyer."

Her words tugged at an old memory in his eart. "She did love spy movies. She'd drag us all to the newest Bond movie as soon as it came out, usually at midnight." He exchanged a sad, commiserating look with Lieutenant Hodges.

The lieutenant checked her watch. "I'm sorry to cut this off, but I have to be in court in twenty minutes."

"What about the case files?" he pressed. "Can you give us anything? It would be really helpful. It doesn't have to be official, just informative."

She hesitated. "Where are you staying?"

"The Bayside Hotel."

"If I can come up with any information, I'll leave it at the front desk. How long will you be in town?"

"At least a few days."

"I'll see what I can do."

"We appreciate that. One last question—was Liliana seeing anyone here in Texas?"

"She went out occasionally but nothing ever led to a second date as far as I know. And she had no problems here at work, if that's your next question."

"But what about the lawyer whose performance was the basis of the appeal?" Alicia cut in.

"Wouldn't that person have been a little upset that their work was being questioned?"

"Well, sure, but appeals are part of the business. You have to learn to not take them personally."

"Who was that attorney?" Michael asked.

"Vince McIntyre."

"Could we speak to him?"

"He was assigned to a carrier three months ago. He's somewhere in the Indian Ocean right now. I know Liliana spoke to him briefly on the phone, but her investigation needed to be conducted without his influence, so she didn't ask him a lot of questions."

"What about now?" Alicia asked. "Who's handling the appeal now that Liliana is missing?"

"It's still in the process of being reassigned. It's possible I may get it, but my boss hasn't yet made that determination. We've all been hoping that Liliana would return." Lieutenant Hodges got to her feet. "I really do have to go. If you have more questions, you have my number."

"Thanks for your time," Michael said as they walked out of the conference room together.

She paused at the entrance to the lobby. "I want you to bring Liliana home. If it were up to me, I'd give you everything."

"I understand."

"Good luck."

"Thanks," he said. "We could use some good luck for a change."

TWELVE

They walked back to the rental car in silence. Michael's brain spun with the information Lieutenant Hodges had presented. There was a lot to think about, which was good. But it was also bad, because there was so much new ground to cover. And were they even heading in the right direction?

He got into the car but didn't bother to start the engine. He wasn't sure where to go next.

Alicia fastened her seatbelt, and then said, "I think we're on the right track."

"Do you?" He cast her a confused look. "I have no idea what to think. If Liliana's disappearance was connected to the legal case she was investigating, why didn't someone go after her here? Why follow her to Miami?"

"Maybe she wasn't kidnapped. Maybe she went into hiding."

He appreciated her suggestion, but he just couldn't believe it. "She wouldn't have stayed hidden for two months. She would have reached out to someone. She hated to wait. It wasn't in her nature to be that patient. It's been too long."

"Okay, so let's go over what we know."

"We don't know anything," he said in frustration, hitting his hand against the steering wheel.

"We know a lot more now than we did an hour ago," she said, a forceful note in her voice. "We know she was investigating a double homicide, that there's a possibility an innocent person is in jail, which, if true, means there's a murderer on the loose. If Liliana got too close to the truth, she could have put herself in danger."

"Again I have to ask, why would the danger follow her to Miami?"

"Why not? What better way to throw off the police?"

She had a point.

"Did the police review airplane passenger lists to see if anyone came from Texas to Miami who was in Liliana's circle?" Alicia asked.

He stared at her in amazement. "How the hell did you think of that?"

"I don't know. Just trying to figure things out. Maybe you could ask Diego."

"I'll do that. But there are other ways to get to Florida. Someone could have come by car or train. Liliana was in Miami for three days before she went missing."

"Good point. But it's still something to think about." She pulled out her phone. "I jotted down some notes while you were talking to Lieutenant Hodges. We need to go down the list and speak to some of these people. I'm thinking we should start with Cheryl Alton, Lieutenant Bryer's sister. She has the most to gain by giving us information that might help prove her sister is innocent."

He was more and more impressed by Alicia's deductive skills and her determined spirit couldn't help but lift him up. "You're making a damn good partner, I have to say."

She smiled. "I'm not as emotionally involved as you are. I saw your face when Lieutenant Hodges spoke about the gift you gave to Liliana. I don't know how Detective Kellerman can't see the truth in your eyes. It's so completely obvious to me that you loved her."

His gut twisted in a knot. "I did love her."

"And she loved you. It didn't matter that you hadn't seen each other in years; you were still in her heart and she was in yours."

"Thank you," he said finally. "I don't know how you always know the right thing to say, but somehow you do."

Alicia laughed at that. "I must be on a roll with you, because I'm usually more likely to put my foot in my mouth."

"I want you to know something, Alicia," he said slowly, watching the humor fade from her eyes with the seriousness of his tone.

"What's that?"

He took a moment to find the right words. "I loved Liliana in the purest way. It wasn't romantic. It wasn't sexual. She wasn't the love of my life, and I wasn't hers. She was a sister to me, and I was a brother to her." He paused. "I need you to know that."

"Okay," she said a little uncertainly. "Why do you need me to know that?"

He couldn't get an explanation out of his mouth, because he didn't quite understand the need himself. "I just do."

Their gazes clung together for a long moment, mixed emotions flowing between them.

Alicia drew in a breath and cleared her throat. "All right," she said. "Should I read through my notes?"

"Let's do that later. I want to go to Liliana's apartment. Can you look up the address on your phone? 112 Pierpont Street?"

"Sure." She went into maps on her phone and found directions. "It's really close, about half a mile."

She gave him directions and a few moments later they pulled up in front of a three-story apartment building.

As he stepped onto the sidewalk, he glanced around the neighborhood. It was a modest block of apartment buildings and quiet for almost four o'clock in the afternoon. He suspected most people were at work.

He led the way into the building, which was not a security building. In fact, it looked more like a motel with exterior hallways and an open stairwell. Liliana's unit was on the second floor.

It was the last apartment at the end of the hall and across from the laundry room. The blinds in the window of her unit were closed, so it was impossible to see inside.

"Now what?" Alicia asked. "I'm guessing you don't have a key."

"No, I don't."

"Does this apartment even still belong to Liliana? Who's paying the rent?"

"I am. After the first month, the landlord sent a letter to Liliana's father saying that if we didn't pay the rent, we needed to pick up Liliana's things, or he would hire a mover and send us the bill. I told them I'd prepay the rent for a year so that Liliana wouldn't lose her home."

"If you paid the rent, then you should be able to get a key. I wonder if the landlord is on site."

"I don't think he is. And we don't need a key." He pulled out his own key ring, on which he had a very small universal tool set. "Keep a look out, will you?"

"You're going to break in?" she asked in surprise. "Do you know how to do that?"

He gave her a dry smile. "I did learn something from my troubled youth, and this lock is child's play."

Within a minute, he had the door open. He stepped inside, Alicia following close behind. He closed the door behind them while Alicia flipped on a lamp to give some light to the shadowy room.

"It smells musty," she commented, wrinkling her nose.

"I should hire a cleaner to come in here once a month."

"Everything is very neat, just dusty."

He walked down the short hallway and into the bedroom. There were only two pieces of furniture: a double bed and a dresser. On the dresser were several framed photographs. He picked up the first one of the Valdez family. "Looks like Christmas last year. David is in the shot with Isabel."

"I no longer think David is a suspect," Alicia said. "I don't think he and Liliana liked each other, but I don't think he was responsible for her disappearance."

"I agree."

Alicia opened the closet door. "Lots of uniforms in here."

He set the photo down and walked over to join her. She was right. There were very few civilian clothes in the closet. His gaze moved up to the top shelf where a box was labeled *Photos*. He grabbed the box and pulled it off the shelf, coughing as another layer of dust swirled around him.

He set the box on the bed and took off the lid. Inside were hundreds of loose photos, many from Liliana's childhood. He rifled through them, pausing when he came to a photo of a group of kids on the steps in front of a church. The boys were dressed in suits and the girls wore white dresses.

"Did you find something?" Alicia asked.

"First Communion. That's me." He pointed to a kid in the second row, third from the left. "And that's Liliana." His finger slid to the cute, dark-haired girl with big brown eyes and a happy smile standing right next to him. "I was two years late for my First Communion, because my mom had gotten sick the year I was supposed to do it. I ended up making my First Communion with Liliana's grade." As he tossed the photo back in the box, he couldn't help thinking how that moment felt like several lifetimes ago. "I'll take these back to the Valdez family. They'll want them."

"Are you okay, Michael?"

"I haven't felt okay in a long time. It's so damned unfair. Liliana should be here, living her life, making her dreams come true. Where the hell is she?"

"I don't know, but we're going to find out."

"Will we find out? We may never know what happened to her." He ran a hand through his hair, feeling overwhelmingly angry and discouraged.

"It's too soon to think that way."

Her optimism only pissed him off. "You may believe in miracles, but I don't, and I think that's what it's going to take. There are no clues here.

There are no clues anywhere. We're chasing dreams just to make ourselves feel better."

"Michael—"

"No," he said, putting up his hand. He saw the plea in her eyes to not give up, but he couldn't go along with that plea, not now, not in this moment, standing in Liliana's bedroom, in the home she would probably never see again. "I have to get out of here."

He was out the door before she could utter a word, and he didn't stop moving until he'd walked past the car and down the block.

Alicia stared after Michael, not sure whether she should go after him or give him a minute. She chose the latter.

Michael needed time to get his head together. Hopefully then he would see that it was too soon to give up. They'd only just arrived in Corpus Christi. There were lots of people to talk to. They weren't at the end—at least not yet.

She walked over to the dresser and opened one drawer after another. The police had no doubt come here during their investigation, but nothing seemed too messy. Whoever had looked around the apartment had not done a very thorough search, or they'd been extraordinarily neat, which didn't seem that likely.

For a moment, she felt a little of Michael's discouragement. Maybe the police had only done a cursory search because there was absolutely no link between Liliana's life in Texas and what had happened in Miami.

Or . . . they hadn't looked closely enough.

She took the box of photos into the living room and set it down on the coffee table, then moved into the kitchen. The refrigerator had been cleaned out. Maybe the landlord had done that.

She opened the cupboards and found boxes of cereal, tea, flour, sugar and canned soups. It was strange to look at someone's life from the outside, think about who they were, how they lived. One minute they were there and the next they were gone.

Liliana obviously hadn't left Texas thinking she wouldn't be back.

As that thought ran around in her head, she wondered where Liliana would keep her work if she brought it home with her. There was no obvious briefcase or computer anywhere in sight.

She walked back into the living room. She tried to see the details, to consider whether there was a clue here in this apartment. Lieutenant Hodges had said that Liliana would have been a good spy, that she was a good judge of people and always dug deeper than anyone else. So where were her notes? Work made the most sense. On the other hand, she had a feeling Liliana took her work home.

There would have been no reason for her to hide her notes. She lived alone. She could have left anything she was working on in plain sight, unless she wanted to hide something away. But Liliana hadn't acted like a woman who was hiding anything. She'd gone to Miami, participated in pre-wedding events, and never mentioned any problems to anyone in her family.

So she hadn't been afraid, but would she still have been careful? Would she have tucked her notes away somewhere?

Alicia let out a sigh. She was trying too hard. Michael was right. There was nothing here.

Her phone rang, jolting her out of her reverie. She expected to see Michael's number. He probably wondered what the hell she was doing and why she hadn't left the apartment yet, but it was her mom's number. She thought about answering but then let the call go to voicemail. She wasn't ready to deal with her mother just yet.

As she slipped the phone back into her bag, her gaze caught on the bookshelf.

Her mom used to hide spare cash in books. She'd said no robber would ever go looking for anything in a book.

It was a long shot, but the memory drew her over to the shelves. She went through the books but quickly saw there was nothing unusual. So much for that brainstorm. She might as well go find

Michael. They needed to move on with their day.

As she went to pick up the box of photos from the coffee table, her gaze fell on a much older book sitting on top of a pile of magazines in a basket next to the couch.

It was *Emma* by Jane Austen—Michael's gift to Liliana.

She picked up the old book and opened the cover to check the copyright. That's when she saw a piece of paper holding a place about midway through the book. She pulled out the paper, her heart beginning to race as she saw Liliana's handwriting. Maybe they were going to get lucky after all.

Michael paced up and down the sidewalk. *Where was Alicia?*

He appreciated the fact that she'd given him a little time to regroup. Seeing that picture of Liliana at their First Communion had hit him hard, but now he wanted to get on with things, figure out what to do next. He was about to go back to the apartment when he saw Alicia come jogging down the sidewalk with the box of photos in her hands.

Her face was lit up like a kid on Christmas morning.

"I found something," she said, coming to a breathless stop in front of him. She put the box down on the ground and handed him a piece of paper. "Take a look at this."

He took the paper from her hand. For a moment, he couldn't figure out what he was looking at. "What—"

"It's notes from Liliana's case. Look at the list of names and notations," she said, moving next to him so she could read them aloud. "Cheryl-sister, doesn't believe affair; BR-ex-husband, temper, jealous? PS-frustrated during court testimony; housekeeper's son-professor cheap; teaching assistants not fans-professor arrogant SOB; Randolph-no friends, why?"

Alicia looked over at Michael, who was studying the paper. "This is a list of who she spoke to regarding the case."

"And where she went," he continued, pointing to the next column. "MDT-fake willingness to help—whatever that means; Flight Deck-meeting place with a question mark—sounds like she was trying to figure out where the professor met his lover."

"There's another reference to the bar on the back," she said as he flipped the paper over.

"Bartender witnessed marital fight days prior," Michael read. "That's interesting."

"And what about this?" she said, tapping her finger at the next line. "Housekeeper overheard loud argument with male outside the house three days before murder." She looked at Michael. "Who was that?"

"Beats me." He sucked in a breath as his gaze

190

drifted toward the bottom of the page. "Did you see this? MDT-RP, Will Jansen," he read aloud. "Then there's an arrow to my name."

"Looks like she did want to talk to you about your grandfather and MDT. I don't know what RP stands for? Maybe someone in the company?"

He stared at his grandfather's name, reeling from the fact that he now had some concrete proof of why Liliana had wanted to talk to him. But what did his grandfather have to do with anything? As far as he knew, Will Jansen had never set foot in Texas. And he was about as low-tech a person as you could find. He barely answered emails. What would he have to do with MDT?

"Where did you find this?" he asked, looking up from the paper to meet her excited gaze.

Alicia gave him a smug look. "Tucked between the pages of a second edition of *Emma*."

"Are you serious?"

"It was sitting on top of a pile of magazines next to the couch. I'm guessing Liliana was making notes and either used the note page as a bookmark or just stuck the notes in there so they wouldn't get tossed out accidentally."

"How did you think to look in the book?"

"My mom used to hide money in books. I looked through Liliana's bookshelves and didn't see anything hidden away. Then I saw *Emma* by the couch. I remembered your sweet story, and I actually just opened it up to see the copyright date. I wasn't really expecting to find anything, but I did."

"That's amazing. *You're* amazing," he said, truly in awe of how Alicia kept finding her way back into the mystery no matter how many doors slammed in their face.

"I am pretty good," she said with a proud smile. "I just found us some more clues to follow."

"You certainly did." He stared into her bright, sparkling eyes and felt an incredible pull. This woman was turning his life upside down, taking him out of the darkness and moving him toward a very hopeful light. His nerves were on fire. His pulse was pounding. And he wasn't thinking about the notes anymore, but about the woman standing in front of him, the woman with the heart of a lion and the mouth of a goddess.

He couldn't fight it anymore. He didn't want to fight it anymore.

He folded the paper in his hand, shoved it in his pocket, and then stepped forward, slid his arms around her waist and kissed the look of surprise right off Alicia's sweet, sexy lips.

THIRTEEN

*M*ichael was kissing her!

Alicia couldn't quite wrap her brain around what was happening. It wasn't just a brief kiss of gratitude. It was filled with emotion and heat.

The sparks that had been smoldering between them burst into flame, and after her initial surprise, Alicia found herself sinking into his kiss. She loved the feel of his mouth on hers, the strength of his hands on her waist. He held her as if he never intended to let her go.

As if she was his, and he was hers . . .

But he wasn't hers.

And this kiss was just an emotional release, a spontaneous idea . . . something . . .

Michael lifted his head, his breath coming hard and fast, his light blue eyes glittering with what looked like hunger.

Her breath caught in her throat. There was no denying the desire in his gaze, the feeling that he needed her as much as she needed him. Licking her lips, she almost went back in for another kiss, wanting to feed that hunger, but Michael abruptly stepped back. It happened so quickly she almost stumbled, but somehow she managed to stay on her feet.

He ran a hand through his hair, his gaze troubled now. "Alicia, I'm—"

"Don't say you're sorry." She put up a hand to ward off the apology she knew was coming. "It's really awkward when someone kisses you and then says they're sorry, they didn't mean it."

He stared back at her, and even though he hadn't said the word, the apology was still in his eyes. "It's not that I didn't mean it," he said.

"Was I a stand-in?" she couldn't help asking.

Shock moved across his face. "What? You mean for Liliana? No!"

His emphatic denial killed that little niggling worry.

"Alicia, I told you that Liliana and I had a brother-sister relationship." He paused. "You asked me why I need you to know that. This is why. I've been attracted to you since we met in the park. There's something about you . . ." He shook his head in bewilderment. "You're honest and brave and sexy as hell, and I find myself thinking about taking you to bed when I should be thinking about the case we're working on."

She licked her lips at his direct words, her entire body lighting up at the idea of going to bed with him. How could that be? She didn't jump into bed with men she barely knew. But Michael was different. She'd learned more about him in two days than she'd learned about her last boyfriend in three months.

"We can't do this now," he said, digging his hands into the pockets of his black jeans, his expression now grim and determined. He'd made a decision and he'd put his walls back up. She was not scaling those walls today.

Not that she wanted to. Well, she did *want* to, but she couldn't. Michael was right. This wasn't the time.

"Are you going to say anything?" he asked, his words tinged with worry as his gaze searched her face for a reaction.

"You know I feel the same connection with you. I keep telling myself it's just the situation. We're both running on too little sleep and too much emotion. This isn't real life, so what we're feeling can't be that real." She paused. "But it feels real."

"Yeah," he said softly, meeting her gaze. "It feels like something—important."

A knot grew in her throat at his words. In the past she'd been a little afraid of feelings that were *important*. She'd made a habit of keeping relationships light, because love terrified her more than anything.

"That scares you, doesn't it?" he asked, cocking his head to the right, a bit of wonder in his gaze. "The girl who chases lightning is afraid of love."

"We're not talking about love; we're talking about sex," she said, feeling a little desperate to remind both of them of that fact. "And we shouldn't be talking about either one. We should be concentrating on the note I just found."

"You didn't deny that you're scared of love."

"And you're not scared of love? I don't see you having a lot of serious relationships."

"A counterattack is always a good defense."

"We're not talking about this now. Let's move on."

He hesitated for a moment, then said, "All right. Let's get in the car. I'll call my grandfather, see if he can shed any light on his appearance in Liliana's notes."

"Good idea," she said with relief.

Michael called his grandfather while she settled into her seat and fastened the seatbelt.

"He's not answering. I'll leave a message." He paused, and then said, "It's Michael. Can you call me back as soon as you can? I have a question for you." Michael set the phone down on the console. "He's probably on the golf course. He has a regular Monday game."

"Does that mean he's retired?"

"No, it just means he plays golf on Mondays and Fridays and usually the weekend," he said with a smile. "But he still goes into his office, and he definitely knows what's going on in his company. I don't think he'll ever retire. He's seventy-six years old with no sign of slowing down yet."

"What's your grandmother like? I've never heard you speak about her."

"She's quiet, always lets her husband do the talking. She's probably what you would call a corporate wife. She has spent her entire life supporting her husband's business efforts. She's always entertaining people, participating in charity fundraisers, that kind of stuff."

"I wonder what kind of relationship your mom had with her."

"My father said that they weren't close. My mother was more of a free spirit. She really didn't have much in common with either of her parents."

As Michael finished speaking, her phone rang. "Speaking of parents," she said with a sigh.

"Your mother?"

"Yep."

"Go ahead and answer it."

"I don't know." She hesitated long enough that her phone went to voicemail.

Michael sent her a thoughtful look. "What's the problem? We can see her for a few minutes. We can make time for your mother."

"She'll ask a lot of questions about why we're here and as soon as lightning comes up, you'll find out just how crazy she thinks I am."

"I don't need her opinion for that," he teased.

She made a face at him. "It's not like you were dying to talk to your dad the other day, so you should give me a break."

"Hey, you can do what you want. I'm just saying that I would support any attempt you want to make to see your mother. What does she do anyway? Does she work?"

"Yes, she works at the university," she said idly, as she considered whether or not to call her mom back.

"Hold on."

Michael's energetic words brought her gaze to his. "What?"

"Your mother works at Texas A&M?"

"Yes, she's in admissions." As soon as she finished speaking, she realized what she'd just said. "She probably knows Professor Bryer."

"I would think so. You need to call your mom back. Sorry, Alicia, but we need to speak to her. She might be able to give us information about the case. You're just going to have to suck it up."

She raised an eyebrow. "Suck it up? That's the extent of your pep talk?"

He gave a careless shrug. "I didn't know how else to put it."

She knew he was right; she just didn't like it.

"Fine, I'll call her back. But I know I am going to regret this." Pulling out her phone, she punched in her mom's number. "I'm not going to give her the whole story yet. We should do that in person."

"Good idea. Let's get in the door first."

Her mother answered on the second ring. "Alicia?" Joanna Monroe said. "It's about time you called me back."

"Sorry. What's going on?"

"Your sister just got a fabulous new job. She's going to be working for Senator Dillon. She's moving to D.C. next month, and I want to have a party for her. I know it's far for you to come, but I think you should make the effort."

"That's great." Her sister Danielle had worked very hard on the senator's election campaign, so it was nice that she'd been rewarded with a good job. Dani had been trying to move up the ranks for the last several years. "What's the date?"

"Probably the last week in October."

"I'll see if I can come," she said.

"I want a yes, not a maybe."

"We'll talk about it." She saw Michael giving her a pointed look and knew she'd stalled long enough. "I'm actually in Corpus Christi right now."

"What?" her mother asked in shock. "What are you doing here?"

"It was a last-minute trip. That's why I didn't call until now. I was wondering if you're free, if I could come by and see you."

"Well, of course. When?"

"Are you still at work?"

"I'll be leaving in a few moments. I should be home in half an hour."

"We'll come by the house then."

"We?" her mother queried.

"I'm going to bring a friend with me."

"A female friend or a male friend?"

"His name is Michael Cordero. We'll see you soon." She ended the call before her mother could ask any other probing questions. "My mom will be home in thirty minutes."

He nodded approvingly. "Good. Let's go back to the hotel and check in with the front desk to see if Lieutenant Hodges has left us anything. Then we'll head back out."

"Before we meet with my mom, we need to figure out how much we want to tell her. She's going to ask questions."

"And some of those are going to be about who I am and why I'm with her daughter," he said knowingly.

"Those will be the first two questions. I know we need to talk to my mother, but I don't have a good feeling about this, Michael."

"Why? Do you think your mother is going to instantly dislike me?"

"Worse. I think she's going to like you too much."

"I can't believe Lieutenant Hodges didn't send over any information," Michael complained after a brief stop at the hotel. "I really thought she'd come through for us."

"It hasn't been that long, and she was on her way to court when we saw her," Alicia reminded him.

"True."

"I'm sure my mother will be able to tell us a lot

about the professor's death," she added as they got back into the rental car and headed to her mother's house. "She's been at the university for fifteen years. She's also the kind of person who knows everything that's going on. In fact, she makes it her mission to know everything."

"You must get some of your curiosity from your mother."

His words surprised her. "I don't know about that. I've always thought I was exactly like my dad. He was more of a dreamer. His curiosity was about the universe. My mom was more interested in gossip—not that gossip can't be entertaining—but her world always seemed a lot smaller than his." As she finished speaking, she felt a little guilty for what she'd just said. "I'm not putting her down or anything."

"Aren't you?" Michael challenged, giving her a quick look.

"Well, maybe I was. Growing up, I was closer to my dad. We had more in common. We loved to spend time together. With my mom, it was contentious. We were always arguing. I constantly disappointed her. She disapproved of most of my choices. With my dad, love felt unconditional. With my mom, love came with achievement."

"What about your siblings? Were they close to your mother or your father or both?"

"Jake was close to both of our parents. He was the oldest, the son, and he was very even-tempered. Danielle was closer to my mom. She's the middle child and two years older than me. She was a girly girl. She and my mom liked to shop, get manicures together, go to the spa, decorate the house, and they spent a lot of time together. My mom is really going to miss Dani. She apparently just got a job that will take her to Washington, D.C. next month. It will be the first time anyone in the family besides me has left Texas for any length of time."

"Why did you leave, Alicia? Was it just for the lightning? Because I know Texas has some big storms."

"The lightning was part of it, but I wanted a change in my life. And I didn't want anyone looking over my shoulder, criticizing my decisions. After I dropped out of college, my mother was constantly harping on me to go back. When the job I'd taken ended, I was at loose ends and decided a change would be good. That was four years ago."

"No regrets?"

"About moving away, no," she said, shaking her head. "My mom has a way of making me feel bad about myself, probably because she's not completely wrong. I haven't been the most ambitious of people, and I've made decisions based on things like lightning patterns instead of career potential. I know that at times my priorities are a little skewed, but I go with my gut. So far it hasn't led me into too much trouble."

"Are you happy with your life?"

"Pretty much."

"Then that's all that matters."

"Is it? I think I'm supposed to want more than a small apartment, an old car, and a job that barely pays the rent and is boring as hell half the time."

"I don't think you have a lack of ambition, Alicia; I just think it's focused on your passion and not on your day job. But the world needs art, and you provide it. There's nothing wrong with that."

"I'm not getting rich."

"I don't get the feeling that money means that much to you."

"I guess it doesn't. I want to have enough to live comfortably, but I've never had any dreams of rolling in a lot of cash. Not that I'd turn the money down if it came my way." She paused. "What about you, Michael? Have you achieved all your dreams?"

"I'm doing well," he said, an odd note in his voice.

She shifted in her seat. "You think you could be doing better?"

"Isn't that always true for everyone?"

"I'm not talking about everyone; I'm talking about you. I bared my soul, Michael. Your turn."

"You didn't have to bare your soul. That's on you."

203

"Come on. Do you have some secret ambition that no one knows about?"

"If I did, why would I tell you?"

"Because we're sharing," she said pointedly.

"All right. I like what I do now, and I see lots of areas that I would like to get better at. Someday I'd like to run my own jobs, be my own boss."

"Would that require you breaking away from your grandfather? I would think you would be in line to inherit his company."

"I'm in line, but only if I prove myself a thousand times over, and believe me, my grandfather is my harshest critic. Even if I did inherit his company, it would still be his. I'd like to have something that's all mine."

"Would you turn it down then?"

He sighed. "I don't know that I could, but I'd also like to design something, not just build to someone else's plan. A long time ago, I thought I might be an architect, but my grandfather thought construction management would make me a more valuable employee. I can't say it was a bad idea, but there's a part of me that still likes to play around with blueprints."

"You have to feed the creative part of your soul. Maybe you could do both."

"Maybe, but so far I haven't had the time."

"Are you sure time is the problem? Or would actually putting your ideas down on paper make the dream too real? Sometimes it's easier to leave things in a dream state. You never fail if you're just dreaming."

He gave her a thoughtful look. "That's a very smart statement."

"Well, I'm a smart woman," she said lightly.

"You are very intuitive," he agreed.

"Are you complimenting me so that I'll change the subject or do you really believe that?"

He laughed. "Just take it as a compliment."

"Okay, I will. Tell me more about your grandfather. Was he born rich or did he make his own fortune?"

"He was born into money. My great-grandfather was an investment banker. He passed on a considerable fortune when he died to my grand-father and his brother. The Jansens have never been short on money or ambition. My grandfather is a ruthless businessman. He has a lot of hard edges, and he scares the shit out of most people. He has no patience for incompetence or lack of drive. He has high expectations for everyone around him."

"It sounds like you're meeting those expecta-tions."

"Some days. Not always." He glanced over at her. "We've spent enough time talking about my family. We're almost to your mom's house. Tell me what I'm about to walk into."

She let out a little sigh. "A lot of drama."

"Just remember this visit isn't only about you and your mom. We need her help."

"I'll try to remember that, but I make no promises. My mom and I seem to butt heads with the least provocation."

"I'll try to be a buffer."

"That would make you a brave or stupid man. Getting between a mother and a daughter can be risky business."

"I'll take my chances."

"Well, hopefully, you won't need to get involved. I just want to ask my mother about Professor Bryer and make this visit as short as possible."

FOURTEEN

Alicia would not get her wish for a short visit, Michael realized about five minutes after they walked through her mother's front door.

After brief introductions, Joanna Monroe waved them into the kitchen and started pulling steaks out of the freezer, telling them she'd been planning to barbecue and was so happy not to be eating alone for a change.

Alicia had given him a dismayed, pleading look, but it was too soon for an intervention. He wanted Joanna on their side so that she would be happy to give them all the information she had on the professor's murder, and that wouldn't happen if she got pissed off at Alicia right from the start.

"Mom, you really don't have to cook for us," Alicia protested.

"Actually, I was hoping Michael might throw these on the grill for me. I do love a man who knows how to barbecue."

"I could do that," he said, picking up on her obvious cue. "I'm not an expert, but I'd be happy to cook for you, Mrs. Monroe."

"Please call me Joanna," she said with a warm smile. "You know, I can't remember the last time Alicia brought a man into this house. I think she was a teenager. And it was probably that awful

Vincent Maloney." She shuddered. "That boy had tattoos of skulls on his arms."

"It was one tattoo on one arm," Alicia corrected. "And, Michael, you don't have to barbecue. We really just came here to talk to you, Mom."

"It's been so long since we've had dinner together, Alicia. Surely you haven't come all the way to Texas not to have an extra hour or two for your mother."

Joanna gave Alicia a pointed look that shot down whatever protest might be coming next.

As the two women stared at each other, Michael was struck by how alike and yet how dissimilar they were. They were both the same height with slender builds, but Joanna had short blonde hair and light green eyes that suggested Alicia's dark hair and dark eyes came from her father's side of the family. Joanna also had a sharper edge to her tone, more angles in her thin face. He had the sense she was always in control of every situation, including this one.

"Of course we have time to have dinner with you," Michael said, stepping into what was becoming a tense silence. "Alicia has told me how much she's missed you. This will be a great opportunity for you both to catch up."

Joanna's eyes softened with happiness at his words, while Alicia sent him a dagger of a look. But in the end, Alicia stepped up to the plate.

"Michael is right, Mom. This would be a good

time to catch up. I'd love to have dinner with you."

"Excellent. I know Dani has a meeting tonight, but maybe I can get Jake to come over. He's usually happy to have someone cook for him."

"Great." It would probably be easier with her brother in the mix.

"I'll give him a call." Joanna glanced around the kitchen. "I must have left my phone in the bedroom. I'll be right back."

"You are such a kiss ass," Alicia told him when her mother left the room.

"You want her to help us, don't you?"

"But dinner with my mom and maybe my brother, too? It's a lot of time to waste."

"Hopefully, it won't be wasted." He paused, seeing her rub her forehead with her hand. Her bruise had faded but there was still slight discoloration on her temple. "Headache?"

"It seems to occur whenever I get within six feet of my mother."

"She seems nice."

"She *is* nice. And I love her, but she also drives me crazy. She has an opinion on everything that I do."

"Better to have an overinvolved parent than one who doesn't care."

"I just hate it when she makes me doubt myself, which is most of the time."

He smiled, thinking her mother had spooked

Alicia more than the lightning she chased. Apparently, Alicia's gutsy fearlessness hit a brick wall when it came to Joanna Monroe.

"If Jake does come tonight, you'll easily be able to see the difference in how my mother treats the son who can do no wrong and her youngest daughter who does everything wrong. And the thing is—Jake isn't perfect. He screws up all the time, but she doesn't see it. Or if she does see it and tries to get on him about something, he just cracks a joke and makes her laugh and all is forgotten."

He gave her a reassuring smile. "It's going to be fine, Alicia. You need to chill."

She shot him a dark look. "I'm going to tell you that the next time we see your father and you get all uptight and twitchy."

"I don't get twitchy."

"You definitely do. In fact, you've relaxed a lot since we left Miami. Maybe Florida has the same effect on you as Texas has on me."

"Maybe we both need to realize that we're giving our families and our pasts too much| power over us."

"Perhaps."

Alicia had no opportunity to say more as her mother reentered the kitchen with her phone in her hand.

"Jake said he'd love to come," Joanna said with a happy smile. "He'll be here in about thirty minutes."

"Great," Alicia muttered.

"Why don't we let the steaks thaw? We'll get some drinks and go out on the deck. It's a lovely afternoon." Joanna opened the refrigerator. "I have white wine, lemonade or water." She glanced back at them. "I'm sorry I don't have beer or anything stronger. I can ask Jake to pick up something on his way over if you like."

"Lemonade sounds good to me," Michael replied, thinking he preferred to keep his wits about him anyway.

She took a pitcher out of the fridge. "Alicia, why don't you get the glasses, and we'll go outside?"

"All right," Alicia answered, opening the cabinet.

As Alicia pulled out the glasses, he followed her mother onto the back deck. Joanna had thought the weather was lovely; he thought it was hot. The temperature was at least in the high 80s but the humidity wasn't as bad as what he'd experienced in Florida all summer. Still, he was happy to see a large shade umbrella over a table on the redwood deck.

The yard was beautifully landscaped, the deck stepping down to a lawn area with colorful flowerbeds and an oak tree, under which hung a decorative bird feeder.

They sat down at the table. Joanna poured the lemonade into glasses and then passed them around.

The cold lemonade was perfect. "This hits the spot," he said, loving the icy tang that cooled his parched throat.

"I'm glad." Joanna turned to her daughter. "So are you going to tell me why you're here in Texas without so much as a five-minute notice, Alicia? I thought you swore you wouldn't be back to this town unless someone was dying," she said with a roll of her eyes.

Alicia grimaced. "I don't think I put it exactly like that, Mom."

"I think you did," Joanna said, not backing down.

"Well, things changed."

"Like what?"

Alicia drew in a breath. He could see the wheels spinning behind her gaze. She was debating how much to tell her mother. He had a feeling the less information, the better. He didn't want the conversation to get derailed by a mother's concern for her daughter.

"I'm helping Michael investigate the disappearance of a good friend of his," Alicia said. "The woman disappeared in Miami, but she was working here in Corpus Christi before that. We came here to see what we could find out about her life, her job, and her friends."

He blew out a breath, relieved that she'd left out the lightning and the fact that he was a suspect.

"Well," her mother said, surprise in her eyes. "I

must say I wasn't expecting you to say anything like that. I'm sorry about your friend, Michael."

"Thanks. Alicia thought you might be able to help us."

"Really? How on earth could I do that?"

"My friend, Liliana Valdez is a JAG lawyer working out of the naval station here in Corpus Christi. She's been reviewing the appeal of a murder conviction. One of the victims was Professor Thomas Bryer."

"Oh," Joanna said, sitting back in her seat, a gleam in her eyes. "Now I understand. You want to know what happened to Thomas."

"Did you know the professor?" Michael asked.

"Yes, of course. He'd been at the university for more than a decade. He was a very well-liked and well-respected teacher. A brilliant man, really. His murder was shocking and sad."

"Did you know his wife or the woman who was also killed?" Alicia interjected.

"I had met Melissa Bryer several times at faculty functions, but I didn't know her well. She was away a lot."

"What about the other woman—Connie Randolph?"

Joanna shook her head. "I had never heard of her until the day they found her body next to Thomas."

"Were you surprised that there was another woman?" Michael asked. "Was Thomas the kind of man to have affairs?"

She hesitated. "I can't say that I know that much about his personal life. He did have a reputation for being a ladies' man, and certainly there were a lot of coeds who flirted with him. I think he was rated very high on the student website called *Hot Teacher*." Joanna gave them a dry smile. "Thomas was attractive in a scholarly way. He had that absentminded professor air about him. He often let his hair grow too long or didn't shave for a few days when he got lost in a project. There were women who found that sexy."

"Do you think his wife was capable of killing him?" Alicia asked.

Joanna gave a noncommittal shrug. "She was a soldier. She was used to guns. It seemed like an ironclad case from what I read in the newspapers and heard around the campus. But you said she's appealing her conviction?"

Alicia nodded. "Yes, and Michael's friend apparently thought there was some basis for appeal. Then she went missing."

Joanna's brows knit together. "Do you believe that the two events are connected?"

"We don't know," Alicia answered. "But it's one theory."

"And you're getting in the middle of this? It sounds dangerous, Alicia." A worried look entered Joanna's eyes as she set down her glass of lemonade. "Should I even bother asking you to drop this, to let the police handle whatever investigation is going on?"

"The police are handling it, Mom. We're just asking a few questions on our own. It's been two months since Liliana vanished. The case has gone cold. Anything we can find out will only help."

"But if you ask the wrong people these questions, you could be in danger. Two people have already died, and if you don't think the professor's wife was their killer, then that person is still out there. I don't like this, Alicia. I don't like it at all." Joanna turned her gaze on Michael, her friendliness cooling. "Why did you get Alicia involved in this? She's a photographer. She's not a police officer or a detective."

"He didn't drag me into this. I volunteered," Alicia said.

"Why on earth would you do that? Are you two involved? What's going on?"

"We're friends. I'm helping a friend."

Alicia's words barely registered with Joanna, whose hard accusatory gaze rested on his face.

"I can promise you that I won't let anyone hurt Alicia," he said, knowing what Joanna really wanted to hear.

"Are you a man who keeps his promises? Because I know lots of men who don't."

"If I make a promise, I keep it." He didn't promise if he couldn't deliver, but he knew without a speck of doubt that he would put himself between Alicia and danger if it ever came to that. Hopefully, it wouldn't.

Joanna searched his face for the truth, and he hoped she liked what she saw.

"All right. I'm going to hold you to that," she said finally, crossing her arms in front of her chest. "My youngest daughter has always been a magnet for trouble, and she rarely thinks before she acts."

He smiled, seeing the discomfort in Alicia's eyes. "Alicia has been quite thoughtful so far."

Joanna gave him a doubtful look. "I hope that's true."

"Would you mind if I ask you a few more questions?" he continued.

"No, but I doubt I can help. I only know what I read in the papers or heard from the other faculty members."

"Then you're ahead of us. We just learned about the case today, so we're trying to get up to speed. Tell us what you know about the actual murder."

"Well, it's my understanding that Melissa Bryer came home, found her husband having sex with another woman, and shot them both. Then she called 911 and pretended that she'd just arrived and that they were already dead when she got there, but no one believed her story. It was much easier to believe that it was a crime of passion.

They were both naked, from what I understand."

"What time of day was it?" Michael asked.

"It was after work, sometime in the evening. I didn't hear about it until the next morning."

"So Melissa is the one who called the police," Alicia said. "Why would she do that if she was the killer?"

"It was suggested that she was trying to cover her tracks by acting like she was completely innocent," Joanna said. "But there were witnesses who came forward saying that they'd seen the woman in Professor Bryer's office and also off campus at a local bar. It appeared that they were having an affair. The only one who would have a motive for killing them would be the betrayed wife. At least that's how it played out in the press. It was quite a scandal for a while."

"The other woman had an ex-husband," Alicia said.

"I didn't know that," Joanna replied.

"Do you know anything about how the two of them met?" Michael asked.

"I believe they met at the tech company where Thomas sometimes worked as a consultant." She paused. "I know that Thomas was lonely when his wife deployed. I guess he found someone else to keep him company. It's very sad. Why did anyone have to die? They could have just gotten a divorce."

He wondered the same thing. Joanna had

certainly made a good case for why Melissa Bryer was in prison for murder. Maybe the claim of incompetent counsel was just a Hail Mary play from a desperate woman who was looking for any technicality to get her off. On the other hand, Liliana's notes had indicated that some of the people she spoke to, including Melissa's sister, did not believe there was an affair at all.

"I still think you should both stay out of this," Joanna added, breaking into the silence. "I'm sorry about your friend, Michael, but I think you should let the police do their job."

He was saved from answering when a male voice rang through the air. "Hello? Anyone home?"

"My brother Jake," Alicia said, getting to her feet to greet the man walking onto the back deck.

Jake Monroe looked more like his mother than Alicia. He wore faded jeans and a navy blue T-shirt, and he had sandy brown hair that was on the long side, as well as a scruffy beard. He didn't have Alicia's dark brown eyes, but rather light green eyes that lit up his face.

Jake gave his sister a hug and said, "This is a nice surprise. Last person I expected to find here was you."

"It was bound to happen sometime," she said lightly.

"They're looking into a murder investigation,"

Joanna put in, as Jake walked over to the table and sat down.

Jake raised an eyebrow. "Really?" He glanced at Michael, then extended his hand across the table. "I'm Jake Monroe."

"Michael Cordero," he replied, shaking Jake's hand.

"So what's this about a murder investigation?"

"I'm looking for a friend of mine, who was reviewing an appeal of a murder conviction," he said.

"Professor Bryer's murder," Joanna put in.

"I remember that," Jake said. "But why are you involved, Alicia?"

"It's a long story," Alicia muttered.

"It always is with you. I've got some time. Maybe over some lemonade?"

"I'll get you a glass," Joanna said, rising to her feet. "Try to talk some sense into your sister while I'm gone."

"I doubt that's possible," he said dryly. "And I can get my own glass."

"I like taking care of my kids." Joanna waved him back into his seat. "I'll bring out some cheese and crackers as well in case anyone is hungry."

"That sounds great. I'm starving."

"You're always starving," Joanna said with a laugh. "I don't know how you eat like you do and it never shows."

As Joanna returned to the house, Jake said,

"Okay, you've got a good five minutes to tell me what's really going on, Alicia."

"I'm helping Michael look for his friend. She went missing during her investigation," Alicia explained. "We're in town to see if we can find out what happened to her."

"Okay," he said, a puzzled look in his eyes. "But are you seriously trying to tell me that this case doesn't involve lightning? Because I didn't think you cared about anything that didn't involve a storm."

"Does it sound like it involves lightning?" she countered.

"That's not an answer." Jake's gaze swung in Michael's direction. "My sister has an obsession with jagged bolts of light coming out of the sky. Did you know that?"

"I'm aware."

"All right. So how does lightning figure into this? If you want to wait until Mom comes back to tell me—"

"Fine," Alicia said quickly. "I was in a Florida park and a lightning strike led me to a military ID tag in the dirt. It belonged to Michael's friend. Since I found the tag, I've been trying to help locate the woman it belonged to."

Jake gave a smug nod. "I knew it had to have something to do with lightning."

"It called me to the tag. You can believe it or not. That's what happened."

"I believe it. You've been chasing lightning for ten years. But I have to say it rarely leads you anywhere good, and this doesn't appear to be an exception. Now you're caught up in a double murder investigation? Don't you have a real job to go to every day? Are you taking time off? If you're not careful, you're going to get yourself fired."

"My job is fine. I know what I'm doing."

"All evidence to the contrary," Jake retorted.

"Alicia has been incredibly helpful," Michael put in, wanting to defend her. "Her discovery jump-started a cold case. She's reinvigorated the police investigation and her insight has brought us as close to finding Liliana as we've ever been. Your sister is very smart and intuitive. I feel incredibly lucky that she's been willing to give up her time to help me. And I couldn't ask for a better partner."

He returned Jake's speculative stare with a hard glint in his eyes, daring Jake to try to convince him otherwise. Jake finally conceded with a nod. "Okay then. So you two are *partners*. Is that all you are?"

"For God's sake, Jake," Alicia said with exasperation. "It's none of your business what we are. Since when do you care who I date?"

"I've always cared. You've just been hard to pin down, but now that you're back in Texas—"

"For a few days. I'm not staying."

"You should stay as long as you can. Mom misses you."

"I don't think so. She has you and Dani."

"You're her daughter, too."

"The one who gives her gray hairs."

"I've put a few of those in her head, too. And if you don't want to tell me what's going on with you two, you should at least think of a better answer for when Mom starts quizzing you. I'm sure she's already got you halfway down the aisle. She is dying to get one of us married off."

"Well, I'm the youngest, so you and Dani should be the ones to go first. Speaking of which, what happened to that woman you were seeing—Brenda, right?"

"That was over six months ago. She's already engaged to someone else."

"Should I say I'm sorry?" Alicia asked. "You don't sound too broken up about it."

"I'm good."

"And the rest of your life is just as good?" she probed.

"Better than good. I started flying for a medical charity that sends doctors into remote locations, and it's been great. You can't believe the places I've been to—villages tucked far away from any sign of civilization. It's like the people are living in another time and place. They have no idea what technology is. They're barely past making fire with sticks and stones. Sometimes they look at us like we're gods coming down from the sky."

"As if your ego needed another stroke," Alicia teased.

Jake grinned. "I can't lie. It's not a bad feeling to be someone's miracle."

"It sounds like you're doing amazing work, Jake. Who would have thought my big brother would end up being a hero?"

"Certainly not me. I have to say some of those small villages make me think about our great-grandmother." Jake glanced over at Michael. "Has Alicia told you about our great-grandmother? She believes lightning is sent down from the gods to show the world something."

"Jake," Alicia said with a sigh. "Michael already knows I'm crazy when it comes to the weather. You don't have to rub it in."

"Sorry. Anyway, I started wondering whether or not she has what she needs. I know she refused to leave her small village and has never been interested in material things, but it's been a long time since anyone spoke to her. I wonder if we would know if something had happened to her. Would anyone even tell us? Would they know how to find us?"

"Mom must keep in touch."

"I don't think so. She never liked Dad's side of the family. Since he's been gone, I don't think she gives any of his relatives much thought."

"Well, you could look into it."

"I might just do that."

"Do what?" Joanna asked, as she returned to the table with a platter of cheese and crackers and a glass for Jake's lemonade.

"Jake is thinking about reaching out to Abuelita," Alicia replied, referring to her great-grandmother.

A shadow passed through Joanna's eyes. "What on earth gave you that idea, Jake?"

"Some of the villages I've been flying into. When was the last time you talked to her, Mom?"

"A year or so ago. We used to exchange letters several times a year, but she developed painful arthritis so she had trouble writing. I have to say she never made much sense, but her last few letters were almost incomprehensible."

"Maybe we should check on her," Jake said.

"She has her family there to look out for her— her younger sister, her nieces and nephews."

"But we're her family, too," Alicia said. "She was Dad's grandmother."

At Alicia's words, Joanna stiffened, and Michael suddenly became very aware of a new tension at the table.

"I know who she is, Alicia. If you or Jake want to reach out to her, feel free, but I don't have a lot of compassion for a woman who never liked me very much or made any effort to welcome me into her family."

224

"Did you make an effort?" Alicia challenged. "Dad said you never wanted to take us to Mexico."

Joanna sucked in a breath. "You think you know everything about your father, but you don't, Alicia. He'll always be your hero, but he was a man, too—a man with flaws. He was nowhere near as perfect as you thought he was."

Joanna's harsh words brought moisture to Alicia's eyes.

"Hey, let's talk about something else," Jake interjected.

"Excuse me," Alicia said, shoving back her chair. She practically ran into the house.

"Always so dramatic," Joanna said with a sigh.

"She wasn't being dramatic. Your words hurt her," Michael told Joanna, not liking this colder side of Alicia's mother.

She stared back at him, as if she were surprised that he'd called her out. "I didn't say anything that bad. She has always seen her father as a hero, and he was that, but he was a lot of other things, too. She's always so sensitive when it comes to him. Did she tell you that he died when she was a teenager?"

"Yes."

"Did she tell you that her father often flew in bad conditions? That he didn't worry at all about his family when he was risking his life, whether it was in the Navy or flying through a bad storm?"

Joanna's lips drew into a line. "Wyatt would be here today if he'd thought more about his family and less about the wild blue yonder and those damned lightning strikes."

"Mom," Jake cautioned. "You don't know what Dad ran into that night. Some storms are unavoidable. He was a good pilot."

"In his younger years, yes, before he let his imagination get the best of him, before he started believing that lightning sprites were sending him messages. That's what he thought," she reiterated, giving Michael a pointed look. "I worry that Alicia takes after her father in that regard. Have you seen her lightning photographs? Has she told you that she jumps into her car and races toward the nearest storm, no matter how dangerous it might be?"

"I've seen some of her pictures. She's an amazing photographer."

"She takes too many chances, just like her father. You'd think she would have learned not to challenge nature after her dad died, but she went the opposite direction." Joanna paused, releasing a sigh. "But I didn't want to start a fight tonight. Maybe I should go talk to her."

"I'll do that," Michael said, getting to his feet.

"Tell her I'm sorry. I won't bring up her father again tonight."

"I'll tell her." He'd just reentered the house when his cell phone rang. He paused at the bottom of the stairs. "Diego, is there any news?"

"Where are you?"

From the tension in Diego's voice, he had a feeling the question was not an idle one. "Who's asking?"

"Kellerman says you're in Texas."

"He had someone follow me?" Michael was angry but not completely surprised.

"What are you doing there? I told you to stay out of the investigation, Michael. And why are you with the woman who found Liliana's ID? Is there something going on between you?"

"She's helping me figure out what happened to Liliana. Did you know she was investigating a double homicide?"

"Yes. Kellerman and Rodriguez reviewed the case and interviewed her coworkers and neighbors. There's nothing in Texas to find. Do you think they didn't ask any questions?"

"I think that they're so determined to find me guilty that anything that doesn't fit that scenario doesn't get looked at closely."

"No one is trying to railroad you, but your actions aren't helping. And none of us, including me, understands why you're suddenly joined at the hip to the only person who might have seen Liliana since she disappeared."

"Alicia wants to help."

"Is that really it? Because most normal people don't suddenly jump into a plane with a man they

227

met a few days earlier and who also happens to be a person of interest in a criminal investigation."

"Well, Alicia would tell you that she is far from normal," he said lightly. "All we're doing is asking a few questions, Diego. There's really no reason for concern. If we find nothing, then all we've wasted is time. And if we find something, we'll get closer to a resolution. Isn't that what we all want?"

"Of course it is. I'm just trying to look out for you."

"Why don't you help me instead? The JAG attorney told us they provided the police with a summary of the investigation Liliana was conducting. Any chance you could send me a copy?"

"No," Diego said flatly. "I've been told in no uncertain terms to stay away from the investigation. They know we're friends. The only time they talk to me is to ask me what the hell you're doing. Sorry."

"I understand. Do you know if the police checked to see if anyone in Liliana's circle bought a plane or train ticket to Florida before or after Liliana left Corpus Christi?"

Diego hesitated. "I'm fairly sure the main players were checked out."

"Fairly sure?"

"Like I said, they don't give me all the details. Do you really think there's a link between this case in Texas and her disappearance?"

"I don't know, but Liliana was investigating a murder appeal, and if the person in jail is innocent, then that means there's someone else who committed murder. And if they've killed two people already, I doubt they'd stop at a third." He hated saying the words out loud, but the truth was staring him right in the face.

"That's why you and Alicia need to come back to Miami. You could be in danger, too. You keep pushing, someone will push back."

"I hope so. That might be the only way we'll get to the truth. Is there anything new on your end?"

"Unfortunately, no."

Which gave him another reason to stay in Texas. At least there were new people to question. "I'll call you if I find out anything. You do the same."

"Be careful, Michael."

"I will."

Despite his promise, he couldn't say that being careful had ever been at the top of his list of things to do, and he wasn't going to put it there now. There was far too much at stake.

But he didn't want to put Alicia in the line of fire and as several people had reminded him in the last few hours, that's exactly what he was doing. He needed to send her back to Florida. While he liked having her as a partner, he didn't have the right to risk her life, and he'd promised her mother he'd protect her. He wasn't stupid enough to think that keeping that promise with a murderer on the loose might be easy. But he also didn't think Alicia would go home without a fight. She was invested in the case. Still, he needed to try to make her see reason. He had a feeling that would not be easy, either.

FIFTEEN

Michael found Alicia in what was probably her childhood bedroom, judging by the floral bedspreads on the twin beds, the matching white desk and dresser, and posters of boy bands from a decade ago. She was sitting on the window bench, and as he entered the room, she wiped her teary eyes before turning to look at him.

He crossed the room and sat down on the bench next to her. "Are you all right?"

"I'm fine."

Despite her words, she stared back at him with hurt in her beautiful brown eyes. He felt his stomach tighten and a knot of emotion fill his own throat. He wanted to make her feel better. He wanted to take care of her. He wanted to protect her from whatever was making her hurt, and he hadn't felt that way in a very long time.

He understood passion and heat. Tenderness and this tightening feeling of affection were much more disturbing.

"You've been crying," he said, wiping a tear off her cheek with the tip of his finger. "Were you thinking about your father?"

"Yes, but that's not why I got so stupid and emotional down there."

"Your mother was hard on you."

"She always is."

"She told me to tell you she's sorry."

Alicia's eyes widened. "Seriously? What brought that on?"

He shrugged. "I might have said something about her being out of line."

"You defended me?"

"I said what I thought. I don't stand by and do nothing when people I care about are being hurt."

Her gaze met his, a question in her eyes. "You care about me, Michael?"

"How could I not?" he countered. "Look what you've done for me."

"Well, thank you."

"You're welcome. So are you planning to come back downstairs or hide out up here for a while longer?"

"I haven't decided yet." She let out a sigh. "I don't like myself in Texas, Michael. I come into this house, and I'm not me anymore. I'm the teenage girl I used to be. I'm the one who disappoints my mother. It's annoying."

He smiled, relieved that she wasn't as emotionally distraught as he'd anticipated. But then, Alicia had a way of rebounding quickly when life knocked her down.

"I like you in Texas, Alicia. In fact, I like you everywhere." He leaned forward and cupped her face with his hands.

Her gaze darkened. "Michael, what are you doing?"

"Nothing yet. But I have some ideas."

"Distracting ideas."

"Oh, yeah," he said, his pulse racing at her sweet scent, the thought of her lips under his again. She was so close, so very close.

"We need to focus," she said, a desperate edge to her voice. "Remember why we're here."

She was only repeating what he'd told himself every time her smile made his heart catch, but he didn't care about why they were here at this moment. He only cared about feeding the desire that was running rampant through his body.

"I remember," he murmured. "But right now it's just you and me—and a moment."

Her lips parted in what he anticipated would be a protest, but he kissed away whatever words were hovering on her lips.

She tasted like lemonade, like summer, like his best daydream. His troubles slid away as he moved his hands from her face to her hair, running his fingers through the thick waves, holding her still so he could kiss her the way he wanted to—the way she wanted him to.

Her arms came around his back. Her tongue invited him in. And he was more than happy to deepen the kiss.

Passion hummed between them, lighting up

his nerves, tightening his body, making him want much more than just a kiss.

Alicia broke away first, her chest rising with each breath as she gazed at him through eyes that were bright and needy. "Michael."

He liked the way she said his name with an intimate sweetness that made him want to make her say his name over and over and over again.

"We can't do this," she added.

Those words he didn't like nearly as much.

"My mom and brother are downstairs."

She made a good point. He sat back, his hands falling to his thighs. "Bad timing, but great kiss."

"Yes," she agreed. "But—"

He cut her off with a shake of his head. "We don't have time for *that* conversation. If we don't go back downstairs, your mother and brother will probably think we're doing what you just stopped us from doing."

Her cheeks reddened at his words, and she jumped to her feet. "Then we better leave."

"One second."

"But you just said—"

"I need a minute," he confessed.

"Oh." She blushed and then sat back down. "I didn't know I had *that* effect on you."

He smiled at the proud gleam in her eyes. "I think you knew very well."

She smiled back and just like that he wanted to kiss her again.

He needed a distraction. "So this was your room?"

"Yes. I shared it with my sister Dani. This window seat was my favorite spot. I used to sit here and read or draw while I waited for my dad to come home. Things were always better when he was in the house."

Alicia's voice filled with emotion as she turned her gaze out the window. "From here, I could see the planes coming in to land at the airport. The night he died, I sat right here, watching the lightning, feeling the thunder rumble through the house. I think I knew there was something wrong. I just didn't want to believe it. Then the police knocked on the door. Even after they told us the horrible news, it seemed like a dream. I don't think it really hit me that he was gone until a week or so later."

"I'm sorry you had to go through that."

"Me, too. I think of my dad often. I wish he could have seen me grow up, graduate from high school, move to a new city. I wish he could have been part of my life for longer than he was, but we don't always get what we wish for."

"No, we don't." He still felt the loss of his mother, and he didn't remember her in nearly the same detail as Alicia remembered her father.

"The hardest part of losing my dad was the mystery around his death. Because they never found his body or his plane, there was always a little seed of doubt in my mind, hope that went on for months. I know that's crazy, because he was over the Gulf of Mexico when his plane went down, and the search area was huge, but it's hard to let go when you don't have proof." She looked into his eyes. "That's why you can't let go of Liliana, because you don't know what happened to her. And I think there's a part of me that wants to find her because I can't find him. That sounds ridiculous—"

"No, I get it," he said, understanding her motives better now. "You're trying to give someone else closure, even if you can't find it yourself."

"Exactly. And I do believe that the lightning led me to the park so I could help. Maybe that's just so I can rationalize my obsession with electrical storms, but that's the way I feel."

"I want to believe it, too, Alicia."

"Really?" she asked doubtfully.

He nodded. "I've never thought much about the weather until I met you."

"Most people don't."

"But my father told me once that people show up in your life when you need them. At the time, he was referring to my grandfather, who hadn't paid me much attention until he decided to bail me out of jail and send me to prep school." He paused. "I feel like you showed up in my life for a reason that I can't begin to understand, but for which I'm incredibly lucky."

She blinked her eyes against a sudden rush of tears.

"Hey, I didn't mean to make you cry again," he said.

"I really don't ever cry—except when I'm in Texas," she said, wiping her eyes.

He smiled at that. "Before we go back downstairs, do you have any photos of your dad?" He glanced around the room. "Or did only boy bands make the wall? The Jonas Brothers? Really?"

"They were cute."

"If you say so."

"I do have some pictures of my dad." She got up from the window seat and walked over to the bookshelf. She pulled a scrapbook off the shelf and brought it back to him. The book was weathered with age.

"This was my dad's book from when he was in the Navy. I took it out of my mom's room after he died, and she never took it back. I don't think she liked looking at it, being reminded of the past, but it brought me comfort." She opened the first page. "Here he is on the deck of a carrier."

"You look like him," he said, noting the man's dark hair and eyes, the lift of his chin, the smile in his eyes. "He looks like he's ready to take on the world."

"He was always ready to do that. He was a fearless flyer." She flipped through several more pages, pointing out important moments from her father's career, including a medal ceremony. "He received the Navy Cross for extraordinary bravery and heroism. He flew his plane into enemy territory to rescue two wounded soldiers. I remember asking him if he was scared, and he said, no, his mind was on the mission. He couldn't afford to be scared."

"Sounds like you get your courage from him, too."

"I like to think so. He was an incredible man. After he left the Navy, people forgot about all that he'd done, especially my mom. She was proud of him when he was serving. But when he got out, he couldn't do anything right in her eyes. They were always fighting." She paused. "I know she said downstairs that I never saw my father for the man that he was, that I only saw the hero. I could say that she never saw the hero; she only saw the man who came home late and didn't help out around the house the way she wanted."

"She also saw her husband. That's a different relationship than the one you had with your dad, Alicia."

"I know, and my dad wasn't perfect, but he was a good man." She turned the page and pointed to four guys standing on the tarmac of a Naval carrier. "These were some of my dad's best friends. Jerry Caldwell, a fellow pilot. Next to him is Randy Cavanaugh, a flight mechanic and on the end is Stan Baker, a radar instrument officer. Growing up, they were Uncle Jerry, Uncle Randy, and Uncle Stan. I was close to Stan's kids when we were little. I have no idea what happened to any of them. It feels like a long time ago."

"Did you move around a lot as a kid?"

"A few times. And there were many months when my dad was deployed, and my mom was raising us by herself. I realize now that that couldn't have been easy. But she's a strong woman."

"That's the nicest thing you've said about your mom."

She made a face at him. "I do love her. She just makes me a little nuts."

"And I have a feeling you do the same to her."

"Yes, I do." She closed the photo album and stood up. "We should go downstairs. You volunteered to grill, remember?"

"I remember." As he got to his feet, he put his hand on her arm as she turned to leave and said, "For the record, Alicia, it doesn't matter what state you're in. You don't need to be anyone other than who you are, because who you are is amazing. Don't let anyone put doubts in your head."

Her eyes filled with appreciation. "That's a really sweet thing to say."

He grimaced. "Sweet isn't what I was going for."

She laughed. "Well, still, it was nice. Thanks for the pep talk."

"Gotta keep my partner happy."

"About what happened before, Michael . . ."

"I know: wrong place, wrong time—again. Someday we'll get it right."

Alicia's nerves were still tingling when she walked out to the back deck. It wasn't only Michael's kiss that had unnerved her, it was also the personal and intimate conversation they'd shared that scared her. She hadn't opened up to anyone the way she'd opened up to Michael. She didn't know why she'd told him so much about her family, her father, and herself, but it felt good to have aired some of the old hurts.

When they reached the table, her mother gave her a speculative look, and she couldn't stop the guilty heat that swept through her body. She really needed to get a grip, remember that she was an adult now and she didn't owe her mother any explanations.

"I was beginning to wonder if you were ever coming back," her mom said as they sat down. "Did Michael tell you I apologized?"

"He did. I was just showing Michael my old room, and some photos of Dad from his Navy days."

"Of course. I'm going to start pulling dinner together," Joanna said, getting to her feet. "Are you still up for grilling, Michael? Jake almost always burns the steak."

"Not true," Jake replied. "But I'm happy to let Michael take over. I've been the only man around this house for too long."

"I haven't grilled in a while but I think I can pull off steaks," Michael said. "Why don't you show me what you have for spices and we'll get the meat ready?"

"Spices?" Joanna asked doubtfully. "I don't have much. I usually just throw the meat straight on the grill."

"Well, let's see what you have."

"You sound like you know what you're doing," Joanna said.

"I was raised by a chef. Some things stuck." He sent Alicia a smile before he followed her mother into the house.

When they were alone, Jake gave her a pointed look. "So what else were you showing Michael upstairs—besides your old room?"

"Nothing that you need to know."

"What's the deal, Alicia? And don't give me the bullshit *just friends* answer. I've seen the way he looks at you, the way you look at him."

She sighed, knowing that she really didn't have a good answer to the question. "I don't know what we are. I've only known him a short time.

241

But I'll admit that there's something there. When I'm around him, I feel dizzy, lightheaded, like I'm walking a few feet off the ground."

"It sounds like you're falling for him."

"Maybe a little."

"Or a lot."

She met his gaze. "Right now we're mostly concerned with trying to find his friend. Anything else that might be brewing is on the back burner."

Jake leaned forward, resting his forearms on the table. "Alicia, you need to be careful. You're getting into the middle of a double homicide investigation."

"I'm just trying to find out whether it's possible someone besides Melissa Bryer could have killed Professor Bryer and that woman."

"The wife had a strong motive, and I'm not sure I even blame her. If I found my wife in bed with another man, I'd feel like taking them both out, too."

"Big talk from a guy who hated to go hunting with Dad," she reminded him.

He grinned. "Well, I don't like to shoot animals for sport. But cheating spouses, that's another matter."

"Speaking of spouses, why don't you get serious about someone, and then Mom will get off my back. You're the oldest. You need to go first, take the heat off me and Dani."

He laughed. "Thanks, but I like my freedom."

"Really? I remember when you were in love with Katherine. I thought you were going to get married before you got out of high school."

A frown drew his lips into a tight line. "Yeah, well, that was a long time ago."

"Do you ever hear from her?"

"Not in years. But Mom likes to keep me up to date. Katherine is a doctor now, a pediatrician."

"That's cool."

"She always liked kids."

"Is she still single? Because I'm guessing Mom is probably hoping you'll get back together. Katherine had a way of calming you down."

"That's not going to happen. We were kids back then. We didn't know what the hell we were doing. Or at least I didn't know."

She heard a note of pain in his voice and felt a little guilty for trying to deflect the conversation away from herself and onto him. "Sorry, I didn't realize you were still touchy about her. That's interesting."

"I think you and Michael are far more interesting. What's your next step?"

"Still trying to figure that out. We're hoping to get more information from JAG. But in the meantime, we're going to try to talk to anyone connected to Professor Bryer. That's one reason I decided to see Mom tonight. I figured she might know him from the university. She told me a little about him, but I need more. You don't know anyone who works at the university, do you?"

"Katherine's younger brother TJ is a grad student in electromagnetic engineering at Texas A&M. Was that Bryer's department?"

"I know he did something in engineering, but there are several departments."

"I think TJ is a teaching assistant there. Mom told me she ran into him a few months back. That's when she caught me up on Katherine."

"Really? I would love to talk to him. I wonder if he still lives at home. He was a lot younger than Katherine, wasn't he?"

"Yes." Jake frowned. "Judging by the gleam in your eyes, I think I'm going to be sorry I brought him up. You should back off of this, Alicia. It's dangerous."

"I don't think talking to TJ is going to put me in danger."

"You're so stubborn. What's really going on here? Are you trying to prove your worth to Michael? Wait—I know the answer. It's the lightning, isn't it? You think you were called to this cause. You're as crazy as Dad was."

"I'm not crazy, Jake, and neither was Dad. If the lightning hadn't shown me that ID tag, I never would have met Michael or come back here."

"That was just coincidence. Look, Alicia, I've flown through some monster storms. I've seen the weather that you love so much from a lot closer than you have, and yes, it's magnificent, but it's nothing more than weather. Lightning is not a sign from the universe. You need to get over that idea. It's not sending you messages. And you're not going to suddenly see what happened to Dad in a bolt of lightning. We know what happened. A storm sent his plane into the sea. That's it."

"I'm just not as sure of that as you are," she confessed.

He raised an eyebrow. "Seriously? You're not sure about what happened to Dad?"

"None of us really know, Jake. We don't have any facts. And there is no body buried in the cemetery under his gravestone."

"He's not still alive, Alicia. You can't think that."

She didn't really think that he was alive, but with no evidence to the contrary, who really knew? "He could be stranded on some tiny island in the middle of the ocean."

"For almost ten years?"

"It could happen."

"But it *didn't* happen. Come on, Alicia. You're too smart to believe that some miracle is going to occur."

She shrugged her shoulders. "It's hard for me to give up on people, especially people I love. I still feel a strong connection to Dad, and I feel it the most when lightning is all around me. Whether he's alive or not, his spirit connects with me. That's just the way it is."

"I'm glad you feel a connection to him, but that's all it is—a feeling. If it makes you happy, fine, but don't get involved in murder investigations."

"Don't you feel anything, Jake? When you're flying the same skies he flew, don't you think about him sometimes?"

"Sure, but I try to remember how he lived, not how he died. Isn't that more important?"

Jake had a point. "I guess," she murmured, happy to see Michael and her mother return. Her conversation with Jake had gone too deep and too serious.

"Cocktail hour has officially arrived," Joanna said, setting down two bottles of wine.

"Sounds good to me," Alicia said. Maybe a drink would calm her nerves.

"Looks like your grill needs a cleaning," Michael said, opening the cover to the barbecue. "Do you have a brush anywhere?"

"In the cabinet underneath," Joanna replied. "I can do that."

"It's fine—I've got it," Michael said.

"You're so helpful, Michael." Her mother gave her a sly look. "Don't you think so, Alicia?"

"I do," she agreed, seeing a smile cross Michael's face. At least he wasn't annoyed by her mother's obvious matchmaking. Still, she decided to change the subject. "Jake just told me that Katherine's brother TJ is a grad student at the university. Do you think he knew Professor Bryer?"

"I'm sure he did. He was in the same department," Joanna replied, sitting down at the table. "He graduated in June. I'm not sure what he's doing now."

"Do the Barretts still live on Shore Drive?"

"Debbie does. Her husband passed away last year, and Katherine has been gone for years. I'm not sure where TJ is living these days. I spoke to him briefly a few months back, and he said he didn't know what he was going to do after graduation."

"I want to talk to Mrs. Barrett, see if she can put me in touch with TJ," Alicia said.

"Leave them alone, Alicia," Jake ordered. "I don't want you getting involved with Kat's family."

"What's it to you, Jake? You and Katherine have been over forever. You just said that."

He gave her an irritated look. "Every time you come home, trouble follows."

"That's an exaggeration."

"Last time you were here for a weekend, you told Hank Peterson that I didn't sell him my entire baseball card collection, that I held back the Ken Griffey Jr. card. He hasn't spoken to me since. I had to find another mechanic. Do you

247

know how hard it is to find a good mechanic?"

"I didn't know that was a secret," she said defensively. "And you're the one who held back the card, so it's your fault."

Jake glanced over at Michael. "I hope you know what you're getting into with my sister. Alicia has a tendency to turn lives upside down."

"I'm beginning to realize that," Michael said with a smile. "But sometimes lives can benefit from a flip."

"Good answer," she said.

He laughed. "I thought so." He'd barely finished speaking when his phone rang. She tensed, wondering if it was news about Liliana. "It's my foreman," he said. "I need to take this. Excuse me."

As Michael returned to the house, Jake said, "His foreman?"

"Michael is managing the construction of a huge new city center in Miami. He works for Jansen Real Estate Developments."

"So he's a builder," Joanna said. "I like a man who's good with his hands."

Alicia rolled her eyes. "I don't think he's the one actually swinging the hammer, Mom."

"Really? Because he looks like he keeps in shape. You could do a lot worse, Alicia. He's attractive, successful, athletic, and he seems to really like you. What more could you want?"

"Do you want any help with the salad?" she asked, ignoring her mom's question.

Joanna sighed. "No, I've seen you chop tomatoes. You sit and talk to your brother. I'll take care of dinner."

"That was not nice," she told Jake after her mother left. "What you said to Michael about me."

"I was joking. But I've always thought you should come with a warning."

"Very funny. You owe me, Jake."

He gave her a suspicious look. "What does that mean?"

"It means you and I are going for a walk." She stood up and grabbed his arm, forcing him to his feet.

"I'm not going to Katherine's house, if that's what you're thinking."

"She doesn't still live there, Jake. It's not like you're going to run into her. And I thought it was ancient history, no big deal."

"It is."

"Then come with me. We'll be back in fifteen minutes." She walked toward the side gate. "Maybe we won't tell Mom where we went until we get back."

"Like I said before, when you come to town, trouble comes with you."

SIXTEEN

Debbie Barrett lived in a modest home three blocks away. Her one-story ranch-style house showed signs of wear, with peeling blue paint and a porch swing that looked like it was about to fall apart at any second. The grass was overgrown and the flowers had died a long time ago.

"Damn. Things have really gone down around here," Jake muttered.

"Debbie probably hasn't been able to keep up the maintenance since her husband died," Alicia suggested. "Ron was such a nice man. He always ran the snack shack at the soccer games and sometimes he'd give me extra licorice."

"Yeah, he was a good guy," Jake said tersely. "This is a bad idea."

"Relax, Jake. It's fine." She rang the bell. "Debbie always liked you—didn't she? Or is there some history with you and Katherine that I don't know about?"

"There are a lot of things you don't know about."

Before she could ask him for more details, the front door opened.

Debbie Barrett stood in the doorway, looking like a hollow shell of the woman she'd once been.

Her blonde hair was gray and stringy. She'd lost at least forty pounds judging by the way her sweatshirt and jeans hung loosely on her body, and there were deep shadows under her eyes.

"Oh, my," she muttered, squinting her brown eyes in disbelief. "Is that you, Jake?"

"Mrs. Barrett," he said. "How are you?"

"I'm—well, I'm all right, I guess."

"I was sorry to hear about your husband," Jake said.

Debbie let out a sigh. "Thank you." Her gaze drifted to Alicia. "You're Jake's little sister Alicia. Goodness, I haven't seen you since you were a teenager. What brings you both to my door?" She turned her gaze back to Jake. "Are you looking for Katherine?"

"No, actually we're looking for TJ," Jake replied. "We thought you might know where he is."

"I'm not sure. I think he's at work."

"Where does he work?" Alicia asked.

"Some technology company. It has initials. I don't remember what they are," she said vaguely. "I haven't been feeling very well the past few months. My memory isn't as sharp as it used to be."

"Do you have TJ's phone number?" Alicia asked.

"I have it somewhere. Oh, wait, it's in my phone." She stepped back from the door and disappeared into the house.

"Should we go in?" Alicia asked a moment later when Debbie didn't return. "Do you think she forgot we're out here?"

"She doesn't look like she's herself," he said grimly.

They waited another minute and then Jake strode into the house and Alicia followed. She was shocked to see that the house was in complete disarray. Trash and dirty dishes littered the coffee table and side tables. There were TVs on in the living room and the kitchen, each one very loud.

Debbie wandered back into the room with her phone. "Here it is. I can't believe I found it."

Alicia smiled at the older woman's look of triumph. "Can I see it?" She took the phone and sent herself a text message with TJ's phone number.

"When you talk to TJ, can you tell him I need some bread and some milk?" Debbie asked. "Oh, and some cat food, too. Lady Blair is around here somewhere."

Alicia didn't see a cat, but she could certainly smell one. "I'll tell him."

"It looks like you need some help here, Debbie," Jake interjected. "Have you talked to Kat lately?"

"She's so busy. She's a doctor now. She works long hours. Such a smart girl, my Katherine. I'm so proud of her, and TJ, too. Both my kids did okay. I did something right, didn't I?"

"I think it's time for your kids to do right by you," Jake said. "This is a big house to take care of. Maybe you could get someone in to clean."

"TJ cleans up for me. He's a good boy. He's just been gone for a few days. I guess I'm not as neat as I used to be," she said apologetically. "Tell your mom I said hello, won't you? Is she doing well?"

"She's fine," Jake said. "And I'll tell her you asked about her."

"And Jake . . ." Debbie began.

When she didn't finish, Jake said, "What?"

"I wish things would have turned out differently for you and Katherine. You were so adorable in high school. I always thought you were the right one for her. I never understood why you broke up."

"That was a long time ago, Debbie. You take care of yourself, okay?"

"I will."

"She's not in good shape," Jake said, as they left Debbie's house. "Where the hell is Katherine? Why isn't she checking on her mother?"

"I'm more interested in where TJ is." Alicia pulled out her phone and punched in his number. The phone went to voicemail with no personalized message.

"Hi, TJ, it's Alicia Monroe—Jake's sister. Your mom gave me your number. I need to ask you something. Could you call me back at this number? It's really important. Thanks." She

253

looked at Jake as she ended the call. "Hopefully, he'll get back to me."

"Thanks for using my name," he said dryly.

"I wasn't sure he'd remember me. And I wanted to sound friendly, like what I have to ask him is no big deal."

"Well, if he does call you back, you should tell him that his mother needs help. I'm worried about Mrs. Barrett. She definitely isn't the woman I remember."

"Maybe Mom can check in on her or get some of the other women in the neighborhood to help her out. You should ask her."

"Or you could."

"We both know any suggestion that comes out of your mouth instead of mine will be better received."

Jake sighed. "You're not going to give me that *Mom loves you best* speech, are you?"

"Obviously I don't need to, because you know it's true."

"When did you say you were leaving town?"

She smiled at his half-teasing, half-serious comment. "Probably not as soon as you would like."

Michael stabbed the raw steak with a fork and turned it over on the grill, and then stepped back from the heat as Joanna came over to check on the meat.

"Those are looking good," she said. "And they smell heavenly, not like any steak I've ever cooked. You said your father is a chef?"

"Yes. He owns a Cuban restaurant in Miami. He taught me the value of spices at a young age. We didn't have a lot of money, but my father could take the cheapest cut of meat and make it into something delicious." As he said the words, he realized how infrequently he thought about his father in a positive light. Maybe it was time to call a truce on all the bitterness and anger.

"And your mother, does she work?" Joanna asked.

"My mother died when I was very young. My stepmother works in the restaurant with my dad. I have three half-sisters as well."

"I'm sorry about your mother."

"It was a long time ago."

"But it's a pain that never goes away. Losing a parent is the worst thing in the world." She paused. "I know that Alicia still aches for her father. I've wanted so much to comfort her, but we usually end up getting in a fight. We've never been able to communicate very well. Sometimes it's like we're strangers instead of mother and daughter."

"Strangers wouldn't feel as much as you two do."

"Has she said anything to you about me?"

He saw the need in her eyes and couldn't help

but fill it. "She told me that she loves you. She said that you were often a single mother when your husband was in the Navy and that she appreciates how well you took care of them."

Joanna's jaw dropped at his words. "I—I have to admit I'm a little surprised. She's never told me that."

"I'm sure there are things you haven't told her, either. It's easier to get angry than to show feelings," he muttered. "At least, it has been for me."

"That's true. You're quite insightful, Michael."

"No, I've just done a lot of things wrong. I'm trying to learn from some of those mistakes." He checked on the steaks again. "These are almost done. Hopefully, Alicia and Jake will be back soon."

"I'm sure they went to see Debbie, to ask about TJ. Alicia is like a dog with a bone. When she wants something, she goes after it."

"I've noticed."

"I'm going to set the table. We'll eat out here. It's cooled off a bit, and I prefer to be outside whenever possible."

"Good idea."

As Joanna disappeared into the house, he took the steaks off the heat so they could rest. He couldn't remember the last time he'd cooked anything. It had all been take-out, home delivery, or gourmet restaurants the last few years. And he certainly hadn't been to a family barbecue in a while.

Alicia's family had its issues but it was easy to see the love underneath the tension. If the going got tough, they'd stand up for one another. He had no doubt about that.

But as much as he was enjoying the grill, he was beginning to wonder where Alicia and Jake had gone and whether or not they'd found out anything helpful.

He looked up as the side gate opened, happy to see they were back, but judging by their expressions, their meeting had not gone very well.

"We went to see TJ," Alicia said, coming over to him.

"I figured."

"He wasn't there. His mother gave us his phone number, but he didn't answer. I left him a message to call me back."

He saw the discouragement in her eyes, but he knew it wouldn't last long. "Well, the steaks are ready."

"They smell incredible."

"They do," Jake agreed, stepping over to the barbecue grill to check out the meat. "What kind of rub did you put on them?"

"Oregano, lime juice, cumin seed, a few other things."

"Impressive," Jake said.

"We'll see how it tastes."

"There you are," Joanna said, as she put the plates down on the table. "Good timing. Did you see Debbie?"

"Yes. She's not well, Mom," Alicia said. "She seemed disoriented, out of it, and her house was a mess."

"Really?"

"The word mess doesn't begin to describe her house," Jake put in. "There was abandoned food on tables, lots of trash, and she couldn't seem to remember where her cat was. She needs help. I don't know where TJ is or Katherine is, for that matter," he added, a hard edge in his voice. "Someone should be taking care of Debbie."

"I had no idea things were that bad," Joanna said. "I'll go over there tomorrow and check in with her."

"That would be good," Alicia said. "It wasn't like we just caught her at a bad time. It looked like she'd been living that way for a while."

"I have to admit I haven't seen her since the funeral. I'll call my friend Lauren. She lives across the street from Debbie. Maybe she can run over there now, and I'll go tomorrow."

"Did you learn anything else?" Michael asked as Joanna went back into the house to make her call.

Alicia shook her head. "No. Debbie said TJ worked for a tech company but she couldn't remember the name. She said it had initials.

258

Maybe it was MDT. We can look him up online after we eat." She let out a breath. "I really thought we were going to catch a break."

"It was a good idea," he said, putting a hand on her shoulder. "And something may still come of it. Right now, you need to take a breath and eat what will hopefully be the best steak of your life."

Her smile made his heart turn over. "You don't lack for confidence, Michael. I hope you can back it up."

"I always can."

"We'll see."

He laughed. "You're going to be tough on me, aren't you?"

"I don't think you'd want it any other way, would you?"

He met her gaze. "No, I wouldn't."

"Hey, you two, are we ever going to eat?" Jake asked.

"Right now," Michael said, taking the steaks to the table.

Dinner with her family was more fun that she would have ever imagined, Alicia thought as they ate Michael's perfectly cooked steak along with salad, green beans, and fruit for dessert. During the meal, the conversation was easy and not filled with criticisms or questions. That was mostly due to Michael's presence at the table.

He certainly seemed to have charmed her mother.

Michael and Jake got along well, too. They both loved sports, and she quickly found out which baseball teams were contending for the play-offs. She also discovered that the Miami Dolphins football team was on an undefeated roll for September, and that Michael still apparently followed his childhood team despite the fact that he'd been living in New York the last ten years.

It was nice to see a more relaxed side of the man with whom she'd spent several intense days. He wasn't thinking about the darkness of the last two months. He was just being himself. He talked, laughed, joked and fit right in with her family. In fact, he made her feel like she fit in, too, and he wasn't even trying to do that. It just happened.

She'd thought it would be difficult to be home, to see her mom and brother, but it was amazingly fun. Either they'd mellowed or she had, or perhaps they'd all changed, but aside from a few digs from her mother about the length of her hair or her unwillingness to call home more often, there was no real tension. It reminded her of the family they'd been before her father died, before the sadness and the uncertainty and then the pain, before they all got tense and angry and dealt with their grief in different ways, often by lashing out at one another.

No one had forgotten, but time had lessened the hurt, and she was grateful for that.

Michael gave her a smile from across the table and she smiled back, thinking how attractive he was in the late afternoon light. His dark hair set off the lightness of his eyes as well as the sun-touched color in his cheeks, the strength of his jaw, the sexy line of his mouth, a mouth she very much wanted to taste again.

He must have followed her train of thought because his gaze darkened and a look of promised intimacy passed between them. They'd been dancing around the sparks of attraction since the first minute they'd met. One of these days, those sparks were going to catch fire, and it was going to take a lot more than a few kisses to put those flames out.

But she didn't want to get burned. She didn't want to get hurt. And Michael had the potential to do that, because she already cared about him, which meant her heart was on the line, and she never put her heart on the line. But Michael seemed to understand her and accept her in a way that no one else ever had. And she thought she understood him pretty well, too. She'd been able to peek past the curtain he probably usually hid behind. He'd opened up about his life, and she doubted he did that often.

But what would happen when all the questions were answered, when Liliana was found?

Would they just go back to their lives? Lives that they led in two different states?

That seemed the most likely scenario.

So why on earth was she thinking about getting more involved with him? There was no future for them. Was there?

"Earth to Alicia," Jake said loudly.

"Sorry, what?" she asked, turning her head to her brother.

"Mom and I would like to send Dani to D.C. with a parting gift. Do you want to go in on it?"

"Sure, of course. What are you thinking?"

"I saw Dani eyeing a lovely tote bag that would fit her computer and be good for traveling," her mother said. "It's several hundred dollars, but I think she'd like it."

"Count me in."

"And Dani's party next month?" her mom said hopefully.

"I will try to come back," she promised.

"Do more than try—come. It's been nice having you here tonight. It feels good to have at least two of my kids here. I wish Dani could have joined us. I can't remember when we were all together."

"It's been wonderful," Alicia agreed. "And now I'm going to do the dishes. You sit, Mom. You worked all day and made dinner. It's the least I can do."

"Well, I won't protest," Joanna said with a pleased smile.

"I'll help," Michael offered.

"You barbecued. You should be resting."

"I don't need to rest," he said, getting to his feet. He grabbed her mom's plate and his own, then headed into the kitchen with her.

"So, my mom likes you a lot," she commented as she scraped and rinsed the plates, then put them in the dishwasher.

"I'm actually pretty likeable, except when I'm in Miami," he said with a wry smile.

"Sounds like you and Miami have the same love-hate relationship as Texas and I do. Maybe we both need to figure out how to live in the place where we grew up."

"Or not. I'll be back in New York by Christmas. And you don't seem to have plans to return here."

"Not any time soon, except for my sister's party." She paused. "I have to say I can't quite picture you in New York. It's so cold there in the winter. Surely you miss the Miami weather. You're a hot-blooded Latino."

He grinned. "I do miss the sun from November to March, sometimes April," he conceded. "But to be honest, I spend only a few weeks a year in the city. Most of the time I'm working on a project somewhere else in the world. Wherever my grandfather needs me to go, I go."

"What's the best place you've gone?"

"I don't know about best, but Panama was a favorite. That was a smaller project, but the country was beautiful. Where have you traveled?"

"Hardly anywhere. I've been to California, New York, Chicago, and Miami, but I've never been to Europe or South America or even Hawaii. Maybe someday."

"Where will you go first?" He smiled. "Wait a second. I know the answer to that question—whichever place has the most electrical storms."

She made a face at him. "I could take a vacation from lightning."

"Could you?" he challenged.

For the first time in a very long time, she actually thought she could. She hadn't checked the weather on her phone in two days, and she couldn't remember when she'd gone that long without knowing the forecast.

Before she could answer his question, Jake came in the back door. "I have to take off, Alicia."

"It was good to see you," she said, giving him a hug. "We should keep in better touch."

"We should. Michael, nice to meet you."

"You, too," Michael said, shaking Jake's hand.

"Try to keep my sister out of trouble—if you can."

"I'll certainly try."

Jake turned back to her. "If you talk to TJ, Alicia, let him know that we're concerned about his mother. Mom said her friend is checking on her tonight, and she'll go over there tomorrow after work, but TJ needs to come up with a long-term solution.

"I will. Maybe you should think about reaching out to Kat," she suggested.

"That ship sailed a long time ago."

Whenever Jake spoke of Katherine, there were always deep shadows in his eyes. Alicia couldn't help wondering if his high school sweetheart didn't still have a piece of his heart.

"Good luck with your quest," Jake continued. "I hope you find your friend, Michael, and the answers you're looking for."

"Thanks," Michael said.

"And come back with Alicia for Dani's party if you can."

"I'll consider it."

"Looks like you charmed my brother and my mother," she said lightly, as she wiped down the counter after her brother left.

"Jake is cool."

"Yeah. He's a good guy when he's not being annoying."

"So tonight wasn't bad."

She shook her head. "Not bad at all."

"Maybe even good?"

"Perhaps. But I think we should call it a night before that changes." As if on cue, her mother walked in the back door with the last of the dishes. "Michael and I are going to take off, Mom."

"I understand. How long will you be in town?"

"We're not sure yet, but we'll probably go back to Miami tomorrow night or Wednesday."

"Well, if you have any extra time—"

"I'll give you a call," she promised. "Thanks for dinner, Mom."

"I'm really glad you came," Joanna said, her eyes soft and a little pleading. "I know we don't always see eye-to-eye, Alicia, but you're my daughter, and I love you."

"I love you, too." She walked into her mom's open arms and gave her a hug. It was probably the first time they'd embraced in ten years.

Michael and her mother said goodbye, and then she and Michael walked out to the car.

It was a beautiful starry night in the quiet neighborhood where Alicia had grown up, but she had the oddest feeling that it was the quiet before the storm. She just wished she knew where that storm might be coming from.

Glancing at her watch, she saw it was after nine. The evening had flown by. "I didn't realize it was so late. So much for my idea of a short visit."

"Yeah, I didn't think that was going to happen," Michael said with a wry smile. "But I love your optimism."

"It doesn't always pay off. So back to the hotel?" she asked as Michael started the car.

"Sounds good to me."

"Even if Lieutenant Hodges didn't drop off the case file information, we should take a closer look at Liliana's notes, see if we can piece together any clues."

"That's an idea."

They arrived at the hotel fifteen minutes later. Checking in at the front desk resulted in disappointing news. There were no messages or packages.

They headed back upstairs, opening the door to Michael's room first. She decided to go inside and just use the connecting door to get to her room, but she hesitated as she saw Michael wander out to the hotel balcony without saying a word.

His mood had definitely changed since they'd left her mom's house, and even more so since they'd received nothing from Lieutenant Hodges. She set her purse on the dresser and walked out to the balcony. Michael was resting his forearms on the rail, staring out at the dimly lit pool and the moonbeams lighting up the waters in the bay.

"You're disappointed," she said, standing next to him.

"I don't really know what I am." He let silence follow those words, then a moment later turned his head and said, "To be honest, I wasn't that disappointed when I realized there was no case file to go over. I was almost relieved, which is not the way I should feel, but I'm tired, Alicia."

"I know." She put a hand on his arm, giving him a sympathetic look. "You need a break."

"I'm not giving up yet, but I don't want to do anything else tonight."

"You don't have to. It's probably better if we look at the notes in the morning when we're fresh."

"I liked being at your house, getting to know your mom and your brother, seeing you with them. It felt almost normal. I'd forgotten what normal was."

"Does your normal usually involve family barbecues where you have to cook, and none of the plates or wine glasses match? I have the feeling your friends are a little more upscale."

"I guess that's true. But I didn't grow up with money, Alicia. I'm more comfortable with the kind of night we just had. I've never really fit in with my grandfather's wealthy friends." He let out a sigh at the end of that statement. "I've always been caught between worlds, cultures, people. My grandfather wants to push down my Cuban side and my father thinks I'll get swallowed up in the Jansen empire and forget my heritage. He wants me to remember where I came from, where he came from."

"What do you want, Michael?"

"I don't know."

"I think you do. You're a man who knows what he wants."

"I want to be myself. I'm a mix of two cultures.

That's never going to change. I'm tired of feeling like I need to choose."

"You don't need to choose. I like your different sides. And we're all a mix, whether it's cultures that influence us or just personality differences. I'm a mix, too. I think it makes me more interesting, not less. And the same is true for you."

"You certainly interest me," he said, brushing a strand of hair off her face.

At the look in his eyes, her heart skipped a beat. "Alicia?"

"Yes?" she asked warily, her blood beginning to rush through her veins with anticipation.

"I know what I want to do tonight."

She stared back at him for a long moment, her brain battling with her body, reason fighting with emotion. Excitement was building within her and he hadn't even touched her. She felt the same anticipation as she did when she heard the rumble of thunder and lightning streaked across the sky.

Michael's words, his mouth, his eyes—pulled her to him. And she wanted to go. She didn't want to resist or think—she just needed to surrender, to feel.

"Alicia?" he pressed.

"I want the same thing," she murmured.

His eyes glittered in response, and his jaw tightened. He looked like he was trying to fight one more battle. "Are you sure?"

"If I wasn't sure, I wouldn't still be standing here. And I sure as hell wouldn't do this." She put her hands on his arms, pressed her body against his and touched his mouth with her lips.

The simmering passion that had been building in intensity exploded in the most deeply intense kiss she'd ever had. Michael wrapped his arms around her body, bringing her into a possessive embrace as his tongue slid between her lips and brought the heat of his body into hers.

One kiss led to another and another.

Michael barely let her breathe between kisses, and she loved his impatient, frenzied moves, making her feel wanted and desired.

They made their way into the bedroom, stripping off their clothes with each step. Part of her wanted to stop and savor every caress, but this wasn't the time for going slow. She had a burning need to have no barriers between them, and Michael seemed to feel the same way.

As she stripped off her bra and stepped out of her panties, she sank into the soft mattress of the bed, Michael's hard body coming down on top of hers. He cupped her face with his hands and stared at her with those beautiful light blue eyes that seemed to see right through her.

Then he kissed her mouth, dragging his tongue along the side of her jaw, licking a path along her collarbone, his head finally moving even lower.

She ran her hands through his thick dark hair as he kissed her breasts, as his hands ventured farther down her stomach to the center of her need. Her nerves tingled and jolted with each touch of his mouth, his fingers, the tension building inside her until she was aching. "I need you, Michael," she murmured.

"I need you more," he said, the truth shining out of his eyes, and it was that truth that shattered her heart.

When they came together, it was better than her best dream, hotter than she'd ever imagined, as magnificent and powerful and life-changing as a lightning strike.

But when her body tumbled down from the peak, Michael was there to catch her, and she was there to catch him.

She had a feeling nothing would ever be the same again.

SEVENTEEN

Alicia woke up, dazed and disoriented, a heavy male arm across her waist. That's when the beautiful memories came flooding back. Michael was on his side next to her, his breathing deep and steady, but even as they slept he was holding on to her, and she liked it. She liked it a lot.

She'd always thought of herself as the kind of person who needed her own space, who was a bit isolated from others, mostly by choice or because she was always charging off to witness nature in its most powerful state.

Since she'd met Michael, she'd had no space for herself, not just in this bed where he was hogging a good three-quarters of the mattress but also in her life. For the last several days, they'd been together almost every minute, and yet she hadn't grown bored with him or tired of his company. She hadn't wanted to put space between them. Instead she'd felt a need to stay as close to him as possible.

Well, they'd certainly gotten as close as they could last night. She'd thought she'd had good sex before in her life, but her past experiences dimmed in comparison. She'd sensed that Michael would bring intensity and passion, and she'd liked his ability to focus exclusively on her. But through the night, she'd been pleased to see another side to him—the side that was generous, adventurous and fun.

As they'd wrestled in the sheets, they'd laughed as much as anything else. She'd never felt so uninhibited, so free to be herself, whether it was in exploring his body or telling him exactly where she wanted to be touched.

She'd liked touching him exactly where he needed it most, too. She'd liked his impatience, his need for her. Even now, the memories were making her heart race. Maybe it was time to wake Michael up. On the other hand, with the sun now starting to stream through the open curtains, she was afraid that the fast-arriving day would change things between them.

Had last night just been an escape, a release from the tension and the worry?

She wasn't sure she wanted the answer to that question.

Glancing at the clock on the bedside table, she realized it was half-past six. Maybe she'd just sleep for a while longer. Closing her eyes, she tried to slip back into happy unconsciousness, but her brain was already coming to life and she wasn't going to be able to settle it back down. Finally, she gave up.

Gently moving Michael's arm off her abdomen, she slid out of the bed and moved toward the open door between their rooms. She walked into her bathroom, smiled at her tousled hair and swollen lips in the mirror and then hopped into the shower.

Thirty minutes later, with her hair blown dry, she wrapped herself in the complimentary hotel bathrobe and moved back into the bedroom to get dressed.

It was then that she noticed the drawers pulled out of the dresser, the closet door open, and the clothes she'd left in the suitcase tumbled on the floor next to it.

Her heart began to beat faster as she gazed around the room. The door to her balcony was ajar. She walked out on to it and realized that there wasn't much space between balconies. It was possible someone could have jumped the low wall between her balcony and the one next to hers.

She moved quickly back into her room and through the adjoining door to Michael's room.

"Wake up," she said, putting her hand on his shoulder.

He blinked in surprise and turned on to his back. "Hey, beautiful. You're up. I thought we could sleep in this morning."

"No, you need to get up."

Her urgent words erased the intimate smile in his eyes. He sat up. "What's wrong?"

"Someone was in my room. My clothes are all over the place and the balcony door was open.

Someone came in while we were out yesterday, or—" She stopped abruptly, suddenly wondering if someone had been in her room while she and Michael had been making love. "Oh, my God, they could have been in the room last night while we—"

He jumped out of bed and put his arms around her trembling shoulders. "It's okay, Alicia. You're okay."

His strong arms and reassuring words helped get her feet back under her. "You should take a look. I'm fine, just a little shaken up."

She let go of Michael.

He grabbed his boxers off the floor and pulled them on, then walked into her room.

She followed him inside, watching his gaze sweep the messy room.

"When do you think they came in?" she asked. "We never came in here last night after we got back from my mom's house."

"I don't know." A grim note entered his voice. "I didn't really look at my room. Did you?"

"Not really. I mean, nothing jumped out at me when we walked in the door, but we got distracted pretty quickly."

As she finished speaking, he went back through the adjoining door, and she followed him. He opened the closet door, and she peered over his shoulder to see his suitcase upended, his clothes on the ground.

"They were here, too," he said, closing the door and looking around the room.

One of the dresser drawers was half-open, but there wasn't anything else in the room that looked askew.

"What would someone be looking for? Do you think it was just a random search for money or jewelry?" she asked.

"I doubt it. It doesn't feel random. Someone was probably looking for whatever we're looking for—evidence related to the case, or Liliana, or something." He glanced back at her. "I think whoever broke in here did so while we were out yesterday."

She looked at his balcony door. "Was it open last night when you went out there?"

"I don't remember. But if they came through your balcony, we had the adjoining doors open."

She felt marginally better with the idea that the break-in had occurred when they were out of the hotel and not while they were sleeping. "We should call the front desk."

"Yes, but I don't think we're going to get too far. Is anything of yours missing?"

"I don't think so. I didn't bring much with me, and I had my purse with me the whole time." Her gaze drifted over to the bedside table. "The red light is lit on your phone. You have a message. I didn't notice that last night, either."

He frowned and walked over to the phone. He

picked up the receiver, pushed the button and listened for a moment. Straightening, he looked at her with a far more energized gleam in his eyes. "There's a package for me at the front desk. Let's get dressed. In fact, why don't you pack up your suitcase? I don't think we should stay here another night."

"Where will we go?"

"We'll figure that out later."

"Okay."

He gave her an apologetic smile. "Alicia, this isn't exactly how I saw the morning going. I had a lot of other ideas, all of them starting with waking up to you in my bed."

"I know. We got off track last night."

"Wonderfully off track," he agreed. "You don't have regrets, do you?"

"No," she said, seeing the question in his eyes. "I had a good time."

"It was better than good," he said, giving her a quick kiss. "I'm going to jump in the shower. I'd invite you, but then we'll never get out of this room."

She smiled. "Go."

Two hours later, they'd reported the break-in to hotel security, waited while the head of security went through their room, then checked out and retrieved a thick envelope from the front desk, which they took to a café.

Before digging into the file they ordered coffee and breakfast, mutually deciding they'd start off on a better note if they ate first.

After a delicious vegetable omelet, Alicia sat back in her seat, feeling more ready to take on the day.

Michael popped the last piece of bacon into his mouth and gave her a smile that was quickly becoming a usual occurrence. She preferred it so much more to the frown he'd worn their first few days together. She wanted to believe that she was responsible for the change in his mood, especially after last night.

"What are you thinking about, Alicia?" he asked, his gaze searching her face.

"That I like your smile, and I'm getting to see it more often now," she said honestly.

"That's in large part due to your presence. I'm starting to feel more like myself again."

"I'm glad, Michael."

"Not that we've solved anything yet, but taking action has been a lot better than standing still." He picked up the envelope from the seat beside him. "Ready to dig in?"

"I think they might want our table. There's a line. Why don't we go somewhere else?"

"Where did you have in mind?"

She thought for a moment. "There's a park not far from here. I used to go there all the time with my dad. They have lots of picnic tables and since it's . . ." She paused to check her watch. "Just after ten o'clock on a Tuesday morning, I doubt there will be anyone else there."

"Sounds good." He grabbed the check. "Looks like we pay up front."

She slid out of the booth and followed him up to the cash register. While Michael was paying the bill, she wandered out to the parking lot. Her gaze caught on a man sitting in a car in front of the café. For a split second, she thought he was looking at her. Then he pulled out his phone and made a call.

"Ready?" Michael asked.

"Uh, sure."

"What's wrong?"

"That guy in the silver Honda," she said as they walked toward their rental car. "I thought he was looking at me. But he's just making a call. I'm getting paranoid."

Michael glanced over his shoulder. "Considering what just happened at our hotel, I don't think you're paranoid. Maybe I should talk to him."

"No, don't," she said, instinctively putting a hand on his arm. "Wait, look. He's leaving."

The man had set down his phone and was backing out of the space.

"It was nothing," she added.

"Well, we'll keep an eye out," Michael said, a hard note in his voice. He put an arm around her shoulder as they walked to the car.

She liked his arm around her—a little too much, she thought. She was used to being independent and on her own, but it was nice to have a protective man by her side for a change.

After getting in the car, they drove toward the park, which was only a few miles away. She'd always liked coming to this particular park because it had a large pond with lots of ducks, a huge play area with ladders and tunnels and slides, and even a climbing wall, which had been one of her favorite things to do. It also had several picnic areas where they'd celebrated more than a few birthdays.

"It's quiet here," Michael commented as he parked in the lot. There were a couple of other cars, one of which probably belonged to an older couple who were strolling the path toward the pond.

"It's busier on the weekends."

"So you used to come here a lot as a kid?" he asked as they got out of the car.

"All the time. It seemed like every other weekend someone in the neighborhood was celebrating their birthday here, and I had at least three parties with all my classmates in this park."

He smiled. "What were you like as a little kid?"

"I was active. I liked to play sports, chase balls and climb trees. I used to follow Jake and his friends around, which they hated. I would have followed Danielle, but she was better at ditching me, and frankly, I wasn't that interested in whatever she was doing." She paused. "Let's go to the picnic area. We can spread out at a table and dig into whatever Lieutenant Hodges has sent us."

"Good idea."

She sat down on one side of a table while Michael took the opposite bench. As he sat down, her gaze swept the area, her nerves still on edge after the break-in at the hotel and the man she'd seen in the parking lot. The deserted area should have made her feel safer, but instead it reminded her that they were alone, possibly being watched at this very moment.

Michael suddenly got up and came around the table. He straddled the bench so he was facing her. She turned toward him, and he put his hands on her shoulders, kneading her tight, tense muscles. "If this is too much, Alicia, we can go back to Miami right now."

It was a tempting offer, but she couldn't take it. "No. If someone searched our rooms, then we must be on to something, right?"

"Probably."

"Maybe it was Detective Kellerman sending someone to check out what we were doing."

"I don't think he'd send someone to search our hotel on the sly. He would have just had the police here in town come and talk to us."

"But he knows we're here, and the only way he could know that is if he's following you or watching your movements."

"Don't worry about him, Alicia. He's not going to harm us."

"I know, but someone else might. Who else knows we're here?"

"Well, Lieutenant Hodges and anyone else at JAG that she might have spoken to, your mom and brother."

"And Mrs. Barrett, but she was so out of it, she might not even remember I was there." She frowned. "We have both a short list and a long list, because we don't know who Lieutenant Hodges talked to about our meeting."

"Maybe you should go home, Alicia. This has never been your fight and I don't want anything to happen to you. I promised your mother I would make sure that you were safe, and I don't want to break that promise."

"I can take care of myself. I've been doing it for a long time."

"That doesn't mean your family doesn't worry about you, or that I don't worry about you. I've put you in the middle of a bad situation." Guilt flittered through his gaze. "I knew I was doing it, but I was so happy to have someone on my side, I didn't want to look too closely at how involved you were getting."

"Stop. I put myself in the middle of this,

Michael. I saw the lightning. I found the tag. I went to the police. And I went back to the park and met you. Everything I've done has been my decision."

"But things are changing. After what happened last night, maybe you should reconsider your involvement. I'm okay with you calling it quits. I wouldn't think less of you, Alicia."

"I'm not a quitter. I don't give up. It's not what Monroes do."

He smiled. "Is that your father or your mother you're quoting?"

She was about to say it was her dad, then realized, somewhat surprisingly, that those words had usually come from her mother's mouth. "I was thinking it was my dad, but it was my mom. She used to buck us up when Dad was deployed for months at a time. We'd get discouraged or be unhappy because we were missing him, and we wouldn't want to do stuff, because he wasn't going to be there; he wasn't going to see us play soccer or perform in the school play. Mom would say that Monroes were not quitters and when things got difficult, we just needed to try harder. It's weird—I don't think I remembered that until just now."

"Coming home can illuminate memories that got twisted over time."

"Did that happen to you in Miami?"

"A little. I'm starting to see that painting my

dad as an uncaring, coldhearted father might have been a little extreme."

She met his gaze. "How could anyone who cooks with so much heat be coldhearted?"

"I think it was easier to deal with his rejection when I thought of him as a monster. Turns out, he really wasn't that at all. But we were talking about you. Your recollections of your mother are softening it seems. What about your father?"

"I don't know that I would ever change the way I feel about him. Obviously, I can't talk to him again or rewrite history. He's frozen in time. My mom can change and our relationship can get better or worse, but the way I think of my dad is always going to be the same. I just wish I knew what had happened to him in the final minutes of his life. I hate that I'll never know if he was scared, if he had any warning, if he had any thought that we would rescue him."

"You'll make yourself crazy if you go down that road too many times."

"I've already worn out the soles of my shoes going down that road. I know I have to accept that I'll just never know, that it was a tragic accident, that there are no explanations. I'm just not there yet."

He nodded, understanding in his eyes. "Do you want to take a walk?"

"No, we have to get to work."

"Let's walk around the pond. Clear our heads. I missed my run this morning."

She got to her feet as he stood up and when he extended his hand, she took it. "Do you run a lot?"

"Five to six times a week."

"That's almost every day."

"It keeps me from overheating," he said with a smile. "Some days the job can be one problem after another, subcontractors not showing up, someone putting a wall where it's not supposed to go, a delay in getting a permit. I have to run a sizeable team and when the team doesn't work well, I've found that I get better results when I'm calm and decisive and not pissed off and stressed out."

"And a run a day does that for you?" she asked doubtfully. "I guess I've never run far enough or fast enough to get those endorphins everyone raves about. I usually find running to be some-what dull, but then I mostly do it on a treadmill."

"You have to get out in nature. Did you bring any sneakers with you? We could go out later."

"Sorry, no sneakers. I wasn't planning on a workout."

"Too bad. We could always get you some."

"I'd just hold you back. I'm sure you would be a lot faster than me."

"I can go slow—when it matters." He gave her a look that took her right back to the night before when he had been painstakingly slow and attentive as he'd kissed his way across every inch of her body.

"Yes, you can," she murmured as his fingers curled around hers. "You know, I can't remember the last time I held hands with anyone and just took a walk. I might have been twelve."

"So do you like it?" He lifted their locked hands and brought hers to his mouth where he gave her knuckles a quick kiss.

A tingle shot through her body. "It's not bad."

"It's better than not bad."

"Maybe."

"So tell me about your friends, Alicia. Who do you hang with in Miami?"

"Well, there's Jeff—he's the weather guy at Channel 2 News."

Michael laughed. "So he's like your dealer. He gives you your weather fix."

She made a face at him. "It's not like that, well, not *exactly* like that. He does tell me when there's lightning headed my way. I also spend time with some of the women at the paper. One of the reporters is a good friend, and I had a roommate when I first moved to Miami who I still see. She got married last year, so her life has gone in a different direction." As she spoke, she realized she could count her good friends on probably one hand.

Turning to Michael, she said, "What about you? Who are your friends?"

"I have some college friends that I spend time with. There's often a bar or a sporting event involved."

"But you live alone?"

"For the last five years yes. Before that, I had some roommates, but I got tired of the keg scene. I prefer being on my own."

"So do I. I can just be myself."

He gave her a funny look.

"What?" she asked warily.

"Just thinking how often you feel like you can't be yourself when other people are around."

"Well, that's probably because I have a hobby most people think is ridiculous. I get judged a lot."

"Or maybe you're judging yourself."

His suggestion hit a little too close to home.

"If you like what you do, then own it," he said. "Be whoever you want to be. The worst thing is trying to be someone you're not."

"I think that's easier to say than to do."

He stopped walking, his pause drawing her gaze to his. "You're not a woman who's afraid of difficult challenges, Alicia."

"I'm not as brave as you think I am."

"Yes, you are."

"How do you know that?"

"For one thing, you'd probably be on a plane home right now if you were the kind of person to get scared off. But you're not. You just have to believe in what I already see."

His words touched her deeply. He seemed to believe in her more than anyone else in her life. "Thanks."

"Just speaking the truth, babe."

They finished walking around the pond and then made their way into the picnic area about twenty minutes later. Alicia was glad they'd taken the time to walk off some of the tension of the day. She felt more ready to dive into the pile of information.

They sat down across from each other. Michael opened the large envelope and pulled out two folders that were filled with papers. He handed one to her and kept the other for himself.

"These look like court transcripts," she said.

He nodded. "Yeah, and I've also got notes from counsel in my batch."

She felt energized by the thick stack of papers, each one of which could serve up a potential clue. They'd been operating on so little information, she felt like she'd just gotten a huge gift. "There has to be something in here," she said excitedly.

"Let's hope so. But remember, Alicia, the police have already looked at this information. It's not likely we're going to find a clue they missed."

"You never know."

EIGHTEEN

For over an hour, they read through the files that Lieutenant Hodges had sent over. Alicia jotted down notes on her phone as she was going through the papers so she wouldn't forget what she wanted to talk to Michael about. By the time she'd finished the file, she had a much better feel for the facts of the double homicide, the witness testimony, and the grounds for appeal.

What she didn't have was a clearer picture of who might have been the murderer if Bryer's wife was indeed innocent.

Michael had been silent during his read-through, although his expression had gotten more serious with each flip of the page.

"Should we compare notes?" she asked when he looked up from his file.

"All right. You go first. What have you got?"

"More questions than answers. In no particular order, here goes: I think we should talk to Melissa Bryer's sister, Cheryl Alton. In her trial testimony, she spoke out quite vehemently about the fact that her brother-in-law was not having an affair. It's possible she lied because she felt that was the best strategy to protect her sister, but my gut tells me she believed what she was saying."

"But she had no proof that he wasn't having

an affair," Michael returned. "She might have believed it because she needed to believe it. That said, I agree that we should talk to her. She has the best knowledge of the key players, which would be Melissa and the professor."

"She works at Bella Beauty Salon downtown as a hairstylist. Maybe she's there today. We should check that out next."

"Okay, what else?"

"I thought it was interesting how little information there was on Connie Randolph, otherwise known as the other woman. While there was extensive background on the Bryers and their personal and work lives, Connie's bio was sketchy. She worked as an engineer at MDT. She was an attractive, thirty-two-year-old woman who divorced her husband about a year before she was killed. Her coworkers said she was hardworking and dedicated to her job and often worked late into the night, but no one socialized with her. She lived alone in a one-bedroom apartment in a building that housed thirty-two units. Her neighbor said they'd never exchanged more than a word or two in greeting in the year that Connie had lived there."

She paused for a moment, thinking that she'd been living a life very similar to Connie's for the past few years. She wondered if something had happened to her if anyone would be able to piece together the real story of her life.

Her frown drew Michael's attention. "What?" he asked.

"Just thinking that I live my life very much like Connie did. You asked me about friends earlier, and I could only come up with a couple. I'm a friendly person. I don't know how I became so isolated." Actually, that wasn't completely true. She'd started distancing herself from people after her father died and somewhere along the way it had just become a habit to keep to herself, to not get too involved, to not put her heart on the line.

She'd broken that habit last night though. Liliana's disappearance hadn't just changed Michael's life; it had also changed hers.

"You're not Connie," Michael said. "You have to keep some emotional distance here, Alicia."

"I know that. It just struck me for a moment, that's all. Anyway, no one seemed to have any idea that Connie was sleeping with Bryer. Everyone who worked with her expressed surprise that she'd been found in his bed."

"Not everyone was surprised," Michael said, glancing down at his notes. "Bryer's housekeeper stated that she'd seen Connie at the professor's house two days earlier. And a teaching assistant at the university—not TJ—said that he'd seen Thomas and Connie having drinks at a bar called the Flight Deck. I didn't see TJ interviewed about the case at all."

"I noticed that. The Flight Deck did come up a

291

few times in the material I read. Bryer met Connie there at least four times in the month preceding their deaths. They also went to Burger Bob's, which is apparently one of Bryer's favorite places. We were just there yesterday." It felt a little unsettling to think they'd inadvertently gone to one of the couple's meeting places without knowing it.

"Just because they ate together or had drinks together doesn't mean they were more than friends and colleagues," Michael said.

"Don't forget the text messages and emails exchanged between the two of them. Those indicated they were having a personal relationship of some nature."

"I don't know," he said, shaking his head. "I read the texts provided in court." He flipped through the pages. "Here they are: *It's important we speak tonight. I need to see you. When can we get together? Are you working late again? When is your wife coming back to town?*" He lifted his gaze to hers. "You could spin those texts but if you just look at them objectively, they don't sound that damning. It's not like they were sexting or sending naked photos to each other."

He had a point. "Well that would support Cheryl's claim that they weren't involved in an affair. But I did read that a bartender at the Flight Deck reported overhearing a loud fight between Professor Bryer and his wife a couple of days before the murder. What were they fighting about?"

"Could have been anything. That same witness—Kayla Robbins—said she'd personally served Connie and the professor at least twice in the weeks preceding the murder and that she wasn't surprised that they'd been found in bed together."

She groaned. "We're going around in circles, Michael. Were they or weren't they? How will we ever know?"

"Good question. I will say that the manner of death felt very cold-blooded and somewhat deliberate. Both were killed with one bullet. Bryer took it in the head; Connie got it in the heart. It felt like a message was being delivered."

"Which played into the prosecutor's case that the scorned wife, who was an excellent marksman, killed them both. But I don't get why she'd kill them in her house or stick around, call 911, and cooperate with the police. She was questioned for an hour before she requested an attorney," Alicia said.

"She could have been trying to prove how innocent she was. She could have thought she was smart enough to beat them. Did you find anyone else with a motive?"

"I wondered about the housekeeper's son, Joey Martinez." She riffled through some papers and pulled out the one with his statement. "He went to the house with his mother the morning after the two were killed. He said he was just dropping her off for work as usual, and they hadn't heard the news until they arrived and saw the crime scene tape."

She paused, turning to the next page. "He told the police his mother had worked for the family for two years and that they hadn't treated her all that well. They often asked her to work late to accommodate their schedules but didn't pay her much." She glanced over at Michael. "That matches what Liliana had in her notes that the son said the professor was cheap. Do you still have Liliana's notes?"

"Yeah, but they're in the pocket of the jeans I wore last night, which are in the car. Should I get them now?"

"We can look at them again later. Was there anything else in your batch of papers that jumped out at you?"

"Yes. Paul Sandbury, Connie Randolph's coworker."

"I read his testimony. What bothered you about it?"

Michael thought for a moment. "It seemed incomplete, as if Sandbury had something to say, but no one was asking him the right questions. He mentioned that Connie and Thomas argued in the office, but he didn't think it was of a personal nature. He thought it was about work.

Unfortunately, he didn't hear the conversation, just the tone. He also mentioned that Connie's ex-husband also had an altercation with Connie several months earlier. It got so heated that the ex-husband was escorted out of the building."

"Yes, but Brian Randolph had an airtight alibi. He was giving a seminar at a conference attended by hundreds of people."

"That doesn't mean he couldn't have set up the murder," Michael said. "We need more information, Alicia. We need to get it from someone who knew the professor well."

"Or Connie. I think we need to put together a list, start at the top and work our way down. Speculation isn't getting us anywhere."

"All right. Let's do it."

As she put the papers back into her file, her phone rang. The flashing number surprised her. "It's TJ."

"Great," Michael said with excitement. "Put it on speaker so I can hear."

"Hello? TJ?"

"Alicia Monroe?"

"Yes, thanks for calling me back. I don't know if you remember me, but I'm Jake's youngest sister."

"Sure, I remember you. If this is about my mother, then I know what you're going to say, the house is a disaster. You have to understand that I have someone coming in once a week to clean, but I can't afford to make it more frequent, and my mother makes a mess ten minutes after the house-keeper leaves. My mother has trouble staying focused on whatever task she's doing. She had a mini-stroke several months ago. She's getting better, and I'm checking on her as often as I can, but I have to work, and she absolutely refuses to have anyone else come into the house."

She heard the frustration and anger in his voice. "What about the neighbors? Or other family members?"

"Katherine is busy at the hospital and is never around. The neighbors haven't been helpful."

"Well, I spoke to my mother. She's going to check in on Debbie today. She said she'd try to pull some people together."

"Really? That would be amazingly helpful," he said with relief.

"Good. I hope your mother gets better quickly. But it wasn't just your mom's situation that I was calling about. I need to talk to you about Professor Bryer's murder. Did you work in his department at the time that he was killed?"

Silence followed her words.

"TJ?" she prodded.

"Why are you asking me about that? I thought you were a photographer living in Miami."

"I am, but I'm also involved in this case."

"I told that lawyer everything I knew. I can't go through it again."

"What lawyer?"

"Lieutenant Valdez. She asked me a bunch of questions a few months ago."

Her breath caught in her chest. "What did you tell her?"

"That I didn't think Professor Bryer was banging that woman who was killed. She wasn't into him at all."

"Are you sure? Several witnesses saw them together at a bar in town and also at his house."

"Everyone at MDT and the university has had a drink at the Flight Deck. It's a hugely popular bar. I don't think it was unusual that they were there."

"So you don't think his wife killed him because he was cheating on her?"

"I don't know what happened exactly, but I think you should leave it alone, and I know I should stay out of it. I work at MDT now. I don't need to get into the middle of anything."

"I understand, but Lieutenant Valdez is missing, TJ. It's been two months since anyone saw her. We think her disappearance has to do with the murders, so if you can tell me anything else, I would really appreciate it."

Silence followed her words and then TJ said, "Lieutenant Valdez seemed to think that someone else killed Professor Bryer and the woman he was with, that there might be a link between his death and someone at MDT."

"Someone like who?"

"She didn't say. She just asked a lot of questions, which was something she and Professor Bryer had in common. He asked a lot of questions, too. I'm beginning to think one of those questions got him killed."

"What kinds of questions would the professor have been asking?"

"Probably something about the technology he was helping them with, and, no, I don't know what he was working on exactly. It's a big company and they have at least a dozen product lines. I'm working on GPS trackers. Professor Bryer was doing something with aeronautical engineering, but everything is highly classified. I don't know what the person in the cubicle next to me is working on."

"Can you give me the name of someone else at MDT I can talk to?"

"The only person I know who worked with Professor Bryer was Reid Packer, one of the co-owners of MDT. Reid and his older brother Alan run the company, but Reid is more hands-on with the technology. I know he testified at the trial, but he's way above my pay grade, so I can't give you any more than that."

"If something else comes to you that might help us follow the same path that Lieutenant Valdez took, will you call me?"

"Sure, I guess. If you're trying to follow her

trail, then you should also go to the Flight Deck. A lot of MDT employees go there. The owner used to work for the company, so he gives everyone with an MDT badge half off their drinks."

"We'll definitely go there. Thanks, TJ."

"You're welcome, and if you can get your mom to help my mom, I'd appreciate that."

"I know she'll help," she said confidently. "Bye." She ended the call and looked at Michael. "Reid Packer could be the name that Liliana referred to in her notes when she wrote MDT-RP. What did he say in his testimony? Do you remember? I have to admit some of it got so tedious, I started to skim."

"He didn't say much of anything. He couldn't disclose what Connie or the professor was working on because of national security. I believe he played that card several times. And I don't think it's going to be easy for us to get the owner of MDT on the phone. I doubt Liliana would have been able to get to him, either."

"Unless she had someone to give her an introduction."

"Like who?"

"Like your grandfather. Maybe he knows him. His name was in Liliana's notes right next to MDT-RP. I think you should try him again."

Michael frowned. "It's a little odd that he hasn't called me back. He's usually good about that."

He pulled out his phone and made the call. He listened for a moment and then hung up. "He's not answering."

"You don't want to leave another message?"

"I already left one. I'll try him again tonight. I think we should go talk to Melissa's sister and then hit the bar up later this afternoon or evening. There will be more people there later in the day."

"Good idea. There might be more information here than we've realized but it's a lot to take in at one time."

"I agree. My eyes started glazing over with the legal language."

"Exactly. I'd rather follow the same trail Liliana was following. If we talk to the same people, maybe we'll figure out what she discovered. Let's start with Cheryl."

Cheryl Alton was a busty, loud redhead, whose voice could be heard clearly above the chatter in the hair salon. After the receptionist told Cheryl that some people wanted to talk to her about her sister, she'd asked them to wait for five minutes, then left her client sitting in a chair with foil-stripped hair and joined them in the lobby.

"Who are you again?" she asked suspiciously.

"I'm Alicia Monroe and this is Michael Cordero," Alicia said. "We're friends with the attorney who was looking into your sister's appeal."

"Which one?" Cheryl asked. "It's been musical chairs where lawyers are concerned. No one seems to care that every time the music stops, my sister's case loses ground."

"Lieutenant Liliana Valdez," Michael said. "She went missing two months ago, and the police believe there was foul play."

"I heard about that, but I don't know what I can tell you. I only spoke to her once. I thought she was going to help me. She actually listened to me, not like the other lawyers who could barely give Melissa the time of day."

"What did you talk about with Lieutenant Valdez?" Alicia asked.

"My sister's innocence." She waved them toward the couch. "Sit down. I've got a few minutes while my client's color sets." After they were seated, she added, "I told Lieutenant Valdez that my sister could have never shot her husband, no matter what she thought he might be doing, and I don't believe for a second he was having an affair."

"What do you think happened?" Michael asked. "If your sister is innocent, who is guilty?"

"I wish I knew, but I think it was someone at MDT. Thomas was working long hours there. He was only supposed to be consulting, but he was there every night in the weeks before he died."

"Are you sure he was there for work and not to

be with Connie?" Alicia asked, thinking that those long hours might back up the affair.

"That's what the prosecutor asked me. No matter what I said, he twisted it to support his theory, but that doesn't make his theory the truth," she said hotly. "He didn't know Thomas; I did. The man was obsessed with work, whether it was teaching or consulting. He was an intellectual. His whole focus was on what he could learn and what he could teach. He barely noticed women on a sexual level. My sister said they'd go months without having sex because Thomas just wasn't that into it. Does that sound like a man who would try to juggle another woman on the side?"

"Maybe he wasn't into sex with your sister," Michael suggested. "That's why he got another woman on the side."

Cheryl shook her head, annoyance in her eyes. "I don't believe that. They were together for fifteen years. They met when they were teen-agers. They loved each other. My sister came home and found Thomas dead. She's not lying about that. And she's been in prison for over a year for a crime she didn't commit. Her first attorney quit. Her second attorney had barely graduated when he got into the middle of the case, and now the attorney who was reviewing her appeal is missing. Doesn't that sound odd to you?"

"It does," Michael agreed. "But the problem is that there isn't any evidence pointing to anyone else but your sister, unless you know something we don't."

"Someone set her up really well," Cheryl said. "But I can't believe whoever did it committed the perfect crime. There had to be a mistake somewhere. I think that Lieutenant Valdez got close to finding that mistake and now she's gone."

Alicia thought the same thing. "Do you know anything about Thomas's work at MDT?"

"I know MDT is a defense contractor, and that they work on systems for the military. Thomas wasn't allowed to speak to my sister about what projects he was working on, but I know there were weapons involved. I believe that whatever Thomas was working on is tied to his death. I told the police that, but they never seemed interested in questioning anyone at MDT. I suspect that's because the company brings a ton of money into the community. I wouldn't be surprised if they bought off the local police." Cheryl paused. "I've tried to get in there and ask questions, but I can't get past the front gate. It's a huge compound with several buildings, an airplane hangar and even a runway for small planes. It's like a small city."

Which would probably make it impossible for them to get in there, either, Alicia thought.

"The other person I thought should have been investigated more thoroughly was Brian Randolph, Connie's ex-husband," Cheryl continued. "Just because he had an alibi doesn't mean he didn't send someone to kill her. I also told Lieutenant Valdez that she should speak to Paul Sandbury. He was one of Connie's coworkers at MDT. I watched him testify, and I thought he was fidgety as hell. I told that to the defense attorney, and he said he thought Mr. Sandbury was nervous because the head of MDT was sitting in the audience watching his testimony."

"The owner?" Alicia queried.

"Reid Packer. He testified, too, but he didn't say much. Every answer was classified for national security." She paused, glancing back at her client. "I have to go. Take my card," she said, getting up to retrieve a business card from the reception desk. "Call me if you have more questions about anything. I don't know what is happening with the appeal now that Lieutenant Valdez is missing. Last I heard a few weeks ago, they were going to get another attorney. I think her name is Erin Hodges. I called her last week, but she hasn't gotten back to me yet."

After Cheryl returned to her client, Alicia and Michael walked out of the salon, pausing on the sidewalk.

"We need to find an in at MDT," Alicia said.

"We already have an in—your friend TJ. He

works there. Maybe he can get us to Paul Sandbury."

"I'll call TJ back," she said, pulling out her phone.

"Alicia, I don't know anything else," TJ said before she had a chance to ask a question.

She cut right to the chase. "I need information on Paul Sandbury. He works at MDT and was in Connie Randolph's department. Do you think you could give me his phone extension?"

"Hang on."

She let out a breath as she looked at Michael. "He's checking."

TJ came on the phone a moment later. "Paul Sandbury doesn't work at the company any-more."

Her heart sped up at that piece of information. "When did he leave?"

"About two months ago."

The same amount of time since Liliana had disappeared.

"Where did he go?"

"Texas A&M. He teaches in the engineering department."

Her nerves jangled at that piece of news.

"I've got to go, Alicia. Don't call me back. I can't get any more involved. I need to keep my job so I can take care of my mother."

"All right." She hadn't even finished speaking when TJ hung up.

"Sandbury quit MDT two months ago," she told Michael. "Now he's working at the university. It feels like a weird circle. Professor Bryer was at the university then MDT. Paul Sandbury goes the other direction."

"And Sandbury quit the company around the time Liliana goes missing. That's a hell of a coincidence. Looks like we're going to the university next."

As they walked back to the car, she said, "What do you think about the ex-husband?"

Michael shrugged. "I'm not sure. But we should talk to him, too."

"So basically we're going to follow Liliana's trail."

"It's the only way we'll figure out what she knew."

"You do realize that if we follow her trail, we could end up—"

"The same way she did," he finished, a hard expression entering his eyes. "It's a risk I'm willing to take, but once again, any time you want out, just say the word."

"Not yet." She fell into step with him as they proceeded to the car. "The other thing I find odd is that Lieutenant Hodges hasn't really gotten into the case. She told us that it was being reassigned to her, and Cheryl had the same information. So why isn't Lieutenant Hodges working on the appeal? Is she leaving it for Liliana? Is she gun-shy? What? And I keep going back to the fact that she's the only one who knew what hotel we were staying in."

"We can't worry about that now. Let's go to the university and see if we can find Paul Sandbury. After that, we'll hit up the bar and then look for a hotel for the night. We can talk to Lieutenant Hodges tomorrow if we need to."

"Okay." As they got into the car, she couldn't help thinking about how many days more she could possibly give to this search. "I hate to bring this up, but I need to be back at work by Thursday at the latest."

"Then we'll get you back. If we're not done here, you can return to Miami without me."

She knew that; she just didn't want to go back without him. She didn't want to go anywhere without him and that was a scary thought for a woman who'd been very comfortable on her own—until now.

NINETEEN

When they got to the university, they stopped in at the admissions department. Joanna looked surprised but also happy to see them. She got up from her desk and came over to the counter.

"I wasn't expecting to see you again, Alicia."

"Unfortunately, we didn't come here just to see you," Alicia said. "We need to talk to Paul Sandbury. He's a teacher in the engineering department."

"Yes, he started a few months ago. Is he involved in this case, too?" Joanna asked, worry entering her eyes.

"He used to work at MDT," Alicia replied. "Do you know if he's here today? We really want to talk to him."

"I can look up his schedule," she said, stepping up to the computer on the counter. She punched a few keys then said, "He's finishing a class at four o'clock."

Alicia glanced down at her watch. "We have about twenty minutes, probably just enough time to get across campus."

"What are you doing tonight?" her mother asked.

"We're not sure yet," she said, seeing the hope

in her mother's eyes. "But I have been seriously thinking about coming back for Danielle's party next month, and I think I can do it."

"That would make me so happy. You come, too, Michael."

"Thanks for the invitation," he said. "I'll do my best."

Alicia appreciated that Michael hadn't said no, because *maybe* always worked better with her mother. "By the way, Mom, did you ever speak to Debbie?"

"Not yet. I'm going to go by on my way home. But I did talk to Lauren, who said the house was as you described, and that Debbie was quite hazy about what was going on."

"I spoke to TJ earlier. He told me he has a cleaning service come in, but that his mom junks things up almost immediately after they leave. He's pretty stressed out about it, but he has to work to pay for help, and he doesn't seem to have much time available for his mother."

"I'm going to put together a group to help," Joanna said. "All the moms who have known Debbie over the years will surely be willing to lend a hand. I won't take no for an answer."

Alicia smiled, believing that her mother had the situation completely under control. Joanna loved to be the boss, and she was extremely capable when it came to managing people and getting things done. "I'll see you later, Mom."

"That wasn't so bad," Michael commented. "Not a speck of family drama."

"That's because I headed her off at the pass."

"I thought you volunteered a return trip fairly quickly," he said with a knowing grin.

"There's still time to back out."

"You shouldn't back out. You should go to the party, wish your sister well."

She nodded, itching to ask him if he might really be interested in coming with her, but the future was looming in a shadowy void, and this was not the time to make plans.

They made their way across the campus. Alicia pointed out some of her old classrooms and told Michael a little about the history of the university. They ended up in the engineering building with about ten minutes to spare. They decided to wait in the hall until the class ended.

"Did you ever take any classes in engineering?" Michael asked, as he leaned against the wall.

"Not a chance. I stayed as far away from this building as I possibly could. I didn't see much of the science lab, either."

He smiled. "I like math and science. Math comes in handy in my job."

"I rarely hear anyone say that math comes in handy in their job," she said with a laugh.

"Construction uses a lot of different math skills—estimating costs, measuring rooms, calculating angles—and that's just the beginning."

"Well, I'm glad to hear that there's an actual reason for anyone to learn geometry," she said dryly. "But to each his own. I'll stick to creative pursuits." She paused. "You said you'd once thought of being an architect. Did you take any classes in drafting while you were in school?"

"As many as I could without actually declaring it my major."

"What do you want to design one day? A building, a house, an apartment complex, a park? What?"

"I'd start with a house."

"Ah—your dream home. Do you already have it planned out?"

"I have some thoughts," he admitted, "but nothing in detail."

"Why haven't you gone further with the plans?"

"It seems ridiculous to build a huge house for myself to live in."

"One day you'll marry, have children, maybe get a dog. Or are you a cat person?"

"Whoa, slow down," he said putting up a hand. "You're getting way ahead of me."

"Don't you want a wife and children?"

"I haven't thought that much about it. What about you?"

"I've thought about it, but I'd have to find a man as crazy as I am to take me on, and he'd obviously have to like lightning."

He grinned. "Obviously. What other require-ments do you have?"

"He'd have to be really attractive, incredible in bed, and completely adore me. That shouldn't be too difficult to find, right?"

"Not for you."

"What's your dream woman?"

"Uh . . ." Before he could answer the door opened, and students began to file into the hallway.

"Saved by the bell," Alicia joked.

"If you want to know what I want in a woman, just look in the mirror," he said pointedly.

Warmth rushed through her face at his words. "Michael."

"What? Don't ask the question if you don't want the answer."

She stared back at him. "Okay, that's fair. Just so you know, when I described my dream man earlier, I was talking about you."

A light jumped in his eyes.

"So we're even," she said. "Are you ready to talk to Paul Sandbury?"

"I'm ready to take you to bed."

His words sent a jolt through her body. "Well, that can't happen now," she said, really wishing it could.

"Maybe later."

"Maybe." She cleared her throat. "Let's do this."

• • •

Paul Sandbury was a short, thin man with glasses and a beard. Focusing on Sandbury brought Michael's mind back into focus, to what they needed to accomplish here. Messing around with Alicia would have to wait.

"Paul Sandbury? I'm Michael Cordero. This is Alicia Monroe," he said as they joined Sandbury at the front of the classroom. "Do you have a moment? We have a few questions for you."

"What's this about?" Paul asked warily.

"The death of your former colleague, Connie Randolph."

Paul started shaking his head even before Michael got his entire statement out.

"I'm done with all that. I talked to the police. I testified at the trial. I even spoke to that other attorney a few months ago. I have no more information to give."

"The other attorney you spoke to—was that Lieutenant Liliana Valdez?"

"Yes."

"What did she ask you?"

"All the questions I'd answered before. Please, just go. I have another class in a few minutes."

"This won't take long," Michael said.

"I can't help you. I'm sorry. I've done every-thing I can do. I've tried to help. I told Lieutenant Valdez that there was more going on between Bryer and Connie, and look what happened."

"What do you mean?" Michael asked.

"I heard the lawyer I talked to disappeared. Isn't that true?"

"Yes, she vanished about two months ago— about the same time you left MDT. Why did you leave the company?"

"I wanted to teach. I have nothing bad to say about MDT." He crossed his arms, then uncrossed them, nervousness emanating from every pore. "I have three kids and a wife in poor health. I need this job, and I need to be alive to take care of them."

Michael tensed at Sandbury's blunt words. "You think you're in danger?"

"Since the last person I talked to is missing, yes."

"Then you don't think the professor's wife was the killer, do you?" Michael asked.

Paul's fidgety gaze jumped at the question. "No, but that's all I'm going to say."

"We're trying to find Lieutenant Valdez," Alicia put in. "You need to help us."

"I can't. I'm sorry. You need to drop this. You ask questions of the wrong people, you're going to end up missing, too." He let out a breath, looking relieved when students for his next class entered his classroom. "Please, leave."

Michael was frustrated by his refusal to help, but he also knew they weren't going to get anything more out of him now.

As they left the classroom, he said, "Sandbury knows something important."

"And it sounds like he told Liliana what he knows," Alicia said.

"Should we stick around until after this class ends? See if we can press for more information?"

"We could, but he seemed pretty scared, Michael. I don't think he's going to tell us anything."

"If he's scared, then . . ." He couldn't finish the thought. Sandbury's behavior had made the danger surrounding Liliana even more real. "I need to talk to him again. I'll shake the information out of him if I have to."

"Well, you can't do it right this second and I'm not sure he's going to crack. He's not just protecting himself. He made a point of saying his family was all he cared about."

"Then what do we do?"

"I think we should get a drink."

Her pragmatic answer left him without words. "Alicia . . ."

"Michael, we can't do anything now. He has a class for at least the next hour. Let's go to the Flight Deck. Hopefully, we can speak to the bartender who testified at the trial. Then we'll figure out what to do about Paul Sandbury."

"All right, but I hope Sandbury doesn't disappear on us."

Worry entered her eyes. "I hope so, too." As

they walked out of the building, she added, "One thing bothers me."

"Only one thing?"

"One of many. I wonder why Liliana is missing and Paul isn't. If he knows something, if he gave her information, why is he still living a normal life two months later?"

He didn't have an answer for that. "You make a good point. Maybe Sandbury gave Liliana a piece of something that she put together with something else. He didn't know everything but enough to help her complete the puzzle."

"We have to figure out what he gave her."

"Well, it would be easier if he just told us."

"It would, but he's scared, Michael, and that makes me wonder if someone at MDT is involved in this. If he needs money to take care of his wife, why would he quit a job that had to pay more than being a university professor?"

"You have to stop asking me questions I can't answer, dammit," he snapped. When Alicia stopped abruptly, he blew out a breath and said, "Sorry, I'm pissed off."

"I get it. Maybe I was wrong to suggest that we leave. If you want to wait until his class is over, then we should do that. It might be the smart move. We surprised him before. He might tell us more if we try again."

He didn't know if Sandbury would tell them more, but he did know he wasn't ready to walk away. "Let's go back. We'll sit in the classroom and wait for him to finish."

When they got back to the classroom, Michael opened the door and stepped inside. He was prepared to take a seat in the last row, but what he saw made him stop in his tracks. A young man stood at the podium now, and there was no sign of Paul Sandbury.

"Where did he go? Where's the teacher?" he asked the nearest student.

"He had an emergency," the young man answered.

His stomach turned over. Sandbury had run. How the hell were they going to find him now?

Alicia felt guilty for her part in encouraging Michael to leave Sandbury's classroom. If she hadn't said they should leave and come back, maybe Sandbury wouldn't have been able to take off. But there was no going back. He was gone, and they had to figure out what to do next. Unfortunately, Michael didn't seem eager to start the car. They'd been sitting in silence for a good five minutes.

"We could try to get his home address," she said. "Maybe my mother would help." When Michael just gave her a shrug of defeat, she took out her phone and called her mom. "It's me again. I need one more favor."

"What now, Alicia?"

"I need Paul Sandbury's home address."

"I can't give that to you, Alicia. It's personal information. I could get fired."

"It's really important, Mom. I wouldn't ask you if it wasn't."

"You're putting me in a really difficult position. It's not that I don't want to help you, but I just don't see that I can."

"We need to go to his house and make sure he's okay," she said, trying a different tactic. "I can promise you that I will not say where I got the address, and I will not do anything that will reflect badly on you. You have to trust me, Mom."

It was a lot to ask someone who'd rarely trusted her, and Alicia waited nervously for an answer. It came a moment later.

"532 Hawker Drive. Don't make me sorry."

"I won't." She set her phone down. "I have his address. Do you want me to drive?"

He looked over at her in bemusement. "You really don't give up, do you?"

"I told you—Monroes don't quit."

He started the engine and backed out of the space.

They made it to Sandbury's house in ten minutes. The modest one-story house showed evidence of kids, with a bike leaning against the porch steps and a doll abandoned on the lawn.

They got out of the car and walked up to the front door. Michael rang the bell, and Alicia moved across the porch to look through the living room window. There was no sign of anyone inside.

"I don't think they're home," she said.

Michael knocked and then twisted the doorknob. He gave her a shocked look when it swung open.

"You can't go inside," she protested, but he was already halfway through the door. She followed him over the threshold, and then stopped abruptly when she saw the chaos inside. "Were they robbed?"

"Or they left in a hurry." He went into the kitchen and then quickly returned. "There's food on the table, a glass of milk and half of a sandwich. The trash can was knocked over, and the back door is ajar."

She moved down the hall and looked into the master bedroom. The drawers were open and empty. The closet revealed dozens of empty hangers. "I think they left," she said, when Michael came up behind her. "That was so fast. How long has it been since we spoke to him? Thirty—forty minutes?"

"Not more than that."

"We terrified him, Michael. Just by showing up, we sent him running." She couldn't fathom that she and Michael had had the power to send a man into hiding with his wife and three children.

"I don't think he was scared of us, but he's scared of someone." Michael shook his head with frustration and anger in his gaze. "He definitely knew something about Liliana, or MDT, or the murders, or hell, I don't know."

"We can go to the police here in town, tell them what we've found out so far. Maybe they can find him and get the truth."

"The way they did before?" he asked cynically. "The cops spoke to Paul Sandbury. He testified at the trial. They didn't get any information then."

"He was still working at MDT at the time of the trial. Liliana hadn't disappeared. Things have changed." She paused. "If you don't want to go to the police, perhaps Lieutenant Hodges can help us. If she's taking over the appeal, she will soon be following the same trail we're on. In fact, we should be working together on this. I don't understand why we're not. I actually don't understand why JAG isn't already working the appeal where Liliana left off."

He put up a hand to stop her ramble. "I know you're trying to help, Alicia, but I need to think for a minute."

"I'm sorry. I'm trying to make this better. I blew it back there. I shouldn't have persuaded you to leave Sandbury's classroom. If we'd stayed, he couldn't have gotten away from us. We wouldn't be in this position."

"You don't have anything to apologize for. You didn't know he was going to run; I didn't know that, either."

"You knew he was hiding something. You knew that we shouldn't leave."

"Well, there's no point in rehashing it. We can't change it."

She was happy he wasn't blaming her, but she was just as discouraged as he was by the recent turn of events. "We should at least go and do our thinking elsewhere, Michael. We don't want the neighbors to see us inside the house. With the way Detective Kellerman thinks about you, if he finds out you were here, he'll probably spin it in a really bad way."

"Good point. We don't know if someone is following us."

It bothered her to think that someone might have followed them to the university—maybe to Sandbury's classroom—possibly even here.

They walked quickly out of the house, pulling the front door closed behind them.

Michael wiped off the doorknob with the hem of his shirt, which made her think the house was a crime scene, but it wasn't. Paul Sandbury had just left. Hadn't he?

TWENTY

Michael's stomach was churning as he drove away from Sandbury's house. He'd come so close to an answer only to be stymied again.

When they got a few blocks away, he glanced over at Alicia. "Okay, let's get back to your ideas on what to do next."

"I think we should wait on the police. The more I think about it, the more I don't believe they'll help, at least not yet. Lieutenant Hodges is probably our best bet."

"Agreed. Let's give her a call." He handed her his phone. "Do you want to find her number?"

"Sure. Do you want to talk?"

"You can do it."

A moment later, she said, "It's going to voicemail." Pausing, she added, "This is Alicia Monroe. Michael Cordero and I have some information we'd like to discuss with you. Can you call us back at this number? Thanks." She set his phone down on the console. "It is after five. She's probably gone home for the day. I doubt we'll hear from her until tomorrow." She glanced over at him. "I think we should go to the Flight Deck. It's after work now. There should be a lot of people from MDT there."

"Good idea."

Fifteen minutes later, they walked into the restaurant. The inside of the bar paid homage to aviation, particularly naval aviation. There were black and white framed photographs taken during WWII as well as color shots of more recent military airplanes. There were also wings and propellers hanging from the ceiling, as well as an entire display case of model aircraft.

"It's crowded for a Tuesday afternoon," Alicia muttered, as they made their way into the large restaurant.

"I see a table in the corner. Let's grab it."

"You don't want to just go to the bar?"

"It's packed up there, and the smell of food is making me hungry. I think we should eat, and then decide who we want to talk to."

"I'm down for that. Breakfast was a long time ago."

He smiled at her easygoing attitude. He was continually surprised by how low maintenance Alicia was. She didn't complain or whine, she just kept on going, no matter how many obstacles got in her way, and she inspired him to do the same.

A waitress dropped off menus and two glasses of water and said she'd be back shortly.

Alicia looked down at the menu. "What looks good to you, Michael? They seem to have a really large selection of pizzas. Want to share one?"

"Perfect," he said, happy to have one less decision to make. "You pick the toppings."

"You don't have any favorites?"

"I love everything. Surprise me."

She smiled. "Okay, pineapple and ham it is."

He smiled back at her. "One of my favorite combinations."

"I was just joking. I can't stand pineapple on pizza. I think I'll just get the combination."

"Perfect. What do you want to drink?"

"Beer and pizza works for me," she said.

"Let's do it."

After the waitress took their order, Alicia said, "I'll be right back. I'm going to wash my hands."

She'd no sooner left the table when his phone rang. It was his grandfather's number. "Hello?"

"Michael. How are you? How's the job going?"

"The project is on schedule," he said.

"Good. I like to hear that."

"I actually called you earlier about a different matter."

His grandfather's sigh was pronounced. "It's not about that woman again, is it? I think you should come back to New York, Michael. They're going to railroad you into prison if you're not careful."

"I can't come back yet—for several reasons. I need to find Liliana and I also want to finish the job I started, which is something you taught me well."

"Very true," William agreed. "But if getting you

out of Miami is better for you, I'll find someone else to take over the project. In fact, to be honest, I'm a little concerned about the job you're doing there. You're very distracted."

"I'm handling everything that needs to be handled."

"I hope so. This is too big of a project to be derailed by your personal problems. I have other people in the company who will give the building project their undivided attention."

"I told you. Everything is good, and we can talk details another time," he said. "Right now I want to talk to you about something in Liliana's notes that was very strange. She'd written your name down next to a company called MDT and some initials that I think belong to Reid Packer. Do you know him? Are you connected to the company in any way?"

"Reid's father, Kent Packer, is one of my friends. I've played golf with him for years. I've met Reid and Alan on several occasions." He paused. "Why would your friend have written my name down?"

"My guess is that she wanted me to ask you about them. Do you know anything about the company?"

"It's extremely profitable. The technology is world class. They get a lot of government contracts. Does that help?"

"I'd like to get more specific. Liliana was

investigating the murder of an MDT engineer and a university professor. It looks like there's a connection between that case and her disappearance."

"How so?"

"Liliana was looking into an appeal of the murder conviction. The guilty person may not be in jail."

"This does not sound good," Will grumbled.

"If I needed to ask Reid Packer some questions, do you think you could get me an appointment with him?"

"I think you should drop this immediately and come back to New York."

"That's not an option. Can you help me or not?" He had a feeling that even if his grandfather could help him, he might choose not to. "This isn't just about Liliana's life but also about mine," he added. "I want to prove that I'm innocent. And I want to get justice for one of the best friends I ever had."

"I suppose I can understand that. Rumors can dog a man for years. I will speak to Kent first. You may want to speak to Alan Packer first. That's Reid's older brother, and I believe he has more power at the company than Reid. Those boys have been competing for their father's attention and his money for as long as I've known them."

"I'll take either Packer. I just need someone high enough in the company to give me access to whoever I need to speak to."

"All right. But I have to say one thing first. Defense contractors like MDT play by a different set of rules. When national security is on the line, laws aren't always followed, information isn't necessarily dispersed, not even to the police. Kent used to tell me that in the end it's always about the good of the country, not necessarily one person. I don't know if that's patriotism or an excuse for doing whatever the hell they want, but I don't want you to get your hopes up. I'm not sure the Packers will honor a request from me if it involves exposing their dirty laundry."

"I'm not going after them; I just want to ask a few questions."

"I'll see what I can do."

"Thank you."

"Keep your nose clean, Michael. I bailed you out of Miami once. I don't want to have to do it again."

He wasn't about to tell his grandfather that he wasn't in Miami at the moment. "I'll talk to you soon."

Alicia returned to the table, giving him a questioning look. "Was that Lieutenant Hodges on the phone?"

"No, it was my grandfather. It turns out he does have a remote connection to MDT. He plays golf with Reid Packer's father. He's going to make some inquiries, see if anyone will talk to me. Apparently, Reid is second in command.

His brother Alan is at the head of the company."

"I'm so glad your grandfather is going to help. That's the first piece of good news we've had in a while."

"We'll see. I'm not sure my grandfather's influence will get Reid Packer to talk about the murder of one of his employees."

"Did your grandfather say anything else?"

"Beyond threatening to replace me if I continue to allow myself to be distracted by Liliana's disappearance? No, he didn't have much else to say." He picked up his glass of water and drank half of it. "Sometimes, I'd like to work for myself."

"I'm sure you could, Michael. But you feel like you owe your grandfather, don't you?"

"He did give me a life I wouldn't have had if he hadn't gotten me out of Miami."

"You're giving him too much credit. He might have gotten you out of a bad teenage situation, but you did the rest yourself."

"True." He let out a breath. "He's going to talk to his friend and see if they'll open the door for me."

"Hopefully, they will."

As they waited for their pizza, his gaze swept the room. He wondered if any of the patrons were employees at MDT. There seemed to be two distinct groups of people: the ripped jeans, T-shirted crowd from the nearby university and the slacks, button-down shirts and casual dresses from the after-work group.

A young blonde bartender worked one end of the bar while a bearded guy covered the other end. He wondered if the female was Kayla Robbins, the woman who had testified at the trial.

An older man came out of a hallway and stepped behind the bar to help with the growing crowd. There was something very familiar about his sandy brown hair, square face, linebacker body and friendly grin. "Alicia," Michael said.

"What?"

"Am I crazy, or is that man behind the bar one of the men in the photograph you showed me the other day—the one with your father and three of his pals?"

She followed his gaze, her eyes widening. "Oh, my God! Yes, that's Jerry Caldwell. I can't believe it. I didn't know he was here in Corpus Christi."

"He appears to work here. Looks like we might have caught a break."

"You're right." She paused as the waitress set down their beers. "Excuse me," she said. "Is the man behind the bar Jerry Caldwell?"

"Yes, he owns this place."

"Could you ask him to come over here when he gets a chance? I'm Alicia Monroe. I'm the daughter of one of his friends."

"Sure."

"I thought it would be better to try to get him away from the bar," Alicia told Michael.

"I agree." The waitress stepped up to the bar to relay the message. Jerry's gaze immediately flew in their direction. He nodded and gave them a wave.

The server came back a moment later to say, "Jerry will be over shortly. He said to tell you dinner is on him."

"Thanks," Alicia said. "I can't believe Jerry works here."

"And he owns the place. Didn't TJ say that the owner of this bar used to work at MDT?"

"Yes. Jerry must have gone to work for MDT after he got out of the Navy."

"I wonder what he did for them."

"It probably had something to do with aviation. Jerry was a fighter pilot. My dad told me that Jerry was good, but sometimes he took too many chances, that there's a fine line between courage and stupidity." She smiled at the end of her sentence. "I think I might have crossed that line a few times myself, especially recently."

He smiled. "Well, for the record, when I look at you I don't see stupidity; I only see a courageous, beautiful woman whose generosity to help others knows no bounds."

"That's . . . I don't know what to say. You've left me speechless."

He laughed. "That might be a first."

"Now you know how to shut me up. Just give me a compliment."

"It might have been a compliment, but it was also the truth."

As Michael finished speaking, Jerry came over to the table. His light brown eyes were warm and friendly and he had a charming smile that grew even brighter as he gave Alicia a hug.

"Is it really you?" Jerry asked, shaking his head in amazement as he and Alicia sat down. "My God, you're all grown up. When did that happen?"

"A while ago."

"I ran into your mom a few years back. I thought she'd said you moved away."

"I did. I'm just back for a visit. I had no idea you were here in Texas."

"I settled in about eight years ago."

"That long? My mom has never mentioned running into you. Have you ever gone by the house to see her?"

"No. Your mom was never one of my fans," he said with a careless shrug. "I took your father out for one too many drinks on a couple of occasions. She thought I was a bad influence. At your father's funeral, she pulled me aside and said she didn't want me around the family, especially Jake. She didn't want me encouraging him to be a pilot, even though everyone could see that's all the boy wanted to do."

"I had no idea my mom had a problem with

you, although it doesn't totally surprise me. I think she grew to hate the Navy and everyone attached to it. But just so you know Jake did become a pilot."

"Good for him."

She glanced over at Michael. "Sorry. I haven't introduced you. This is Jerry Caldwell, otherwise known as Uncle Jerry, and this is Michael Cordero. I told Michael that you were great friends with my dad."

"Wyatt was one of the best pilots I ever flew with," Jerry said. "He was a brilliant flyer and an even better man. I still miss him."

"I do, too," Alicia said, meeting his gaze. "I can't believe it's been ten years since he died."

"Time flies. So you're home for a visit. Did your mom remarry? And how is your sister?"

"Mom never remarried. If she dates, she doesn't tell me about it. Danielle is working in politics. She's still single, as are Jake and myself."

"What are you doing for a living?" Jerry asked.

"I'm a photojournalist for a newspaper."

He nodded. "You always loved to take pictures. Your brother and sister would be playing outside, and you'd be shooting the action. Nice you could make a career out of it."

"Yes. So how did you come to own a bar?"

"I had to trade in my wings a few years ago. I had a hard landing and it affected my vision. It was time for another career. I was done with service. Now it's all about the fun," he said with a grin.

"Looks like business is good," Michael interjected.

"It's always crowded here. The best place to have a bar is near a university or a military base. I hit the jackpot and got both." He paused. "How long are you going to be in town, Alicia?"

"A few days. Michael and I are actually doing some research on a criminal case. We're hoping you might be able to help us."

He raised an eyebrow. "Really? What kind of case?"

"The double homicide involving Professor Thomas Bryer and a woman by the name of Connie Randolph. We understand they used to come here and that one of your bartenders testified at the trial."

"That was Kayla. Why are you looking into that old case? I thought it was long done."

"A friend of mine was the lawyer working on an appeal," Michael explained. "She disappeared a few months ago. We're trying to find her, and we think her disappearance might be connected to the case."

"She was one of the JAG lawyers?" Jerry questioned.

"Lieutenant Valdez," Michael said. "Did you talk to her?"

"I probably did. I talked to a bunch of lawyers

and a lot of cops. Are you saying the wife didn't kill her husband and his lover?"

"We're not saying anything. We have more questions than answers," Alicia said. "What can you tell us about the professor? Did you know him?"

"He liked his vodka neat," Jerry said with a wry smile. "I know more about my customer's drink preferences than their personal lives. I can tell you that he came in here with a hot blonde at least three times in the month before they were killed. She always ordered a cabernet and never more than one."

Alicia smiled. "You do remember drink orders. What about the professor's wife, Melissa Bryer?"

"I saw her once, a few days before the murder. She and the professor were having a loud argument. Kayla went over to talk to them, ask them to take it outside. That was the last I saw of them. I told the police all this and the lawyers, too. Kayla isn't in today, but if you need to talk to her she'll be working tomorrow night."

"That might be helpful," Alicia said.

"Did you work for MDT?" Michael asked. "Someone told us you give a discount to MDT employees because you used to work there."

"I did. I worked for them after I left the Navy. I was a test pilot for their aviation division. They are making some really cool weapons. They're first in technology as far as I'm concerned.

They have some of the best people in the world working for them. It was an honor to be part of the team."

"Why did you quit?" Alicia asked.

"That hard landing I mentioned was in one of their planes. It wasn't my fault. We had some mechanical problems, but I had a concussion and some vision problems afterwards. It was rough to give up my wings, but life goes on. You do what you have to do. You start over." He paused. "I tried to get your dad to work for MDT when I first started there."

"I didn't know that."

"At the time, the aviation division was working out of their offices in Arizona. Your father would have had to move there, and he didn't want to leave Texas. He told me his wife and his kids were happy here, so he turned me down. I always thought he was a better pilot than what he settled for, flying tourists around, but we all make our own choices."

"I didn't know that he'd made that choice for us," Alicia said, her gaze filled with admiration for her dad.

"Wyatt said his family had sacrificed enough while he was in the Navy. Luckily, I didn't have any family to consider."

"You never married?" Alicia asked.

"That institution is not for me. I'm a free spirit. I go where the wind blows."

Michael could see that Alicia was enjoying her conversation with her dad's friend, that it was probably making her feel close to her father again, and he didn't want to interrupt, but he was also afraid that the crowded restaurant would quickly draw Jerry back to the bar.

"Getting back to MDT," he said. "Did you happen to know Connie Randolph, the other murder victim or her coworker Paul Sandbury?"

"Names don't ring a bell. I might have met them. Half the people in here right now work at MDT. It's a huge company. I don't know all their names. Most people seem happy enough with their jobs, but I've served a few people drowning their sorrows after getting laid off. Every now and then, cuts come down from the Pentagon, funding gets decreased and people get fired. I've seen it happen a lot. I was in a specialized position when I worked for them, so I wasn't as vulnerable, but I'm happy now to be my own boss."

"Do you have any contacts at MDT who might be willing to speak with us?" Michael asked. "Maybe someone in the same department as Connie Randolph?"

Jerry thought for a moment. "I could ask around if you want. Why don't you give me your number, Alicia? I'll see what I can do."

"I'd really appreciate your help," Alicia told him as she gave him her number.

"Well, I hope I can come up with something that will help you find your friend. There's nothing worse than a missing person."

"That's for sure," she said with a heavy sigh. "Those first few months after Dad died were the worst. The uncertainty of not knowing made everything more difficult. It was hard not to keep hope alive."

Jerry nodded, a somber look in his eyes. "I remember. I took a plane up a couple of days to do my own search for Wyatt, just to be sure. I knew it's what Wyatt would have done for me. We always watched each other's backs." He paused. "Wyatt would probably want me to tell you to be careful, Alicia. I don't think he'd want his baby girl getting mixed up in a murder investigation."

"I'm not a baby girl anymore."

"Well, I know that, but I wouldn't want you to get hurt."

"I can take care of myself."

"Just as stubborn as your father." He pushed back his chair. "Sorry to cut this short, but I need to get back to work. Dinner is on the house. Make sure you order dessert and another round of drinks."

"Thanks, Jerry." She got up and gave him a hug. "It was really good to see you again."

"How long will you be in town?"

"A few more days. I'm not sure yet. It depends on what we find out."

"Well, don't be a stranger. Come back if you have more questions. In the meantime, I'll ask around and see if anyone at MDT would be willing to talk to you. I have to tell you I'm not that optimistic. MDT makes everyone sign a confidentiality agreement."

"We figured that," she said. "It's a long shot, but if you do run across anyone, please give me a call."

"I will. Nice to meet you, too," Jerry said to Michael, extending his hand. "You take care of this woman here, all right? She's a special girl. Her dad used to tell me that and from what I've seen, it's true."

Michael nodded. "I'm doing my best."

"Good. She deserves a man who's worthy of her."

"Jerry, it's not like that," Alicia protested. "We're friends."

Jerry just gave her a knowing smile. "Sure you are. But that was for your dad. I know he'd want me to say something to any man you brought around. That's the least I can do for him. Enjoy your meal."

"Sorry he put you on the spot, Michael. Everyone seems to get the wrong idea about us," Alicia said as Jerry returned to the bar.

"It's not the wrong idea, and you know it, Alicia."

"Okay, fine," she conceded. "So that wasn't totally helpful, was it?"

"Jerry might come through with more information. He seems willing to help you, and that's more than we're getting from other people. He also backed up what we read in the transcripts about the fight between the professor and his wife. I'm just not sure that fight was about Connie."

"You have another theory now?"

"Based on Sandbury's flight, I'm thinking that maybe Professor Bryer and Connie were working on something together that might have threatened someone or something at MDT. Maybe the wife thought there was an affair, but it was not that."

"But Thomas and Connie were found in bed together."

He tipped his head to her point. "Perhaps they were sleeping together and also working on something against the company."

"Are you suggesting that they might have been whistleblowers?"

"It's a possibility. Sandbury seemed to hint at the fact that there was something besides sex in the mix."

"That would mean someone at MDT killed them to protect a secret."

She was right. If someone at MDT had killed two people to keep a secret, they'd have no hesitation to stop at a third. His stomach clenched at the thought.

Alicia must have read something on his face. Her gaze narrowed. "Don't go there."

"Too late. We both know that the outcome after so long will probably not be good."

"We don't know that," she argued. "Sandbury disappeared really fast. Maybe Liliana did the same."

As much as he wanted to believe that, it just didn't ring true in his head.

He sat back in his chair as the waitress came by to deliver their pizza, along with plates, napkins and peppers.

"This looks good," Alicia said.

It did look good; he just wasn't that hungry anymore.

"You have to eat," Alicia told him, grabbing the first slice of pizza. "You need to keep your strength up."

"I will," he said, taking a sip of his beer.

"I know it's harder for you, Michael. I can focus on the mystery, but you have a lot more emotions involved," she said, compassion in her eyes. "Is there anything I can do to make it better?"

"You're already doing it," he said, thinking that Alicia had a way of both firing him up and calming him down. She always seemed to be able to read his mood, to know the right thing to say. "Thanks."

"You're welcome. And take your time, but just know that I'm really hungry, so if you want any of this, I wouldn't wait too long to dive in."

He smiled as she took a large bite of pizza. Then he grabbed his own slice and found his appetite again.

An hour later, they left the Flight Deck. They'd talked to the waitress and one of the bartenders before leaving but hadn't gotten any more information than they'd received from Jerry. The bartender remembered the murdered couple but didn't witness the fight with the wife, and the waitress said she had trouble remembering anyone, as there was always a full crowd every night.

"Well, that wasn't a total waste," Alicia said, hooking her arm through his as they walked into the parking lot. "The food was good, and it was nice for me to see Jerry again. There are so few people I can talk to who knew my father; it feels good to hear someone say his name."

"It sounded like they were good friends."

"Like brothers, Dad used to say. I think that's the way the military is. When I asked my father what the military was fighting for, because I didn't understand why he left for weeks at a time, he told me that he was fighting for the men who were next to him, his radar instrument officer, his mechanic, the pilot flying at his wing and the people back home who were depending on him to keep them safe. I guess there's a unique bond for people in service to their country. They're making a sacrifice that most people wouldn't make. It certainly wasn't anything I ever wanted to do. I feel a little guilty saying that out loud."

"Don't. We all have our calling. And yours is lightning."

She grinned. "Yeah, like that's going to do much good for the world."

"You never know. Your pictures are good. You capture moments in life, on this earth, in the sky that are incredible. You're leaving a legacy behind."

Pride entered her eyes as she gazed back at him. "You're going to leave me speechless again."

He laughed. "And yet you still managed to find words." He unlocked the car, and they got inside.

"You're leaving a legacy, too, Michael. Your buildings will be around for a long time."

"True, but they don't always feel like *my* buildings. They're more of a collaboration."

"You still put your mark on them. So where are we going now? It's almost eight. I know we still have some people on our list to contact, but it's getting late. We haven't tracked down Connie's ex-husband yet."

"We'll leave that for tomorrow. Let's find a hotel and then we'll figure out a plan."

As he pulled out of the parking space, he saw a man sitting in a vehicle a few spots over. It looked like the same man and the same car Alicia

342

had seen earlier in the day. He'd no sooner passed the vehicle when it roared to life, backed out and went in the opposite direction. It sped away so fast he didn't have a chance to get a license plate number.

"Damn," he muttered, his gaze on the rearview mirror.

"Problem?" Alicia asked curiously. She turned to look over her shoulder.

He debated whether or not he should tell her. He didn't want to worry her unnecessarily. "No problem."

"Michael. No secrets between us, remember?"

"All right. I thought I saw that guy you noticed earlier outside the breakfast café. But he went in the other direction."

"Really?" She turned her head again, but the car was gone. "I don't see anyone."

"I'm not sure it was the same person, but I am going to make certain that no one is following us to our new hotel."

"I'll help. I'll keep an eye on the side-view mirror."

After they exited the parking lot, he made several quick turns, keeping an eye out for the car he'd seen earlier. After twenty minutes, he felt comfortable that they were not being followed. When he saw a hotel with an underground parking garage, he decided to turn in. It might be good to get their car out of sight.

They gathered their bags and walked into the elevator and up to the lobby.

A few minutes later, they entered their hotel room on the fourth floor. Michael immediately turned the deadbolt and put on the safety chain while Alicia moved toward the window.

"It doesn't open," she said, relief in her voice. "And there's no balcony."

"Then we're good."

"Yeah." She blew out a breath and sat down at the small table by the window.

He tossed his keys onto the dresser and took a seat on the edge of the bed facing her. "Are you all right?"

"I have to admit my heart started racing a little after you saw that man again."

"Like I said, I don't know for sure—"

"Yes, you do," she said, cutting him off. "You don't make mistakes, Michael. And you notice details. I've spent enough time with you to know that. You don't have to pretend for my sake. Obviously, someone has been watching us. I just wish I knew who it was and why. I also wonder how they found us again at the Flight Deck. If it was the same man we saw after breakfast, how did he catch back up to us?"

"I should have been paying more attention." He paused for a moment. "I wonder if Liliana was being followed during her investigation, if she had any idea she was in danger."

"She didn't act like she was in danger when she got to Miami. And I don't think she would have brought danger to her family. She stayed at her parents' house. She spent time with her sister and her brothers, her friends, even her old friend Brad. I don't believe she had any idea that she was in trouble."

Alicia's words made a lot of sense. "I agree. And whatever her feelings were about David, she didn't go to Miami to break up the wedding."

"And David didn't have anything to do with her disappearance. I believe she asked you to meet that night, because she wanted to get in touch with your grandfather. And she probably just really wanted to see you again. She was only there for a short time and didn't know when she'd be back or when you'd ever have the chance to reconnect."

"I believe that, too."

"It's good that she reached out to you, Michael, because if she hadn't tried to meet you, you wouldn't have been a suspect, and you might not have gotten as involved as you have. Not that you wouldn't have searched for her, but she put you in the middle of her problems, and having seen how good you are at problem solving, I think things worked out as best as they could. Not that I don't wish she'd never disappeared, but—I don't know, I'm making a mess of this."

"No, you're not," he said, shaking his head.

"You're right—about everything, except one thing."

"What's that?"

"I didn't come to Texas because I was a person of interest, I came because of you. You're the one who sent the dominoes flying. You're the one who got me to start looking in a new direction." He paused. "I just don't think we can save her, Alicia. I haven't wanted to say that out loud, but it's been going around in my head for a long time. I think it's too late."

Alicia got up from her chair and sat down next to him, putting her hand on his arm. "If we can't save her, we'll get her justice. We'll make sure the truth comes out."

He saw the fight in her eyes and it lifted him up. "You never quit."

"Not when something is important. Liliana matters. And you matter. You matter a lot to me, Michael. I think you know that I'm not just here because of Liliana, but also because of you."

"I wish . . ." he began.

"What?"

"That we'd met under other circumstances. I wish we weren't spending every second of every day worrying about Liliana or investigating a double murder of two people we never met before. I want to have a normal day with you. I want to make you happy, see you smile, hear you laugh."

His words brought a smile to her lips. "We'll get there, Michael, if you want to get there."

"I do. Jerry said you were something special, and he was right."

"You're something special, too. I've never felt so connected to anyone like I do with you. And it's scary. I'm brave when it comes to nature, not so much when it comes to people who touch my heart. After my dad died, I didn't want to ever feel that kind of pain again. Loving someone—losing them—it's just so awful. And I know you know that, because you've been through what I've been through."

"Maybe that's why we're so connected," he said, feeling a little of the same fear she'd just expressed. Alicia might be worried that he could hurt her, but he knew for sure that she could hurt him. He'd known her for less than a week, and yet he couldn't imagine a day without her in it. How the hell had that happened? How had they gotten so close so fast, and yet it wasn't even close enough?

"Alicia?"

"Yes?"

"I want to make tonight about you."

Gold flecks of desire filled her brown eyes. "I was thinking we make it about us." She kicked off her shoes and scooted back against the pillows. "Show me what you've got."

"I intend to do just that."

TWENTY-ONE

Alicia woke up to sun streaming through the windows. One of these nights, she was going to have to remember to pull the curtains before she lost her mind in Michael's arms.

She glanced over at the man sleeping next to her, her heart filling with love and tenderness as she looked at his face. He had such strong features even in sleep, as if he instinctively tried to keep up his guard when he knew he would be vulnerable. But he'd let down his guard with her.

Making love with him had been a soul-shattering experience. They'd come together three times, each one better than the last, each one showing her a different side of the man she was falling in love with. He was a man who could be intense and driven, but also lighthearted and playful, a man who could make her toes curl with every touch of his hands and taste of his mouth.

She'd fallen hard. There was no point in pretending otherwise.

She didn't know what came next, but she knew that she couldn't turn back the clock, couldn't pretend that she didn't love him.

Love. Such a scary word, and she was definitely scared now, because the future was so uncertain.

Michael's real life wasn't in Miami; it was in New York.

And her life was in Miami—wasn't it?

Although, she could live anywhere. She could do anything. As long as there was lightning, or maybe not. She smiled to herself, thinking that the electricity between her and Michael was as powerful as any lightning bolt she'd ever seen.

"I can hear you thinking," Michael said, interrupting her thoughts.

She rolled onto her side to face him, happy to see his light blue eyes filled with the same happiness she felt. "That's my stomach."

He grinned and brushed her hair off her face. "I heard that, too. I need to feed you."

"You do. We worked up quite an appetite last night."

"Why don't you order room service, and I'll grab a shower?"

She wasn't sure she wanted him to leave the bed, but when her stomach growled again, she decided it was a good idea. "Okay."

He sat up in bed. "Unless you want to join me in the shower."

"Then we won't eat until lunch time."

"Good point." He leaned over and kissed her. "There's always after breakfast."

"And after lunch and after dinner," she said, as he took his beautiful naked body out of bed.

He laughed. "I'm going to remind you that you said that."

"Don't worry, I won't forget."

After Michael went into the bathroom, she wrapped the sheet around her body and padded over to the table to grab the room service menu. She ordered eggs, hash browns, pancakes and threw in some bacon, because she was starving. She also ordered two glasses of orange juice and a pot of coffee.

Then she walked over to the window and stared out at the street. Everything looked normal, but she couldn't help wondering if whoever had been following them was out there somewhere. And if he was, why was he just following them? Why not confront them or threaten them or something . . .

Maybe it *was* the cops watching them, one of Detective Kellerman's contacts in the Corpus Christi Police Department, although that seemed ridiculous. If Kellerman had done his job right in the first place, he would have spent more time in Texas following Liliana's steps in the days before she went to Miami, instead of dismissing her life here with less than a cursory glance. But he'd been so fixated on Michael that he hadn't been able to see anyone else.

She couldn't wait for the day when Michael's name would be completely cleared. She would do everything she could to make that happen.

Michael came out of the bathroom, a towel hung low on his hips, his broad chest still glistening with water, his dark hair damp, his cheeks freshly shaved.

He put his arms around her and nuzzled her neck. "Your turn, babe."

"You smell good," she said, taking a deep breath of his musky scent.

"So do you."

"That's not possible," she said with a laugh. "I like you like this."

"Wet? Half-naked?"

"That, too. But I was talking more about your mood. You seem happy."

"It's hard not to be happy when I'm with you."

She probably took his light words more seriously than he'd intended, because they warmed her all the way down to her heart and her soul. She should come up with some equally good words, but she couldn't seem to find any. Like before, his compliment had stolen her words. Finally, she said, "I should take a shower. I ordered breakfast, and I have to warn you, I might have gotten a little carried away."

"I think we can handle it. Hurry back."

"I will." She paused, needing to lighten the tension swirling inside of her. "I almost forgot. I won't need this in the bathroom." She tossed the sheet she had around her naked body on the bed and gave Michael a good view of her bare ass as she walked toward the bathroom.

"You're killing me, Alicia."

She flashed him a smile and then slipped into the bathroom.

As she took her shower, she couldn't help thinking how much more fun it would be to have Michael under the hot spray with her. *Next time,* she told herself.

But even as the thought crossed her mind, she wondered when next time would be. They stil had a few people to talk to in Texas, and she had to get back to her job by tomorrow, which meant she really needed to get on a flight tonight. She could probably push her job to Friday, but even if she did that, they'd have to leave by tomorrow. There was a lot to do, and she didn't want to go back to Miami without a few more answers.

Rinsing the shampoo from her hair, she got out of the shower and dried off. She ran a comb through her wet hair and wrapped herself in a towel. If breakfast hadn't arrived yet, maybe they could find some way to pass the time.

With a smile, she opened the door and walked into the bedroom.

Michael had put on clothes and was on the phone.

He lifted his gaze to hers, and there was so much pain in his eyes, it rocked her back on her heels.

He said, "Thanks" and ended his call.

"What happened?" Judging by the look on his face, she thought she knew, but she had to hear him say the words. "Michael?"

He drew in a shaky breath as he put his phone down on the table. "They found Liliana's body in the park."

Her heart stopped. "But they looked there before."

"Not in the right place." His chest heaved again as if it were difficult for him to get in air. "She's dead, Alicia."

She ran to him, hearing the raw agony in his choked voice. She put her arms around him, holding him as tightly as she could. "I'm so sorry, Michael."

"I knew it," he said in a dull tone. "I've known it for weeks." He pulled away from her. "I need to go back to Miami."

"Of course. We'll go now, as soon as we can get on a plane. I'll make reservations."

"That would be good. I—I need to take a walk."

"Do you want me to come with you?"

"No, I need to be alone." He grabbed a hotel key and left.

She stared at the door for a long moment, wishing she could have gone with him, but she understood that he needed a moment for the news to sink in.

She needed a moment, too. Even though she'd

thought as Michael did that Liliana was probably dead, hearing it confirmed was still shocking.

She slowly got dressed, then packed up the few things she'd taken out of her bag. Breakfast arrived, and she picked at the food, just because she knew she needed some energy to get through the day.

While she was eating, she got on the phone to look for flights. She found one leaving around eleven. It was eight now. If Michael came back in the next hour, they could make it.

Thirty minutes later, the door opened and Michael walked back in. His hair was tousled as if he'd run his fingers through it a dozen times and there were tense lines in his face, dark shadows around his eyes.

"Hey," she said softly. "There is a flight to Miami leaving in about two and a half hours. You have time to eat and then we should go."

"I'm not hungry. I'll get my stuff." He went into the bathroom to retrieve his shaving kit, then tossed it into his bag and said, "I'm ready."

"Okay." She wanted to say more, but he was so closed off, she thought anything she tried to say would just annoy him, so she kept quiet.

The ride to the airport was also silent. They returned the rental car and made it to the plane about twenty minutes before the flight was due to take off.

Michael grabbed the window seat while she

sat in the middle, an elderly woman on her right.

As the plane took off, she put her hand on Michael's leg. He tensed, and for a moment, she thought he might shake her off, which surprised her. They'd gotten so close over the last few days and even closer the night before. But now he seemed very much like a stranger, which was an unsettling thought.

She removed her hand from his thigh and clasped her hands together in her lap.

Michael turned his head to look out the window.

With someone else in their row it wasn't possible to have a private conversation, not that Michael seemed interested in having any conversation. He was completely locked up in his head.

Hopefully, when they got back to Miami that would change.

Images of Liliana floated through Michael's mind on the three-hour flight from Texas to Miami. He replayed moments from their childhood that he'd thought he'd long forgotten: Liliana as a little girl sitting on the steps of her house with a book in her hands while the rest of them played baseball in the street and Liliana as a thirteen-year-old saying goodbye to him when he left Miami for prep school. She'd told him he was going to do amazing things. She couldn't wait to see what he turned out to be.

There were no recent images of Liliana in his

head. He wished he'd made time to see her in the last eight years, but he'd never imagined that time would run out so fast. He'd always figured they'd run into each other again one day.

Well, he was going to find her killer, no matter how long it took. He would get her justice if it was the last thing he did. He had no idea how he could make that happen, but somehow he'd find a way.

He didn't realize the plane had landed until Alicia called his name.

He looked up, seeing everyone on their feet, pulling their luggage out of the overhead bins. Unbuckling his seat belt, he stood up and followed Alicia out of the plane.

They'd carried on their bags, so they headed straight to the exit and hailed a cab. It was three o'clock in the afternoon, but there was very little sun today. Another storm was blowing in off the coast, and the gloomy skyline seemed a perfect backdrop for the terrible news they'd recently received.

"I need to talk to Diego and see the Valdez family," he said, as the cab pulled away from the curb. "I'll drop you at home first, then go to my place and get my car."

"All right," she said slowly, giving him a thoughtful, measuring look. "Do you want me to come with you?"

"No, I think I should talk to Liliana's family

on my own. They're going to be devastated."

"I understand. Michael, I haven't wanted to press, but can you tell me who called you to tell you about Liliana and what exactly did they say?"

"It was Diego. He said someone called in an anonymous tip last night saying that Liliana's body was in the park. They gave specific directions on how to find her."

"An anonymous tip after all this time?" she asked doubtfully. "I thought they had just done another search of the park and stumbled upon a grave or something."

"No, it was a phone call. Diego said they have not been able to trace the call. I'll know more after I touch base with him."

"Who would call in a tip? The person who kidnapped her—killed her?"

He stiffened at the reminder that Liliana had died a violent death. He almost couldn't bear to think of how that had happened. "It's possible it was an accomplice or someone the kidnapper spoke to."

"I wonder why that person called the tip in now."

"Maybe with the constant press, the candlelight vigils, the person developed a conscience."

"You don't really believe that, do you?"

"No, but I have no other answers, Alicia." He drew in a breath. "Sorry. This is why I need to be alone."

"I'm just trying to help."

"I know you are." He put his hand on her leg. "Just give me a little time."

"Of course," she said, as the cab pulled up in front of her building. She gave him a compassionate smile as she opened the door. "I'm really sorry that it ended like this. Call me later, okay?"

"I will."

She hesitated, and it looked like she wanted to say something more, but in the end she just got out of the cab and said, "Goodbye, Michael."

There was a finality to her words that he didn't like. He wanted to call her back or get out of the car and follow her inside. There were things he needed to say to her, things that had nothing to do with Liliana, but that conversation would have to wait. He had no ability to think beyond what he needed to do next, and that was to find out what had happened to Liliana.

Diego met Michael in the parking lot outside the medical examiner's office an hour later.

"You can't go inside," Diego said, his gaze grim. "You can't see her body. I'm sorry, Michael. It's family only. And even if it weren't family only, Kellerman wouldn't allow you to see her body."

"I need to see her, Diego."

"No, you don't," his friend said forcefully. "You

don't need to see her the way she is now. Remember her as she was. Trust me, it's better that way."

He wanted to argue, but judging by the steel in Diego's eyes, any further fight would be pointless. "What can you tell me about the tip or what evidence you've collected so far?"

"I'm not supposed to tell you anything."

"I'm still a suspect? How is that possible?" he asked in frustration.

"We have her body; we don't have her killer. And you've been out of town for three days."

He shook his head in amazed anger. "You think I called in the tip?"

"I don't, but there are others who consider it a possibility."

"Kellerman is crazy." He blew out a breath. "When was she killed? Can you tell me that at least?"

"We don't have a specific timeframe yet."

"But you have something. Come on."

"Judging by the condition of the body, it's been a couple of months," Diego admitted. "It's my belief she was killed shortly after she disappeared."

He stared back at Diego for a long moment. "All this time she's been dead?"

"It looks that way."

"Have you spoken to her family?"

"I talked to Isabel earlier; she couldn't stop

crying. She'd been so hopeful for a different outcome. Kellerman spoke to her parents. Their house is now filled with relatives and friends. They're in shock."

He couldn't even imagine the pain they were going through.

"What about you, Michael? What did you find out in Texas?"

"That the case Liliana was working on is tied to her death. Kellerman did a piss-poor job following up on that end."

"What do you mean?"

"Liliana was investigating a double homicide, and it looks like the woman convicted of those murders is innocent. I think Liliana got too close to the real killer. They followed her back to Miami and killed her here. That put the police investigation into her disappearance miles away from her life in Texas. It was a good idea, too. Because no one has been looking in Texas for her killer."

"We did look in Texas."

"Not very well."

"You have every right to be angry, Michael, but we only have so many resources. We had to look in Miami first. As for what was going on in Texas, do you have any proof to back up your theory?"

The blunt question made him realize he had nothing concrete to turn over. "I have some notes Liliana made and some information I've gathered from people who had more to say than they were asked."

"What are you talking about?"

"I spoke to a coworker of the woman who was killed. He told me that he spoke to Liliana, that he gave her important information and then she disappeared. He was scared out of his mind when I showed up to ask more questions. When I went to follow up with him, he'd grabbed his wife and kids and left his house in a big hurry. So tell me I'm not on to something."

Diego stared back at him with concern. "You should have gone to the police in Texas."

"I was considering it. Then you called. Maybe I shouldn't have left Corpus Christi, but all I could think about was coming home, seeing Liliana." As he finished his explanation, it occurred to him that maybe that's why someone had called in the tip. They'd wanted to get him and Alicia out of Texas. Had that person been Sandbury? Had he wanted to get rid of them so he and his family could go home? "Damn," he muttered.

"What?" Diego asked.

"I just realized that there's a good chance someone called in the tip about the body to get me and Alicia out of Texas. Think about the timing—we're down there asking questions, stirring up an old crime and suddenly someone steps forward with critical information."

"We need to sit down and go over everything you learned down there," Diego said. "I'm on duty until seven. Why don't we meet later tonight? I'll come by your place."

"I thought Kellerman told you to stay out of this."

"He did, but I'm no longer listening. I'll see you around eight."

"All right. I'm going to see Liliana's parents now. I need to say something to them."

"Good luck. It's rough over there."

TWENTY-TWO

A licia tried to take a nap when she got home. She hadn't gotten a lot of sleep the night before, but her mind wouldn't let her rest. She kept thinking about Michael, about how he was feeling, what he was going through.

It bothered her that he'd shut her out. He'd barely spoken three words to her after he got the news. She'd told herself it was just the shock, the grief, that had made him withdraw from her, but there was a little nagging worry deep inside that she couldn't seem to shake. She didn't know what she was so concerned about. They hadn't made any promises to each other. It was just a strange and abrupt ending to an intense relationship.

They'd been living in each other's pockets for almost a week and now she was alone in her house. It felt weird. She needed to go back to work tomorrow. She needed to get back to her life, but how could she do that? She needed something from Michael—at the very least a *goodbye, see you later*.

Not that goodbye would make her feel a lot better, but it would be better than this feeling of uncertainty. She'd had a place by Michael's side in the investigation. She'd been a trusted partner. They'd bounced ideas around and supported and taken care of each other. They'd laughed and they'd loved, but now what?

With a frustrated groan, she gave up on a nap and got to her feet. She went into the kitchen to make tea. She needed a wake-me-up.

While the water was heating, she sat down at her kitchen table and opened her computer. Pulling up a blank page, she started to make her own notes. Michael still had Liliana's notes in a pocket somewhere, but she remembered a lot of what was on there. Plus, she had some ideas of her own to add.

She typed in suspects, then put in Paul Sandbury. Was he really a suspect? Or was he more of a witness to something? Deleting the word *suspects,* she changed it to *people to follow up with*. After Paul, she added Lieutenant Hodges to the list. They needed to fill her in regarding Sandbury's quick exit from town.

Next came Jerry, who still owed her a call back, and Cheryl, who might have more information or at the very least a way to contact the Bryers' former housekeeper. She'd liked to talk to that woman and possibly her son, too.

Who else? She tapped her keys lightly as she thought about everything she'd learned.

Brian Randolph, Connie's ex-husband came to mind. He might have an alibi, but he was still worth some follow-up questions, especially in regards to his blow-up with Connie at the MDT offices. Which brought her back to the company where both Connie and the professor had worked. Michael's grandfather had said he might be able to get Reid to speak to them.

But as she finished typing in Will Jansen, she wondered if she was just spinning her wheels for no reason. Maybe the police already had clues to Liliana's killer. Maybe Michael would prefer to be done investigating since there was no hope of bringing Liliana back alive.

Alicia still wanted to keep going, but would Michael feel the same after going through what would probably be a very sad funeral?

She also had to consider why she wanted to continue. She'd neglected her life the past week. She hadn't even framed her most recent batch of lightning shots to hang in the gallery. Wasn't it time to get back to reality?

But they didn't have an answer, a killer. They didn't have the justice she had promised Michael she would help him get. If he wanted to continue, there was no way she would say no.

Her phone rang, and she jumped for it, hoping it was Michael. It was crazy how much she missed him, considering they'd only been apart for a few hours, but it wasn't Michael. It was a Texas area code.

"Hello?"

"Alicia? It's Jerry."

"Hi, how are you?" she said, relieved to have

someone else to talk to so she could get out of her own head.

"Not bad. I have some news for you."

"Really? That's great. What is it?"

"I spoke to one of my bartenders, and she told me that the woman from MDT who was killed had told her that a coworker was following her, taking pictures of her and it creeped her out."

"Did she know who that coworker was?"

"It was the same name you asked me about— Paul Sandbury."

Her stomach twisted into a knot. "Why would he take pictures of Connie?"

"Beats me, but I thought you might want to know."

"Why didn't the bartender testify about Paul at the trial?"

"Kayla was the one who testified. This was another woman. She said no one asked her, and she didn't want to get involved. But, of course, she was willing to talk to me, since I'm the boss."

"Of course."

"Do you want to come by the bar and talk to her?" Jerry asked. "She's working tonight."

"No, actually, I'm back in Miami."

"Oh, I didn't realize you were leaving so soon."

"They found the lieutenant's body last night, so Michael and I came back."

"Well, I guess it's over then."

"Not entirely. We still don't know who killed

her. I may be back to Texas soon. But in the mean-time, could I speak to your bartender over the phone?"

"I'll give her your number and have her call you. Her name is Monica."

"Great. Thanks, Jerry."

"I don't know that you should be thanking me. It sounds like you need to get out of this situation, Alicia. It's dangerous. Three people are dead already. I think your father would tell you to leave it alone."

"But he wouldn't have left it alone. He was all about justice, standing up for what is right."

"Well, that's true," Jerry said, a heavy note in his voice. "But that got him into trouble, and I'd hate to see the same thing happen to you."

"I'll be careful."

"Sometimes that's not enough."

"Thanks for calling, Jerry."

"I'm almost sorry I did. I'm worried about you."

"You don't have to worry. I'll be fine."

"Well, take care."

"I will." After hanging up with Jerry, she called Michael. She'd intended to give him space, but she really needed to talk to him about Sandbury. She could take the information she'd gotten from Jerry to the police, but she'd prefer to consult with Michael before doing that.

His phone went to voicemail. She decided to leave a message. "Hi, it's me. I hope you're doing okay. I just talked to Jerry. One of his bartenders, not the one who testified, told him that Paul Sandbury was following Connie and taking pictures of her. I know you're in the thick of things, but we really should think about talking to the police in Corpus Christi. They might be more receptive than Detective Kellerman. Anyway, call me back."

She'd barely set down the phone when it rang. Again, her heart jumped in anticipation, and again it was let down. It was her friend from Channel 2 News. "Hi, Jeff. What's up?"

"A new storm. Looks like we're going to get a show tonight."

His words drew her gaze to the window. The clouds had grown thicker and darker since she'd gotten home. "I haven't been paying attention to the weather report. What's the forecast?"

"Heavy electrical storm activity headed our way in the next hour. I'm shocked you don't know that," he said. "Are you sick?"

She was a little shocked, too. "I've been distracted."

"You must have been."

"Thanks for letting me know."

"No problem. Talk to you soon."

She got up and turned off the tea kettle, realizing it had been singing for several minutes. She poured the hot water into a mug, dipped the tea bag up and down a few times, and then walked over to the window. The approaching storm clouds reminded her that less than a week ago a similar storm had turned her life upside down.

What would this one bring?

As she thought about the last storm, her mind drifted back to the illuminating flash of lightning that had highlighted a struggle in the park and then the tag by the carousel. Had Liliana's body been found near there?

She wished she could see where her body had been found. Maybe it would give her some closure, because right now she felt restless and charged up and it wasn't just the possibility of more lightning jangling her nerves, it was the feeling that she was so close to solving the mystery, but she didn't know how to put all the pieces together.

Liliana had obviously found one more clue than she and Michael had, something that made everything make sense. And it was more than likely that that clue was going to die with her.

Alicia stood at the window for another ten minutes. Then on impulse, she grabbed her rain gear and her cameras and headed out the door. She needed a distraction and there was one coming just over the horizon . . .

After twenty minutes with the Valdez family, Michael felt overwhelmed with sadness and anger, and he was not alone. Liliana's parents were devastated. Her mother Theresa couldn't stop crying. Her father Dominic looked like he'd aged twenty years since he'd gotten the news about his daughter. Rico was getting drunk. Juan had gone silent, barely able to speak to anyone as he cooked in the family kitchen, doing the only thing he could do that would help anyone.

Michael's father was also at the house along with his stepmother Veronica and two of his sisters. Like Juan, his dad had gone straight to the kitchen, bringing more food from the restaurant to the already overflowing kitchen counters.

The neighbors had come in a steady stream, some of whom Michael remembered from the old days, others who were new. An entire community was suffering a huge loss, and it made him realize how many lives besides his own that Liliana had touched.

The living room in the Valdez house had become ground zero for planning funeral arrangements, the women in the neighborhood already getting down to practical matters. They couldn't change what had happened, but they could send Liliana off with all of their love.

The younger kids were in the yard or in the dining room, snacking off the platters on the dining room table.

The men seemed to move restlessly in all directions. It was a feeling he understood quite well, because now that he was here, he was torn between wanting to stay and wanting to go.

He didn't want to plan Liliana's funeral. He wanted to find her killer. He just didn't know how to do that.

Alicia would probably have an idea. He needed to call her back, which he would do as soon as he left here. He just didn't know how soon he could leave. He felt like he needed to pay his respects with time. It was the least he could do.

"Michael," his father said, drawing him into the hallway. "I'm glad you're here."

"I came as soon as I heard the news."

"Where have you been the last few days?"

"Trying to find Liliana. Obviously, I wasn't successful."

His father nodded, a weary, sad recognition in his gaze. "It is a tragic outcome, however, I am grateful that Dominic and Theresa can now bury their daughter. I hope that will bring them some peace," Ernesto said.

He didn't know how a headstone would bring peace, but maybe it would. "We still need to find out who did this."

"I hope that will happen," Ernesto said. "Sometimes life doesn't give you all the answers you want."

"That's not acceptable to me."

His father smiled. "No, it wouldn't be. You've always needed to know everything. You were so angry when your mother died. You asked me a million questions about how and why it happened, and none of my answers satisfied you. They didn't satisfy me, either." He paused. "I don't want Liliana's death to follow you the way your mother's did. I don't want you to waste years looking for the truth and not live your own life. Your mother wouldn't have wanted you to grieve as long as you did for her, and Liliana wouldn't want that, either."

"I don't know how to stop looking for answers. To forget what happened."

"You'll never forget, but you'll go on. You have to forgive yourself, Michael. What happened to Liliana is not your fault. If you can learn anything from this terrible tragedy, learn that life is precious, that each day means something. You don't want to waste a minute. You don't want to put off relationships for another day. You don't want to let anger keep you away from people who love you."

He knew his father was talking about their relationship, and for the first time in forever he actually agreed with him. "I have let anger and resentment keep me away from the family," he said.

His words brought surprise to his father's face. "I'm a little shocked you'd admit that, but then it's been a long time since you shared your thoughts with me. You've been closed off for so many years."

His father was right about that, too. "I had to close off. It was the only way I could survive. When you sent me away to school, it felt like you were throwing me away," he said harshly. The words he'd been holding back for fifteen years suddenly came flooding out. "You were so disappointed in me. I didn't think you cared if I came back or not. If you didn't care, why should I?"

Pain filled his father's eyes. "I was disappointed in myself, Michael. I had let you down. You'd gotten into trouble, because I wasn't paying enough attention to you, because I couldn't figure out how to reach you after your mom died. I felt guilty for marrying Veronica, for having more children, for not being able to make you see that I loved you, because I always loved you, Michael, and I loved your mother. You're my firstborn, my son."

Emotion put a knot in his throat and a tightness in his chest. He'd been holding on to the negative feelings for so long, it seemed impossible to let them go.

His gaze drifted past his father's face to the portrait on the wall. Liliana's thirteen-year-old face stared back at him. Her eyes pierced his soul. The day he'd left for prep school, she'd told him that one day he'd forgive his dad and say he was sorry so that they could be a family again. He'd told her that day would never come.

But maybe it had come. Maybe Liliana had brought them back together again.

"Michael?" his dad asked, a question in his eyes.

He turned his gaze to his father. "I'm sorry."

His father's eyes widened. "I'm sorry, too."

"Then why don't we call it even?"

"Yes, yes," Ernesto said, nodding excitedly. "You'll come to the house and see your sisters?"

"As soon as I get a chance." He let out a breath. "Right now, I need to find Isabel. She's the only one I haven't spoken to yet."

"She's upstairs."

"Thanks." He put his hand on his dad's shoulder and they looked at each other eye-to-eye, man-to-man. "I'll talk to you soon."

"I look forward to it."

After leaving his dad, he went up the stairs to the room Isabel had once shared with Liliana. The room no longer had the twin beds that he remembered, but rather a queen. In the middle of that mattress surrounded by loose photographs was Liliana's sister, Isabel, her cheeks streaked with tears.

"It's too hard," she said, her voice breaking.

He moved quickly across the room and put his arms around her. "You shouldn't be doing this alone."

She sniffed and pushed him away. "I'm okay. I sent everyone away. I wanted to be alone with her one last time."

He sat down on the bed across from her. "These are from a lifetime ago." He picked up a childhood picture of Liliana. She was sitting on the top of a picnic table at some camping spot with her brothers and sister. Liliana couldn't have been more than eight.

"I'm putting together a poster and a slide show for the service."

"I'm sorry, Isabel."

She nodded. "Me, too. I kept hoping she'd just come back and everything would be all right. I knew I was lying to myself, but I had to keep hoping. I just wish I hadn't asked her to come back for my wedding. Then she'd still be alive."

"We all wish we'd done something differently, but the only one responsible for what happened to Liliana is the person who killed her. And to be honest, Isabel, I've learned some things in the past few days that lead me to believe Liliana's trouble followed her from Texas. You're not responsible for her death. If she hadn't come here, she would have still been in danger."

Isabel looked like she wanted to believe him. "Is that really true?"

"It is. I can't prove it yet, but I will. I will find the person who took her away from us."

There was doubt in her eyes. "It's been so long." She shivered and wrapped her bare arms around her waist.

"Are you cold? Can I get you a blanket?"

Her eyes watered as she pointed to the light-weight white coat hanging over the desk chair. "I'll take that."

He grabbed the coat and handed it to her.

"This was Liliana's," she said as she slid her arms into the coat. "I got cold when we were waiting for the valet after the rehearsal dinner, and she took this off and gave it to me. That's the kind of sister she was; she'd give me the coat off her back."

He could feel her pain as keenly as his own. "She was great."

"So smart, too. I was really proud of her. She made so much of herself. Look at me—I cut hair for a living. I never had the kind of ambition she had. I need a tissue," Isabel said, sniffing again. She reached into the pocket, her expression changing as she pulled out a small white envelope. "What's this?"

His pulse quickened. "Did that belong to Liliana?"

"I think so. I didn't notice it before. I guess I never put my hand in the pocket." She stared at the envelope as if it might bite her.

"May I see it?"

She handed it to him. "There's nothing on the front."

He could see that. He opened the envelope and pulled out three photographs. It took a minute for him to realize what he was looking at—the bar at the Flight Deck. A blonde woman he recognized as Connie Randolph was handing an envelope to Jerry Caldwell.

His brows knit together as he moved to the next photo. It was another shot of Connie and Jerry. This time they were in the parking lot behind the bar. Judging by the change in clothes, it had been taken a different day. Connie was reaching into her bag, another envelope visible inside her purse.

The third photograph showed Connie and Jerry back in the bar again. As Michael peered at the picture, he realized that the mirror behind the bar had captured the person shooting the photo. It was Paul Sandbury.

His heart started beating incredibly fast.

Sandbury had shot these photos of Connie and Jerry, which meant that whatever was going on was happening between Jerry and Connie, not between Connie and the professor, or at the very least, in addition to that relationship. This was the information Sandbury had given to Liliana. It probably explained why he was suddenly so scared and quite possibly why he'd quit his job after speaking to Liliana. Had someone at MDT known he was spying on Connie? And why had he been spying on her? What was in the envelopes she and Jerry were exchanging?

"Who are those people?" Isabel asked in confusion. "I don't recognize them."

"They're involved in the case Liliana was working on. I'm going to take these, all right?"

"Okay," she said in confusion. "Are they important?"

"They might be."

"I feel so stupid. I never thought to check her coat. When the police asked to go through her personal belongings, we showed them her suitcase and her clothes hanging in the closet in Juan's old room. She was sleeping in there while she was here. I never gave them her coat. I never thought about it."

He could see how easily it had slipped her mind. She probably hadn't worn the coat since that night. "It's okay," he assured her. "Showing these photos to the police wouldn't have helped save Liliana. You know that she was killed almost immediately after she disappeared."

"I know, but—"

"No buts. You couldn't have stopped what happened, but maybe now we'll be able to find who killed her." He jumped to his feet and strode quickly out of the room, jogging down the stairs. He didn't bother to say goodbye to the family. He needed to take the photos to Alicia and get her take on them. She was not going to be happy to hear that Jerry might be involved.

It seemed difficult to believe. The man had been so cheerful and friendly. But he'd lied when he'd told them he didn't know who Connie was and had no idea if he'd ever met her. So what else was he lying about?

And Sandbury? He was another big question mark. He must have told Liliana something about the photos, so why hadn't he been willing to tell him? Was it fear that had now kept him silent?

But there was something else Michael didn't understand. Why get rid of Liliana and leave Sandbury walking around to tell his story? There had to be a piece of the puzzle that he was missing. Sandbury knew something but not enough to make him that dangerous. Liliana must have known more than Sandbury.

He doubted that she'd put it all together, though. She hadn't acted in fear while she was home. Maybe she'd thought she was safe in Miami.

When he reached his car, he pulled out his phone and called Alicia. He frowned when the phone went to voicemail. *Damn. Where was she?*

A rumble of thunder drew his gaze to the sky. A flash of light to the east sent a chill down his spine. He had a feeling he knew exactly where she was.

TWENTY-THREE

Alicia felt an eerie sense of déjà vu as she parked in the lot at Virginia Key National Park a little after six. Just like the last time she was there, the lot was empty and a light drizzle was dampening the ground. She took her backpack and headed down the trail toward the carousel, using the flashlight on her phone to see where she was going. She had no idea where Liliana's body had been found, but she suspected she'd find some evidence of crime scene tape somewhere in the park.

When she reached the carousel, goose bumps ran along her arms, and she shivered as a gusty wind lifted her hair off her neck. It wasn't just the approaching storm that had her nerves on edge; it was knowing that a murder had happened in this park.

She was probably crazy to be out here alone, but she doubted that Liliana's killer was lingering in the park or that he was even in Miami. Liliana's problems had started in Texas. Maybe they'd followed her here. But there was no reason for anyone to be here now.

Lightning streaked across the sky, too far away to make a real impact. But the rumble of thunder that came a few minutes later told her it was getting closer. The lightning had called to her before. It had shown her what she needed to see. Maybe tonight it would do the same. Even if she couldn't find the place where Liliana had been buried, she could still get some stunning photographs. It didn't have to be a wasted trip.

She walked around the carousel, thinking that one day she'd like to see the merry-go-round filled with laughing, happy children, instead of looking like a ghostly, spooky structure in the woods.

Her nerves got tighter, and she was suddenly assailed with the urge to leave, to go home, to get back to her real life—a life she needed to live instead of just spectate. She'd spent too many days taking pictures of other people's important moments. Where were hers?

After her father had died, she'd tried not to be happy for a long time, but she didn't want to live the rest of her life in sadness. He wouldn't want that for her. He'd been an even bigger dreamer than she was. If she could believe that the lightning called to her, then she had to also believe that her dad was in a better place, that he was watching over her. And if he was watching over her, she wanted him to be proud of what he saw.

More importantly, she wanted to be proud of herself.

She'd felt good the last few days, more in

charge, in control, using her intellect to make a difference. She wasn't just a photographer, an observer of life. It was time to be who she was meant to be. It was time to go home and live her life.

Lightning streaked across the sky, illuminating the park, and she didn't even raise her camera. "I know," she said aloud. "I know what you're showing me now—myself. Why didn't I see it before?" Her words echoed in the blustery wind that rattled through the surrounding trees.

A crack of wood brought her head around. She was shocked to see a man approaching. He wore jeans and a dark sweatshirt with a hood over his head.

Was it Michael?

No, something wasn't right. It wasn't Michael, but she'd seen this man before—the night of the last storm. *It was the man by the carousel, the one fighting with Liliana.*

She turned to run, but he was already upon her. He grabbed her by the arm. She struggled against his iron grip, but he was bigger than her, taller, broader, and stronger.

He pulled something out of his pocket. The metal flashed as lightning lit up the sky again. It wasn't a knife; it was a gun.

It was just like the last time, only she was the one who was struggling.

She kicked out at him and jerked hard to release

382

herself from his grip. He didn't let go, but the hood came off his head.

She stared in shock at a face she knew. "Oh, my God, you! How can it be you? I just talked to you on the phone. You're supposed to be in Texas."

"I didn't want to do this," Jerry said, staring back at her. "But you didn't give me any choice, Alicia."

"What are you talking about? What are you doing here?"

"You're a smart girl. Surely, you've figured it out by now."

She'd figured one thing out. "You killed Liliana? Why?"

"Because she was on to me. She was one step away from the truth. I couldn't let her take that step."

"I don't understand. Are you saying that you killed Professor Bryer and Connie Randolph?"

"The bitch got caught."

"Who? Connie?"

"Bryer was on to her. She came to me and told me that I needed to do something, make sure we weren't caught. I told her I'd take care of it. I'd make sure Bryer never bothered her again."

"But you killed them both?" She still couldn't quite comprehend what he was saying.

"I had to take them both out. She would have been a loose end."

She couldn't believe the man she'd known as

Uncle Jerry had just confessed to killing three people. And he was going to kill her, too. She could see the intent in his eyes.

Who was going to save her? She'd foolishly come to the park by herself.

"How did you know I was here?" she asked, stalling for time while she tried to figure out how to get away.

"I was outside your apartment when I called you. I hoped you'd tell me that you were dropping the investigation now that the body had been found, that it was over, but you didn't say that. You were going to keep going. When you left to come here, I couldn't quite believe how easy you were going to make it for me. I'm only sorry your friend isn't with you. I'll have to take care of him later."

"You can't kill everyone," she said, terrified that he would go after Michael next.

Jerry's smile was more evil than she'd ever imagined.

"It's really not that hard after the first one."

"How can you kill *me?* You were best friends with my father. He loved you. He thought of you as a brother."

A shadow crossed his face. "I'm going to regret this one, but I have too much to lose, Alicia."

"What were you and Connie doing together? If I'm going to die, at least you can tell me what was going on."

"She was stealing classified specs from MDT. She passed them on to me, and I sold them for some nice cash. It was how I got the Flight Deck. MDT owed me. After my crash, they hung me out to dry. Just like the Navy did. I was tired of working for people who didn't appreciate me. So I found some who did."

"What was in it for Connie?"

"Money. Her ex-husband bled her dry. That's how it started anyway. She didn't realize that once you know anything, you know too much."

"And Paul Sandbury? What was his part in all this?"

"I wasn't actually sure he knew anything until you came to the bar and told me about him. I'll deal with him later." He paused. "This wasn't your problem, Alicia. You shouldn't have gotten involved. But you're just like your father. You like to stick your nose where it doesn't belong, and then you're surprised that you're in danger."

"What are you talking about? My dad didn't do that. He didn't meddle. He wasn't in danger."

"You know so little about your father," he said in amusement. "He was always the hero for you—for many people."

"I know everything about my dad," she said heatedly. "He was a good man."

"Yes. He was good—too good. It was sad . . . what happened to him."

There was something in his tone that made her

think he was talking about more than a plane crash. "You know something about that crash, don't you?" Her stomach twisted into knots. Anticipation ran down her spine as Jerry stared back at her.

"I'm done talking," he said. "You and I are going to take a walk. You came out here to see where she was buried, didn't you? I'm going to show you."

Before he could force her down the path, a brilliant, blazing flash of lightning struck the top of the carousel, blinding them with its powerful light.

Jerry let go of her hand to cover his eyes. She took advantage of his distraction and gave him a hard shove.

As he stumbled backward, she ran as fast as she could. But the lightning was gone as fast as it had come, and she tripped in the now overwhelming darkness.

She screamed into the wind, hoping someone somewhere could hear her. She had to save her life, because if she didn't, Jerry would go after Michael next.

She scrambled to her feet and ran as fast as she could, but Jerry was closing in on her. She could hear his heavy steps, his quickened breathing. His hand swiped at her back, his fingers grabbing her arm, almost pulling it out of the socket.

And then another man shot out of the trees.

Michael!

She was both relieved and terrified to see him.

Michael launched himself at Jerry, tackling him to the ground.

"Run," he shouted at her.

But she couldn't run away, not while Michael was fighting for his life with a madman.

Jerry was incredibly strong, and he was a trained soldier. He might have spent most of his days in a plane, but he knew hand-to-hand combat, and with each punch of his fist, she could see Michael losing ground.

She had to find a way to help him.

The lightning struck again as if in answer to her prayer. Just like the last time, it hit the ground, lighting the trees on fire, sending heavy branches to the ground.

She grabbed one of those flaming branches. As Jerry threw Michael to the dirt, she rushed forward and swung the branch as hard as she could at Jerry's head.

He screamed in pain, the fire from the branch lighting up his hair, his clothes.

She backed away, keeping an eye on Jerry as Michael staggered to his feet.

She thought Jerry might beat the fire out, but then the flaming tree above his head showered more fire down upon him. It was as if Mother Nature had joined in the fight.

Alicia stared at him in shock as he was enveloped in the blazing heat.

Michael came over to her, blood dripping down his face. "Let's get out of here."

"But—"

"You try to help him, he'll take you with him," Michael said harshly. "He'll kill you, Alicia."

She had no doubt that was the truth. It was still hard to watch a man being burned to death.

Sirens lit up the night, and a wave of relief ran through her.

"I called Diego on my way over here," Michael said. He pulled her further away from the fire as he yelled, "We're over here."

A moment later, three cops rushed down the path, two of them immediately heading to Jerry. They pulled him free of the fiery branches and rolled him on the ground as firemen now rushed toward the fire, followed by the paramedics.

The third police officer came over to them.

"Are you two all right?" he asked.

"We're fine now, Diego. Thanks for getting here in the nick of time." Michael put his arm around Alicia's trembling shoulders.

"You need to go to the hospital, Michael," Diego said, his gaze concerned. "You're bleeding."

"I'm fine," he said, swiping at the blood on his face with his fingers.

"You're not fine," Alicia told him. "Your face is all beat up. And I saw Jerry kick you in the ribs."

"They're bruised, that's it. You saved my life, Alicia." He turned toward Diego. "You should have seen her. I told her to run, and she hit him with a flaming branch."

"I wondered how he got caught up in the fire."

"It was the lightning. It hit the tree. I just used what it gave me," she said. "Is he going to live?"

"I don't know," Diego replied. "He doesn't look good."

"Damn. Is that Kellerman?" Michael interrupted, tipping his head toward the two non-uniformed men making their way down the path.

"I had to tell him you called me," Diego said. "Let me fill him in first, give you a chance to catch your breath. Stay here."

Michael nodded, turning to her with concern in his gaze. "Did Jerry hurt you, Alicia? Before I got here?"

She shook her head. "No, but he was going to kill me the same way he killed Liliana. He did it, Michael. He confessed everything to me. He also murdered Professor Bryer and Connie Randolph."

Michael looked as stunned as she felt. "Why?"

"Jerry was working with Connie. They were stealing secrets from MDT and selling them to someone. Bryer found out. Connie asked Jerry to take care of him, but he killed both of them instead." She swallowed, her voice hoarse from the smoke.

"So that was what was in the envelope," he murmured.

"What do you mean?" she asked in confusion.

"I went to speak to Liliana's parents. After I paid my respects to them, I went upstairs. I was talking to Isabel, and she asked me to get her a coat, because she was shivering from the shock. I reached for the first one I saw. It was Liliana's. She'd lent it to her sister the night of the rehearsal dinner. Isabel had forgotten all about it. She'd never given it to the police. In the pocket of the coat were three photographs, all showing Jerry and Connie exchanging an envelope. In one of them, the photographer was captured in the mirror. It was Sandbury. He must have given the photos to Liliana. He must have told her what Connie and Jerry were doing. I don't know why he didn't tell us."

"He was terrified when Liliana disappeared. The thing is Jerry didn't know that Sandbury had photos or information. He said he got suspicious when I brought up the man's name yesterday. He said he would take care of him later."

"Well, Sandbury was right to run then. I know he gave Liliana the photos, but I don't believe he told her the whole story. She didn't know how close she was to the truth. If she had, she would have taken precautions."

"One of these days, maybe we can get him to tell us what exactly he told her." She let out a breath. "Jerry called me this afternoon. He acted friendly and helpful, but he was just feeling me out. He wanted to know if we were done asking questions. I told him we wouldn't be done until we got justice. I didn't know he was outside of my apart-ment. I guess my words made him realize that I was going to be a problem. He told me you would be next." She shook her head, choked up at the thought.

He tightened his arm around her. "I'm still here, and so are you."

"I never should have left my apartment, but I was feeling restless, Michael. I didn't know what to do with myself. The lightning was coming, and I wanted to see where Liliana's body had been found, so I came here. I couldn't imagine Liliana's killer would still be here. Jerry followed me. He said I made it easy for him."

"You didn't make it easy. That's why he's fighting for his life."

"Because of you. If you hadn't come when you did . . ."

"You're safe, Alicia. That's all that matters now."

It felt so good to have his warm strength sur-rounding her. She wanted to stay there forever, but she could see the paramedics strapping Jerry to a gurney and she needed to know if he was still alive.

As the paramedics wheeled Jerry down the path, she moved forward. "Is he going to make it?"

"We have to get him to the hospital," the paramedic said. "You can talk to him later."

"It's over," Michael said to Jerry. "You're going to pay for what you did."

Jerry lifted a badly burned hand and pulled the mask away from his burned face with whatever strength he had left. He was fighting to hold on, but he was slipping away.

"Over for me, not for you." He looked at Alicia with evil in his eyes. "Someday you'll know what happened to your father. It's not what you think." His hand fell to the side, and his eyes closed.

"He's crashing," one of the paramedics said.

"Wait," she shouted, wanting to know what Jerry had meant, but the paramedics were rushing him to the ambulance waiting in the parking lot. The vehicle took off a moment later, sirens blazing.

"What did he mean? Why did he say that about my dad?" she asked, a feeling of dread running through her body.

"He was messing with you."

"No, it was more than that." She tried to remember Jerry's earlier words about her father. "Earlier tonight, he said something about me being just like my dad, sticking my nose where it didn't belong, and then being surprised there was danger." She clapped a hand to her mouth. "He knew something about the plane crash. What if it wasn't an accident? We have to go to the hospital. Jerry has to make it. He has to tell me what he meant."

"We'll go to the hospital," Michael reassured her. "But you can't believe anything he said, Alicia. He's a pathological liar, a killer. He can't be trusted."

Everything Michael said made sense, but she wasn't entirely convinced.

"We'll talk it all out," he added. "We'll go over every word that you and Jerry exchanged. Okay?"

"Okay." She let out a breath. "It's really over, isn't it?"

"It is."

"And the lightning showed us what we needed to see," she murmured. "It's actually how I got away from Jerry. A bolt hit the carousel rods and the flash blinded him for a second."

"Sounds like divine intervention."

"It felt like it. It was so much like the last time: the lightning, the carousel, the struggle. He was going to kill me the same way he killed Liliana. He must have dragged her into the woods when I was knocked down by the lightning."

"No, Alicia, I'm sorry. I should have told you earlier. Liliana wasn't killed last week. She was killed two months ago, right after she disappeared."

She stared back at him, more shock running through her body. "But I saw her."

"You didn't see her. You couldn't have."

"Then who did I see?" As they exchanged along look, the unbelievable answer came to her. "Oh, my God! I didn't see her; I saw myself. It was me fighting with Jerry. I wasn't seeing the present; I was seeing the future. It was my scream that was ringing through my head. It was a premonition."

"Have you had those before?"

"Never. But how else can you explain what I saw last Friday?"

She could see that the rational part of his brain wanted to deny her theory, but he had no other idea to offer.

"I don't know," he said. "But I think we should go home and figure it out."

"I need to speak to you both," Kellerman interrupted. "To get your statements." His tone was harsh and somewhat doubtful, as if he didn't know what to make of the situation and still couldn't quite believe Michael wasn't guilty of something.

"I'm taking Michael to the hospital," she told Kellerman. "You can talk to him later. I'd start working on an apology, because the man who killed Liliana was just taken away in an ambulance. He confessed everything to me. He also killed two other people in Texas. So maybe you should talk to him."

Kellerman gave a short nod. "We'll do that. But we will speak to both of you later."

She put her arm around Michael's waist as they

walked back to their cars. "I'll drive," she said when they got to the parking lot. "We'll get your car tomorrow."

"I can't believe you got us past Kellerman."

"After facing down Jerry, Kellerman was easy."

He gave her a somewhat weak smile as he got into the passenger seat. "Have I told you that you're amazing?"

"Yes, but you can tell me again when it doesn't look like you're hallucinating. I should have made the paramedics take a look at you."

"I just have a headache. It's no big deal."

She suspected that the adrenaline was wearing off and now the pain was settling in. She hoped a headache would be the worst of it.

Michael had suffered a mild concussion. After undergoing tests at the hospital, he was released two hours later with the caveat that he needed to rest for the next twenty-four hours. Diego told them that Kellerman would see them in the morning, for which Alicia was immensely relieved. She couldn't get into a lot of explanations tonight.

While waiting for Michael, she'd learned that Jerry had died before arriving at the hospital. She would not get any answers from him about the cryptic statements he'd made to her. And as Michael had reminded her, Jerry was a psychopath, so why should she believe anything he'd said to her?

Maybe because it had felt . . . true. There had been something in Jerry's eyes every time he spoke about her dad.

But how on earth would she ever find out now? Jerry was dead. And he'd killed everyone who knew what he was doing.

Perhaps not everyone . . . but she suspected he'd covered his tracks extremely well.

It was after midnight by the time Alicia got Michael home and into bed.

Michael had no fight left in him to protest. His face was a mix of black and purple bruises with a good-sized cut on his forehead. Judging by the way he winced every time he moved, she suspected he had some aches elsewhere.

"Did they check your ribs?" she asked him as he slid under the covers wearing boxers and a T-shirt.

"Just bruised, like I thought." He gave her a tender smile. "I've been beat up worse than this."

"When was that?"

"When I was a kid."

"I don't think I believe you."

"The important thing is that I'm okay and you're okay."

"I came out way better than you."

"I'm glad about that. I couldn't stand the thought of him hurting you. When I got out of the car, I heard you scream. I was afraid I wasn't going to get to you in time." His jaw tightened. "It was unthinkable."

"I was stupid to go to the park alone."

He ran a finger down the side of her face. "Stupid or brave? Remember that fine line?"

"I crossed it again."

"You showed enormous courage, babe. And let's be honest. If you hadn't gone to the park, Jerry would have found another opportunity to get to you and probably also to me."

"I wish he would have lived. I know that sounds strange to say, but I really wanted to ask what he meant about my father. Now I'll never know."

"He wanted to hurt you. He couldn't kill you, so he gave you as much pain as he could."

"That makes sense. Jerry told me that MDT owed him. That they'd grounded him after his crash, threw him away like a piece of trash. I guess that was his motivation for stealing their secrets and selling them."

"Revenge and greed are a dangerous combination. Why was Connie involved?"

"He said it was for the cash. I guess Bryer caught her doing something. And obviously Paul Sandbury also figured out she was stealing secrets from the company."

"He should have come forward when Connie was killed. Then Liliana would still be alive," Michael said harshly. "What a coward."

She nodded. "I have a feeling that it wasn't cut and dried."

"What do you mean?"

"Sandbury's wife is sick. He needed the insurance. Maybe he wasn't going to turn Connie in, perhaps he was going to blackmail her."

"Or get a cut of the action," Michael said. "It makes sense, but then Connie died."

"He kind of tries to imply that she wasn't having an affair at the trial, but he gets shot down by the prosecutor who doesn't want any other versions of the story."

"Then when Liliana goes to see him, he decides to free himself of his guilty conscience."

"I don't think his photos got her killed. Jerry said that she was making too many waves, talking to too many people."

"I wonder why she got in the car with him," Michael said.

"He might have told her that he'd come to Florida to tell her what really happened. If she didn't suspect him, she would have wanted to hear what he had to say."

"Yeah. So I guess that's it."

"Except for the part about my dad."

He gave her a compassionate look. "I know it's going to be difficult to let that go, maybe impossible, but nothing will change what happened to your father."

"If it wasn't an accident, then I need to get my dad justice."

"If Jerry was the one who made sure your

father's plane went down, then justice has already been served, Alicia."

She hadn't thought about it that way. "That's true. Jerry was always such a friendly, outgoing guy. When we saw him yesterday, he was so nice to me. He was like my uncle. But he was so evil and twisted. I wonder if my father ever saw that side of him."

"He was very skilled at hiding his true nature." Michael paused. "I know you wish you could have five more minutes with Jerry, but his death means Liliana's parents and family won't have to live through a trial. They won't have to look at his face. They won't have to relive it all again."

"You're right about that."

"Theresa and Dominic will probably want to talk to you, though. They'll want to know what Jerry said about her murder."

"He really didn't tell me anything specific, and when he did speak of her, he had no humanity in his voice. She didn't matter to him. She was just an obstacle. I would never want to tell Liliana's family that."

"Then don't. All they need to know is that their daughter was trying to stop a killer. And in a way, she did that, because if she hadn't gone missing in Miami, we never would have gone to Texas. In the end, we stopped Jerry from hurting anyone else."

She did feel good about that. "That's what I'll tell

them." She paused. "How are you doing, Michael? And I'm not just talking about your injuries. You've had a lot of emotions to deal with today."

"Too many to make sense of tonight. We can talk about it tomorrow." Michael patted the bed next to him. "If you're staying, I think you should get into bed."

"I would like to stay, but . . ." She didn't know exactly what she wanted to say.

"But I need to apologize," he finished.

She looked at him in surprise. "I wasn't going to say that. I just want you to rest."

"No, I need to say I'm sorry. I pulled away from you after Diego called with the news about Liliana's body. I barely spoke to you on the way home. You called me earlier, and I didn't call you back."

"You were upset."

"Don't make excuses for me."

"Okay, I won't," she said, meeting his gaze. "You did cut me out, and it worried me. I knew you were upset, but I wanted to comfort you, and you wouldn't let me. That hurt."

"I felt an enormous wave of guilt when Diego told me Liliana was dead. I'd actually forgotten about her last night. I was so happy with you. She didn't cross my mind once. Then I got the call, and I felt bad for feeling good."

"I guess I can understand that," she said slowly.

"I felt like I had to distance myself from you,

so I could focus on what I needed to do and that was to find her killer. But I have to tell you that it felt really strange to be without you. After I dropped you off at your house, I missed you."

"I missed you, too, Michael."

"Good, because I have something important to tell you. I love you, Alicia."

A tingle of surprise shot through her body. "You love me? Are you sure it's not the pain medication talking?"

He smiled. "Not a chance. Love was an emotion I locked away a long time ago. But somehow you broke that lock. You pushed past my walls. You made me feel free again." He picked up her hand and tightened his fingers around hers. "You're the one, Alicia."

"It's fast."

"Like a lightning bolt," he teased. "But you love lightning, so maybe you can love me, too."

"No maybe about it. I do love you, Michael. Like you, I wasn't sure I could give in to love, because the thought of losing someone else I cared about was too frightening. But when you and Jerry were fighting, I was overwhelmed by the need to protect you, to save you."

"I told you to run."

"I couldn't leave you. I didn't want to live, if you weren't going to live, too."

"Well, we both made it."

"So what happens next?"

"I'm thinking you get under the covers with me," he said. "And I'll show you exactly how I feel about you."

"With a concussion? No way. I will sleep with you, but that's it."

"I'm fine, Alicia."

"I intend to make sure of that." She stripped down to her underwear and got into bed with him, resting her head on his shoulder as he put his arm around her and pulled her close.

"We can take things slow," she told him. "We can get to know each other better. I won't hold you to anything if you change your mind."

He laughed. "I won't change my mind, and I'm very clear on how I feel about you, but slow is good. I want to get to know you when we're not trying to track down a killer, when our life is normal and maybe even a little boring."

"True."

"But knowing your penchant for chasing lightning, I have a feeling life is always going to be exciting where you're concerned," he said.

"I don't think I'll be chasing the lightning anymore."

"Why not?"

She lifted her head so she could look into his eyes. "Because I know now why I ran toward it. I was looking for you. I found you, and you're all I need. The lightning didn't call me to see that tag in the dirt; it called me to you."

He smiled at her. "I actually believe that, too."

"And just so you know, I don't have to stay in Miami, Michael. I can go wherever I need to go, wherever you need to be."

"I'm open to the possibilities. I talked to my father earlier. We called a truce. I wouldn't mind being closer to him, to my sisters and Veronica. I don't know if I want to live next door, but I definitely want to spend more time here."

"Liliana's disappearance brought us both closer to our families. I'd really like you to come to Texas with me next month for my sister's party. My mother will be thrilled to see you."

"I like your mother and your brother, too. I'm interested to meet your sister as well, so I'd love to go. Family is important, but what's most important is that I love you and you love me. We'll figure out our future together."

"I like the sound of that."

"And I like the sound of your voice, the sweet curve of these lips." He touched her lips with his finger. "The silky feel of your hair, your beautiful brown eyes, always filled with curiosity and fearlessness, and then there's your body."

"Michael," she said, a little breathlessly as his body began to harden against hers. "You need to rest."

"Later," he said, moving so suddenly she was on her back before she knew it. "But right now, I'm going to love you."

"And I'm going to love you back."

x

403

EPILOGUE

Two weeks later

Liliana's memorial service was held at St. Peter's Church with the burial of her ashes in a beautiful cemetery overlooking the Atlantic Ocean. A reception at Paladar for family and friends followed the service.

Alicia held Michael's hand throughout the emotional day. While there were sad moments, there were also happy memories shared. By the time they settled in at a table in the restaurant for a late lunch, the pain was gone from his eyes. He was free now—from fear, suspicion and guilt.

"That wasn't as bad as I expected," Michael said. "It felt like we were celebrating her life, instead of mourning her death."

"It was really well done. I know her family will grieve for a long time, but I hope they can start to move past the worst of the pain."

"It helps for them to know that Liliana was trying to stop a killer. She was a hero. And her death wasn't in vain. It's not much compensation, but it's something." Michael paused as Detective Kellerman and Diego walked into the room. "I can't believe Kellerman is here."

"Maybe he finally wants to apologize to you."

Despite all the meetings they'd had with the police since Jerry's death, Detective Ron Kellerman had never admitted he'd been wrong about Michael.

"I doubt it," Michael said.

While Diego stopped to chat with Theresa Valdez, Kellerman saw them and walked over to their table. "Mr. Cordero, Miss Monroe."

"You surely can't have more questions for me," Michael said.

Kellerman sat down in the chair next to Michael. "No. I wanted to tell you that I was wrong about you."

Michael looked stunned by his words. "Seriously? You're finally going to admit that?"

Kellerman nodded. "I should have done a better job looking into the criminal case in Texas, but the police in Corpus Christi assured me that the right person was in jail for the double homicide. Obviously, they were wrong. I was, too. I didn't think people could change. It certainly hasn't been my experience, but you did change. You're not the punk I remembered."

"No, I'm not," Michael said, not letting Kellerman off the hook.

Alicia couldn't blame him. The detective had put Michael through hell the past two months. "Has Mrs. Bryer been released from prison?" she asked.

"Yesterday," Kellerman answered. "It took a

few days to work through the system. The Corpus Christi district attorney is now satisfied that Jerry Caldwell killed Thomas Bryer and Connie Randolph, thanks to your statement, Miss Monroe, as well as the pictures found in Lieutenant Valdez's coat and a statement from Paul Sandbury."

"What's going to happen to him?" Michael asked.

"I'm not sure yet. The extent of his involvement with both classified information and obstructing justice is still under review. However, he's being quite cooperative now that Jerry Caldwell is dead."

"Was there anyone else at MDT involved?" Alicia asked.

"According to Sandbury, no. He said Connie and Jerry were working together. Bryer found out what she was doing. Then Sandbury got suspicious and started following Connie around. He was thinking of blowing the whistle on her or blackmailing her for a cut of the action. He was desperate for money. His wife needed some experimental medical treatments not covered by insurance."

"So he does a bad thing for a good reason," Michael said. "Doesn't excuse what he did."

"He'll pay," Kellerman said. "But I have to warn you that he'll probably plead out, because corporate theft of classified information that could affect national security probably won't go to trial. At any rate, it's over now. It wasn't the outcome any of us wanted, but I always think knowing the truth is better than living with uncertainty." Kellerman tipped his head, got up and left the table.

"At least he apologized," Alicia said.

Michael shrugged. "His apology means nothing to me." He turned in his chair to face her. "I think we should get out of here."

"Really? We just got here."

"We've talked to everyone. We've paid our respects. It's time to move on."

She liked that idea a lot. "All right," she said, getting to her feet. "Where are we going?"

"It's a surprise."

"You're being mysterious."

He gave her a wicked smile. "I know how you love a mystery, and I like to keep you on your toes."

"Yes, you do," she said, grinning back at him. "Let's go."

They managed to slip out of the restaurant without having to say too many goodbyes. They got into Michael's car, and he lowered the convertible top for the first time, which gave her another reason to smile.

She really liked the carefree side of Michael, and she intended to see more of it in the days, weeks and years to come.

They drove for a good twenty minutes before turning down a long driveway. At the end of the road was a very old, run-down two-story house. The land was beautiful and the view of the bay in the back of the house was even more amazing, but the structure itself was practically falling down.

"What's this?" she asked.

"A steal," he said, as they got out of the car. "The house was recently vacated by its elderly owner. As you can see, it's a tear-down, but look at the land it's on."

"It is beautiful."

"Let's walk around the back. As you can see, it also needs an upgrade."

She had to agree. The grass was dead and overgrown with weeds. The swimming pool had been emptied, probably years ago, and the tiles were cracked. An old gazebo was barely standing in the far corner of the grass.

"What do you think?" he asked.

"Well, it has possibilities, but it looks like it needs a lot of work."

"Definitely, but it could be something spectacular, wouldn't you agree?"

She could see by the gleam in his eyes that he really wanted her to agree. "Did you buy this house, Michael?"

"I've put in an offer," he admitted.

"Really?" She was stunned. They'd started to

talk about the future and going to New York had definitely been part of the discussion.

"It's a great location. You'll be able to see the lightning storms coming off the coast, and you won't have to drive to a park to get your pictures."

"That's true." She was touched by how much he'd thought about her needs.

"And the house itself will be amazing." He pulled a piece of folded paper out of his pocket. As he unfolded it, she could see a drawing. "It's not a blueprint, but it's my design, one I've been working on for a while."

She was impressed by the beauty and detail of his sketch. "When did you have time to do this?"

"I've actually been drawing this house for years. I just didn't know when or if I'd ever build it, and if I did, who would live in it with me. Now I do."

"It's a beautiful home, Michael. You're so talented."

"I'm glad you like it, because I want you to live in it with me. I want to marry you, Alicia."

"I thought we were going to date for a while, go slow."

"We can date as long as you like, but I want you to know this is where I'd like to end up, if that's what you want, too."

Images of a future with Michael filled her head: the beautiful new house, the swimming pool brimming with water, the gazebo refurbished and romantic, kids playing around the pool, a boy with Michael's blue eyes, and a girl with her unruly brown hair, maybe another baby girl sleeping in a playpen.

"Alicia, what do you think?" he asked, a worried note in his voice.

"It's perfect. I want to marry you, too, Michael. I want to have kids and live here and be really, really happy."

His smile was bigger than she'd ever seen it. "Kids, too?"

"You want children, don't you?"

"Sure. I would love a little crew of lightning chasers."

She laughed. "I don't need to chase the lightning anymore. I told you that. I've seen what I need to see—you. I only chased the light because there was a hole in my heart. It's not there anymore."

"I'm glad." He lowered his head and gave her a long, loving kiss. "But I would never try to stop you from being yourself, Alicia. That's all you ever need to be with me."

Tears pricked her eyes at the statement of unconditional love. "I feel the same way about you, Michael. I know you've felt torn between cultures and cities and families, but your home is with me, whether it's here or anywhere else."

"So here is good, don't you think?"

"Yes, here is wonderfully good."

Michael put his arms around her and they stared

out at the view. She sighed with contentment. "I don't think I've ever been this happy."

"It's only going to get better."

"I don't know how it could."

"When do you want to tell your family about us?"

"When we go back to Texas for Danielle's party," she said. "But be prepared. My mother will start planning the wedding as soon as we say we're getting married."

"I'm ready. I'm going to give you a ring, too, Alicia. But I want you to pick it out with me. I want it to be everything you've ever wanted."

She turned in his arms to face him. "You're everything I ever wanted, Michael. Thank God for the lightning. It brought me the perfect man."

He smiled. "I wouldn't say perfect, but I also am thankful for the lightning because it brought me my own very beautiful storm."

Dear Reader:

I hope you enjoyed reading *Beautiful Storm*, the first book in my new Lightning Strikes Trilogy.

While Michael and Alicia solved the mystery of Liliana's disappearance in *Beautiful Storm*, that's just the first part of a bigger mystery that will continue to unravel in *Lightning Lingers* (#2) and *Summer Rain* (#3). *Lightning Lingers* features Alicia's brother Jake with her sister Danielle taking center stage in *Summer Rain*.

Along with this new trilogy, I'm continuing to write the *New York Times* Bestselling Series: The Callaways. The most recent book, *If I Didn't Know Better* is now available with more books coming next year. If you'd like to be alerted to new book releases, please sign up for my newsletter!

Following this letter is an excerpt from one of my standalone bestselling romantic suspense titles, *Don't Say a Word*.

Until next time, happy reading!

Barbara

ABOUT THE AUTHOR

Barbara Freethy is a #1 *New York Times* Bestselling Author of 44 novels ranging from contemporary romance to romantic suspense and women's fiction. Traditionally published for many years, Barbara opened her own publishing company in 2011 and has since sold over 5 million books! Twenty of her titles have appeared on the *New York Times* and *USA Today* Bestseller Lists.

Known for her emotional and compelling stories of love, family, mystery and romance, Barbara enjoys writing about ordinary people caught up in extraordinary adventures. Barbara's books have won numerous awards. She is a six-time finalist for the RITA for best contemporary romance from Romance Writers of America and a two-time winner for *Daniel's Gift* and *The Way Back Home*.

Barbara has lived all over the state of California and currently resides in Northern California where she draws much of her inspiration from the beautiful bay area.

For a complete listing of books, as well as excerpts and contests, and to connect with Barbara:

For information: barbara@barbarafreethy.com

Follow Barbara on Facebook at
http://www.facebook.com/barbarafreethybooks

Sign up for Barbara's Newsletter at
http://eepurl.com/f7Ymr

Join Barbara's Private Fan Group at
https://www.facebook.com/groups
/BarbaraFreethyStreetTeam/

Visit Barbara's website at
http://www.barbarafreethy.com

Center Point Large Print
600 Brooks Road / PO Box 1
Thorndike, ME 04986-0001 USA

(207) 568-3717

US & Canada:
1 800 929-9108
www.centerpointlargeprint.com